Praise for Alan Furst

'Furst never stops astounding me' Tom Hanks

'Furst's ability to recreate the terrors of espionage is matchless'
Robert Harris

'The writing in *Mission to Paris*, sentence after sentence, page after page, is dazzling. If you are a John le Carré fan, this is definitely a novel for you' James Patterson

'Furst's tales . . . are infused with the melancholy romanticism of *Casablanca*, and also a touch of Arthur Koestler's *Darkness at Noon*'
Scotsman

'Your heart will be pounding with tension' *Guardian*

'The most talented espionage novelist of our generation' Vince Flynn

'[*Spies of the Balkans*] is a delight from first page to last . . . Seductive, unexpectedly sexy . . . It is quite superb' *Daily Mail*

'Furst's research is such that one gets the impression he hasn't just travelled, he has *time*-travelled. He evokes beautifully the haunted precarious existence of Europeans caught up in the march of war'
Financial Times

Alan Furst is widely recognised as the master of the historical spy novel. Now translated into eighteen languages, he is the author of thirteen novels including *Mission to Paris*, *Spies of the Balkans*, a TV Book Club choice, *The Spies of Warsaw*, which became a BBC mini-series starring David Tennant, and *The Foreign Correspondent*. Born in New York, he lived for many years in Paris, and now lives on Long Island.

Also by Alan Furst

Mission to Paris
Spies of the Balkans
The Spies of Warsaw
The Foreign Correspondent
Dark Voyage
Blood of Victory
Kingdom of Shadows
Red Gold
The World at Night
The Polish Officer
Dark Star
Night Soldiers

MIDNIGHT
IN EUROPE

ALAN FURST

W&N
WEIDENFELD & **NICOLSON**

A W&N PAPERBACK

First published in Great Britain in 2014
by Weidenfeld & Nicolson
This paperback edition published in 2015
by Weidenfeld & Nicolson,
an imprint of the Orion Publishing Group,
Carmelite House, 50 Victoria Embankment,
London EC4Y 0DZ

An Hachette UK company

10 9 8 7 6 5 4 3 2 1

A CIP catalogue record for this book
is available from the British Library.

ISBN 978-0-7538-2900-4

Printed in Great Britain by Clays Ltd, St Ives plc

The Orion Publishing Group's policy is to use papers that
are natural, renewable and recyclable products and
made from wood grown in sustainable forests. The logging
and manufacturing processes are expected to conform to
the environmental regulations of the country of origin.

www.orionbooks.co.uk

*'The lamps are going out all over Europe.
We shall not see them lit again in our lifetime.'*

Sir Edward Grey,
British foreign secretary,
on 3 August 1914,
the eve of the First World War

EUROPE
1938

Danzig (Gdansk)
LITH.
E. PRUSSIA (GER.)
Berlin
Bydgoszcz railyards
Warsaw
Praga
POLAND
Carlsbad
Karviná
CZECHOSLOVAKIA
Brno
AUSTRIA
Budapest
HUNGARY
ROUMANIA
YUGOSLAVIA
ALBANIA
GREECE
Salonika
Piraeus
Licata
Route of the SANTA CRUZ
ITALY
U. S. S. R.
Odessa
Constanta
Black Sea
BULGARIA
Istanbul
Bosphorus Channel
TURKEY
Mediterranean Sea
AFRICA

© A. Karl/J. Kemp. 2014

THE
PARIS
FRONT

ON A SOFT, WINTER EVENING IN MANHATTAN, THE FIFTEENTH OF December, 1937, it started to snow; big flakes spun lazily in the sky, danced in the lights of the office buildings, then melted as they hit the pavement. At Saks Fifth Avenue the window displays were lush and glittering – tinsel, toy trains, sugary frost dusted on the glass – and a crowd had gathered at the main entrance, drawn by a group of carollers dressed for a Dickens Christmas in long scarves, top hats, and bonnets. Here then, for as long as it lasted, was a romantic New York, the New York in a song on the radio.

Cristián Ferrar, a Spanish émigré who lived in Paris, took a moment to enjoy the spectacle, then hurried across the avenue as the traffic light turned red and began to work his way through the crowd. In a buckled briefcase carried under his arm, he had that morning's *New York Times*. The international news was as usual: marches, riots, assassinations, street brawls, arson; political warfare was tearing Europe apart. Real war was coming, this was merely the overture. In Spain, political warfare had flared into civil war, and, the *Times* reported, the army of the Republic had attacked General Franco's fascist forces at the Aragonese town of Teruel. And, you only had to turn the page, there was more: Hitler's Nazi Germany had issued new restrictions on the Jews, while here was a photograph of Benito Mussolini, shown by his personal railcar as he gave the stiff-armed fascist salute, and there a photograph of Marshal Stalin, reviewing a parade of tank columns.

Cristián Ferrar would force himself to read it, would ask himself, *Is there anything to be done? Is it hopeless?* So it seemed. Elsewhere in the newspaper, the democratic opposition to the dictators tried not to show fear, but it was in their every word, the nervous dithering of the losing side. As Franco and his generals attacked the elected Republic, the others joined in, troops and warplanes provided by Germany and Italy, and with every victory they boasted and bragged and strutted: *It's our turn, get out of our way.*

Or else.

He'd had a long, long day. A lawyer with the Coudert Frères law firm in Paris – 'coo-DARE', he would remind his American clients – he'd spent hours at the Coudert Brothers office at 2 Rector Street. There'd been files to read, meetings to attend, and confidential discussions with the partners, as they worked on matters that involved both the Paris and the New York offices, whose wealthy clientele had worldwide business interests and, sometimes, eccentric lives. Coudert had, early in the century, famously untangled the byzantine affairs of the son of Jacques Lebaudy. Lebaudy *père* had earned millions of dollars, becoming known as 'the Sugar King of France', but the son was another story. On receipt of his father's fortune he'd gone thoroughly mad and led a private army to North Africa and there declared himself 'Emperor of the Sahara'. In time, the French Foreign Legion had sent the emperor packing and he'd wound up living on Long Island, where his wife shot and killed him.

But the difficulties of the Lebaudy case were minor compared to what Coudert had faced that day: the legal hell created by the Spanish Civil War, now in its seventeenth month; individuals and corporations cut off from their money, families in hiding because they were trapped on the wrong side – whatever side that was – burnt homes, burnt factories, burnt records, with no means of proving anything to insurance companies, or banks, or government bureaucracies. The Coudert lawyers in Paris and New York did the best they could, but sometimes there was little to be done. 'We regret your misfortune, monsieur, but the oil tanker has apparently vanished.'

Ferrar had left the Coudert office at five-thirty and headed uptown to his hotel, the Gotham, then, as a favour to a friend at the Spanish embassy in Paris, he'd walked over to the Spanish Republic's arms-buying office at 515 Madison Avenue. Here he'd picked up two manila envelopes he would take back to Paris – the days when you could trust the mail were long gone. He went next to Saks, meaning to buy Christmas presents – a hammered-silver bracelet and a cashmere sweater – for a woman friend he was to meet at seven. This love affair had gone on for more than two years as, every three months or so, he flew to Lisbon, where one could take the Pan Am flying boat to New York.

Actually, Ferrar was not precisely a Spaniard. He'd been born in Barcelona and so thought of himself as Catalan, from Catalonia, in ancient times a principality that included the French province of Roussillon. A Castilian from Madrid might well have recognized Ferrar's origin: his skin at the pale edge of dark, a gentle hawkish slope to the nose, and the deep green eyes common to the Catalan, with thick, black hair combed straight back from a high forehead and cut in the European style; noticeably long, and low on the neck. In June he'd turned forty, went horse-riding in the Bois de Boulogne twice a week, and stayed lean and tight with just that exercise. Heading towards the entrance to Saks, he wore a kind of lawyer's battle dress: good, sober suit beneath a tan, delicately soiled raincoat, fedora hat slightly tilted over the left eye, maroon scarf, and brown leather gloves. With the briefcase under his arm, Ferrar looked like what he was, a lawyer, a hardworking paladin ready to defend you against Uncle Henry's raid on your trusts.

As he reached the entry to the department store, Ferrar saw once again a thin little fellow who wore gold-rimmed spectacles, hands in the pockets of a blue overcoat, shoulders slumped as from fatigue or sorrow, who had followed him all day. This time he was leaning against the door of a taxi while the driver read a newspaper by the light of a streetlamp. The man in the blue overcoat had been with Ferrar at every stop, waiting outside at each location but not at all secretive, as though someone wanted Ferrar to know he was being watched.

Now who would that be?

There were many possibilities. For the secret services of Germany, Italy, and the USSR, the civil war in Spain was a spymaster's dream, and attacks were organized against targets everywhere in Europe: politicians of the left, diplomats, intellectuals, journalists, idealists – all much-favoured prey of the clandestine forces, be they fascist or communist. At embassies, social salons, grand hotels and nightclubs, the predators worked day and night. As for the man who followed him, Ferrar suspected he might be a local communist in service to the NKVD, since the USSR – the Republic's crucial, almost its only, ally – famously spied on its enemies, its friends, and everybody else. Or could the man be working for Franco's secret police?

Ferrar was determined not to brood about it, he could think of nothing to do in response, and he was not someone easily intimidated. He dismissed the man's presence with an unvoiced sigh, pulled the massive door open, and entered the store. Barely audible above the din of the shopping crowd, yet another band of carollers was singing 'joyful and tri-umm-phant'. Momentarily adrift in an aromatic maze of perfume and cosmetics counters, Ferrar searched for the jewellery department. The man in the blue overcoat waited outside.

P. J. DELANEY it said on the window. Then, below that, BAR & GRILL.

The very perfection of what the gossip columnists would call 'the local saloon'. It had been there forever, on East Thirty-Seventh Street in Murray Hill, a neighbourhood of boarding houses and small hotels, a low rung on the middle-class ladder where office workers, shop assistants, and people who did God-only-knew-what lived in genteel poverty. But their lives were their own. The neighbourhood had, for no particular reason, a seductive air of privacy about it. You could do what you liked, nobody cared.

Delaney's, as it was known, was down four steps from the pavement, open the door and the atmosphere came rolling out at you; decades of spilled beer and cigarette smoke. Cristián Ferrar sat in a booth by the wall; a stout wooden table – its edges scarred by cigarette burns – was flanked by benches attached to high backs, the tops handsomely scrolled. He had his *New York Times* spread out before him, ashtray to one side, whiskey and soda on the other.

Ferrar tried to read the newspaper, then folded it up and put it back in his briefcase – at least for the moment he would spare himself the smoke and fume of Europe on fire. He was in Delaney's to meet his lover, Eileen Moore, so turned his thoughts to the pleasures they would share. As he thought of her, his eyes wandered up to the window and the pavement outside where, since the bar was below street level, he could see only the lower halves of people walking by. Could he identify Eileen before she entered the bar? In his imagination he could see her strong legs in black cotton stockings, but she might be wearing something else. Outside it was still snowing, a little girl paused, then bent over to peer through the window until her mother towed her away.

Ferrar had a sip of his drink; then, when he put the glass down, there she was. 'Hello, Cristián,' she said, hands in the pockets of her wool coat. He stood, his smile radiant, and they embraced – a light, public embrace which lingered for the extra second that separates friendship from intimacy. Then he helped her off with her coat, finding ways to touch her as he did so, and hung it on a brass hook fixed to the side of the booth. She sat, slid next to the wall, he settled beside her, she rested a hand on his knee, there were droplets of melted snow in her hair.

'It's been too long,' he said.

'It has.'

'We'll make up for that,' he said.

Her hand tightened on his knee. Their eyes met, followed by a pair of knowing smiles. Grins, almost.

She had auburn hair, parted in the middle and falling in wings to her shoulders – easy to brush into place, cheap to maintain – and a pale, redhead's complexion with a spray of freckles barely visible across the bridge of her nose: an Irish girl, raised in the Bronx, now, in her early thirties, living a Manhattan life. She wouldn't be called *pretty,* but her face was animated and alive and good to look at. She wore a grey wool sweater that buttoned up the front, little gold earrings, no makeup, French perfume he'd bought her in August, black skirt, and the black cotton stockings with a seam up the back.

'Seeing you made me forget,' she said. 'I meant to say *buenas noches*. Did I get that right?'

'You did,' he said. Then, 'The old greeting – they don't say that these days.'

By this she was startled. 'And why not?'

'It would mean that you were of the upper classes and someone would arrest you. Now they say *Salut,* or *Salut camarada*. You know, "comrade".'

'I'm not much of a comrade,' she said. 'I marched here, back in November, and we have a *Help Spain* coin jar at work, that's about as far as I go with the politics.' *At work* meant, he knew, at the

Public Library, where she shelved books at night. By day she wrote novels – cheap paperbacks with lurid covers.

'Have you eaten?' he asked.

'No, I'm not all that hungry. What's on the blackboard?'

' "Chicken à la king", it said. Which is . . . ?'

'Pieces of chicken in a cream sauce on toast. If the cook is feeling his oats there might be a pea or two in there.'

'And what king ate this?'

Her laugh was loud and harsh. 'You,' she said.

'Let me get you a drink.'

'What've you got there?'

'Whiskey and soda.'

'Rye whiskey, in here. Yes, I'll have that.'

He went to the bar and returned with the drink. Eileen took a pack of Chesterfields from her purse, smacked it twice on the table to firm up the tobacco at the smoker's end, then peeled back the foil. Ferrar drew a Gitane from his packet and lit both their cigarettes. She raised her glass and said, '*Salut*, comrade,' then added, 'and mud in your eye' and drank off a generous sip.

'In my *eye*?' He was being droll, which she really liked. And it sounded good in his accent – vaguely foreign, with a British lilt, because he'd learned his English in Paris, where the teachers were British expatriates.

'Are you still living at the same place?' Ferrar said.

She nodded. 'The good old Iroquois Hotel. A room and a hotplate, bathroom down the hall.'

And a bed, he thought. A fond memory, that narrow bed with a lumpy mattress and iron rails at head and foot. Not much of a bed, but wonderful things happened there. With Eileen Moore he shared two great passions; they loved to laugh, and they loved sex – the more they excited each other, the more excited they became. Attraction was always mysterious, he believed – he didn't really know what drew her to him – but for himself he knew very well indeed. Yes, he had a fierce appetite for her small, curved shape, for her round bottom in motion, but beyond that he was wildly provoked by her redhead's colouring: her white body, the faded pink of her nether parts. He believed, deep down where his desire lived, that redheads had thinner skin, so that a single stroke went a *long* way. In Ferrar's imagination, amid the crowd in the noisy bar, he recalled how, when he first touched her nipples, her chin lifted and her face became taut and concentrated. *Stop it,* he told himself – it was too soon to leave. He finished his drink and went off to get two more.

Waiting at the bar, Ferrar remembered the first time he'd seen her. She'd been working as a clerk in a warehouse near the Hudson River, there'd been a sudden fire, two of the workers had been injured and were carried out as the building burned to a shell. The owner, a German Jew who'd fled to Paris, had filed a claim with his insurance company, the company stated that the fire was arson and refused to pay, the owner retained Coudert and sued. When Ferrar, in New York for meetings, had interviewed some of the workers, Eileen Moore sat across from him at a desk while a secretary recorded the deposition in shorthand. She did not record, but may have noticed, that attraction between Eileen Moore and Ferrar was instantaneous and powerful. Three months later – the insurance company had settled – he was back in the city; he called her, they met at Delaney's, they went to her room.

Returning to the table, a drink in either hand, he said, 'Are you writing a new book?'

'Yeah, I am. *Fatal Friday* did OK, so my editor wanted another. My working title is *Death of a Dame*, what do you think?'

'Well, I'd read it.'

'Aw, go on,' she said.

'I would read it because you wrote it.'

She snorted. 'No trace of me on the cover, as usual, at Phoenix Press only men write naughty crime books – that's the rule.'

'Do you mind?'

'A little, maybe. My friend Dawn thinks I should.' By Dawn

she meant Dawn Powell, the reigning novelist of Murray Hill.

'Would you try one with your name on it?'

She shrugged. 'I don't know. Maybe some day.'

'I think you will, Eileen,' he said, touching her thigh beneath the table.

Suddenly she leaned over and kissed him on the cheek. 'Damn, I'm happy you're here.'

He took his hand from her thigh and ran his fingers up under the silky hair on the back of her head. 'Have what you want of that,' he said, indicating her glass. He left the rest unsaid, she knew what he wanted.

She finished her drink and then, with mischief in her smile, and that quick nod and glance towards the door which meant *let's get out of here,* she sped them on their way.

Outside, the snow was sticking here and there as the night grew colder but was no more than a coating on the pavement. As they climbed the steps in front of the bar she took his arm and then, as he transferred the Saks bag to his other hand, he noticed, a little way up the street and on the side opposite Delaney's, a taxi with its lights off, engine thrumming, two white faces in the front seat.

'What's in the bag, Cristián?'

'Presents for you, but you'll have to . . . earn them.'

'Oh no,' she said. *Not that.*

Madrid, 17 December, 1937. Castillo wasn't the bravest man in the world but he was probably somewhere on the list. No movie hero, Castillo – he was a pudgy fellow, fiftyish, who might have been taken for a bookkeeper at a small factory. On the night of the seventeenth he found himself in the besieged city of Madrid, where he shouldn't have been. Madrid was a bastion of the Republic, but the city was run by the Communist party; cold, hard, suspicious people uninterested in explanations or excuses, and very dangerous. But Castillo was trying to do a good deed and, as far as he knew, had managed it. Now he had to get out of Spain and go home to Paris.

A freezing night in Madrid, bitter cold, and where the water pipes had been ruptured by bombs or artillery shells, rivers of ice ran across the paving stones. Castillo was on his way to the Hotel Florida, haunt of American celebrities, writers and journalists from everywhere, and stray dogs like himself. To keep the hotel from being bombed, the top floor had been crowded with fascist hostages so it was, for the moment, safe enough. Eager to be out of the weather, Castillo took a shortcut through an alley that led onto the Calle Victoria. There was a bar tucked into a tenement building in the alley, a poster taped to its cracked window – there weren't many whole panes of glass left in the city – showed a man with a green face, listening intently, his hand cupping his ear. A spy! A young woman next to him held an index finger to her lips. Above her head, the message: 'Sh! Comrades, not a word to brothers or friends or sweethearts.' Spy mania had become a passion in the city.

When Castillo was halfway down the alley, there was a white flash above the Calle Victoria and the concussion blew his hat off. Other bombs followed, and when their explosions lit the sky, a thousand roosters, mistaking the light for dawn, began to crow. Dust filled the air and something, a metal something, clanked on the street as it came down from wherever it had been. A woman screamed, the dogs began to bark. Castillo stood still – should he run? Throw himself to the ground? Realizing he was bareheaded, he looked around for his hat and finally saw it, upside down, a few yards behind him. Suddenly he shivered with fear and frantically searched his shirt and trousers for bloodstains, but found none.

He took a deep breath, steadied himself, and retrieved his hat. Now, how to get back to the hotel. A crowd would gather in the Calle Victoria; people – looking for survivors – digging frantically in the rubble, soldiers, police, ambulances with blue paper concealing their headlights from Franco's spotter planes. And officials, with authority from some bureau no one had ever heard of, whose sole purpose on earth was to demand to see one's papers, which would lack a validating stamp that no one had ever heard of. For Castillo, a frightening prospect. So he began to walk back the way he'd come. This was a mistake, the sort of decision that seems obvious at the time but then turns out to have been wrong, when it's too late. He had almost reached the end of the alley, then a voice in the darkness said, 'You, *camarada.*'

Castillo stopped dead. From the shadows came a child with a rifle. He had a long look at Castillo: heavy overcoat, blue suit, white shirt, a tie, maybe one of those upper-class Franco sympathizers caught in the city by the war.

'Your papers,' said the child. Who, Castillo now saw, wasn't a child at all. He was small and dark, maybe fifteen, with a child's face. His feet were wrapped in rags.

As Castillo reached for his passport and permits, he said, 'Who are you?'

'I am the sentry for this alley.'

Castillo handed over the documents, the sentry held the papers upside down and pretended to read them. 'Are these *your* papers?' he said.

'Yes.'

They weren't.

'Are you a spy?'

'No. Certainly not.'

That was a lie.

The sentry was trying to decide what to do, Castillo could see it in his face. A few, very long seconds went by, then the sentry said, 'I will take you to the officer.'

'Of course,' said Castillo. 'Which way do we go?' He almost pulled it off – the sentry hesitated because Castillo had done the trick very well, his confident voice just faintly suggesting that the officer might not be pleased when he discovered what the sentry had done. Finally the sentry said, 'I'll take you there, it is not far.' He had best be polite, this man in a suit could be somebody important.

The walk took fifteen minutes and ended at the service entrance to the Palace, the largest hotel in Europe, which had been converted to a hospital. Before the war, most of the hospital nurses in the city had been nuns but they had fled to Franco-occupied territory and the wards were now staffed by the prostitutes of Madrid – their hair growing out black because the city's supply of peroxide was needed as antiseptic for the wounded.

The sentry led Castillo down one flight of stairs, then another, to a room that had once been part of a kitchen; zinc tubs lined the walls and the still air smelled of grease and sour wine. When his eyes adjusted to the darkness – the room was lit by two candles at either end of a table, electricity being an occasional thing in the city – Castillo could see the forms of men standing in line. As he took his place at the end of the line his stomach clenched with fear, because the man seated at the table was in civilian clothes and he was wearing glasses. *Officer of what?*

Castillo had come to Madrid eight days earlier. He'd taken the night train from Paris to Toulouse, then flown Air France to Barcelona. From there, he'd caught a ride to Madrid with British volunteers fighting for the Republic. Thus he found himself standing, hanging on for dear life, in the back of an old Bedford truck – old enough so that it had to be started with a crank – brought to Spain by the volunteers, who were dockyard workers from Liverpool. To reach Madrid they had to take the single open road, held by the International Brigades, which could only be used at night because of the bombers.

They drove fast, with lights off. After two breakdowns and a flat tyre, they made it to Madrid, and Castillo found a room at the Florida.

In the room: one bed and four guests. Two of them, French journalists, slept in the bed while the other two, a Polish Jew who did not precisely say what business he had in Madrid, and Castillo, slept on the floor. The room had a hole in the ceiling – an artillery round had hit the room above theirs – that had been patched with a piece of cardboard on which somebody had written 'Art as practised by General Franco'.

Castillo had come to Spain on his own initiative, using a false identity, because he worked in Paris for the embassy of the Spanish Republic and they would never have allowed him to do what he was doing now. Thus his papers, using the name Cruz, had been provided by a professional forger in Paris. The barman at his café had sent him to see a room clerk at a small hotel in the Marais, who knew a dependable forger – a *cobbler,* in Parisian criminal argot. With so many émigrés from so many countries flooding into France, business was good for the cobblers.

Now Castillo should have sought help from the diplomats in Paris – some of them surely knew *helpful people* in Madrid – but the situation at the embassy was beyond complicated: after the attempted coup d'état by Franco and his fellow generals in 1936, the embassy diplomats were asked to declare their loyalty to the elected government of the Spanish Republic, or to resign. Almost all of them stayed, but only some of them were loyal. For others, their hearts with the Franco forces, it was wise to keep quiet and wait to see who would win. So, naturally, looking to the future, some of them had the occasional chat with Francoist operatives in Paris.

Thus, when it became obvious to Castillo that his agent in Madrid, codename Dalia, was in trouble, he had no one to turn to for help, knew that if word of Dalia's predicament got around the embassy it wouldn't stop there. An inner voice told Castillo that going to Madrid was a bad idea, but a deeper voice sent him south – he could not leave her to her fate, simple human decency said that this was wrong, and Castillo was perhaps a little smitten by her. But then, who wasn't?

No conventional beauty, Dalia, but striking beyond description – people stared at her. She didn't especially care. In her indefinite forties, she was ruled by nobody but herself, could be charming in an honest way, could be abrasive, feared nothing. But none of this would save her if she were arrested. And, worse yet, *interrogated*. To himself Castillo said, *No, this must not happen*. Just who was hunting her, and why, he could not even guess. All he knew was that the political cross-currents of the Spanish Civil War were ferocious and now Dalia was caught up in them. So, he would save her.

Poor Castillo – his life never meant him to have been anything like a secret agent. When the war started he'd been a curator at the Prado – Spain's national art museum – a curator of nineteenth-century painting, the modern era as far as the museum was concerned. Castillo happened to be in Paris when the civil war broke out in 1936, where he had been trying to establish the provenance of a prince's portrait left to the Prado by a rich noblewoman. One hot day in July he returned to his hotel, having spent the afternoon at the Bibliotheque Nationale, and there received a telephone call from a friend in Madrid: do *not* come back here, they are going to shoot the intellectuals. Castillo stayed where he was but a month later, marooned in Paris, money running out, and wanting to support the Republic any way he could, he went to the embassy and asked the second secretary if they needed help.

What happened next was a shock. The diplomat, a second secretary called Molina, offered him a job at a nearby office which worked under the rather opaque title of the Oficina Técnica – the Technical Bureau – which tried to buy armaments for the Republic on the international arms market. Was this a job for a museum curator? Soon enough Castillo learned that the previous incumbent in his job had been a gynaecologist from Barcelona, while the new director of propaganda was the Surrealist film director Buñuel. Under attack, the Republic had to improvise: educated and presumably loyal volunteers were welcomed, hired, and told to do their best.

Three months later, a stranger – soon to be known as Dalia – appeared at the bistro where Castillo had lunch and, without a word of explanation, sat down at his table. She did not introduce herself, said simply that she was a Spanish patriot, and had secret information that could help win the war. 'And you are . . . ?' he asked. She shrugged and gave him a name, the shrug implying that it wasn't hers. Very well, Castillo said, such information should be passed along to one Colonel Zaguan, who, um, handled that kind of thing.

'No, not him,' she said casually. 'I do not trust him.'

In truth there were *questions* about Zaguan, head of the embassy office of the Republic's secret service, known as the SIM, but they were rarely asked out loud. Castillo offered to speak to one of the diplomats. Again she refused. She would give the information only to Castillo himself, and he would have to figure out who could be trusted with it. 'Why did you choose me?' Castillo asked. 'How do you even know who I am?' She responded with a wicked smile, saying, 'I know who everyone is.' Castillo gave in.

Victorious, she unsnapped a slim gold clasp on her purse, drew out an envelope, and handed it over. The unsealed envelope had the printed name and Sixth Arrondissement address of the Hôtel Lutetia in the upper-left corner. Castillo put the envelope in the inside pocket of his jacket, then asked the woman if she would care for a glass of wine. 'Next time,' she said. Then, using her wicked smile to say goodbye, she stood abruptly and left the bistro.

When Castillo returned to his office, he looked to see what was in the envelope – he would not have been surprised to discover that the woman was mad as a hatter and had brought him a sheaf of senseless newspaper clippings. But this was not the case. What he found, typed on three sheets of hotel stationery, was a list: German names and ranks grouped under the headings *Pilots, Flight Crew, Ground Crew* and *Administration*. He had in his hand the identities of at least some of the personnel who served with the Condor Legion – German fighters and bombers sent to Spain by Hitler, a ready-made air force for Franco's fascists.

Ten minutes later he was in Molina's office at the embassy. The diplomat had a corner office with two windows. The second secretary was a professional, seasoned diplomat with the pince-nez and trimmed Van Dyke beard to prove it. Technically second-in-command, Molina in fact ran the embassy – the ambassador was remote and unapproachable, a classic bureaucrat who made sure that nobody knew what he thought about anything. Instructions to the staff were communicated through Molina, or Molina issued them himself and left the staff to assume they came from the ambassador.

Castillo told Molina about the woman in the bistro, then handed over the envelope. Molina adjusted his pince-nez in the fussy way he had and read for a time. Finally he said, 'This looks real enough.'

Castillo was relieved. He trusted Molina and was almost his friend and didn't want to appear naive in his eyes. 'What's to be done with it?'

'It should go to the army general staff in Valencia,' Molina said. As Franco's siege of Madrid intensified, the government of the Republic had fled en masse to the city on the Mediterranean coast. 'There are people there who will make use of it, if they can. And maybe this information should come from me, because if they find out you're involved they'll put pressure on you for more, and that will be the sort of pressure you won't like. Or, if this turns out to be some sort of poison . . . a game, you know, then you'll come under suspicion and you'll like that even less.' Molina was for a moment reflective, then said, 'But perhaps you wish to have the credit.'

'I don't,' Castillo said emphatically.

'For the best, I think. Castillo, please don't *tell* her anything, because we don't know who she is and . . .' Molina paused, then said, 'Because this may be some kind of bait, an attempt to acquire secrets from us. Do you see?'

Castillo nodded. He did see, and fervently wished he didn't. This horrid war would be the end of him. He was a museum curator, not an arms buyer, and surely not a spymaster. In the centre of his chest he felt anxiety squeezing him with its nasty, powerful little fingers, so took the first of what he knew would be a future of deep breaths. He chatted with Molina for a time, then returned to the Oficina Técnica.

In time, he found her. He'd begun to think it was hopeless, but then, after six days in Madrid, he found her. Her plea for rescue had come to him written on a bar napkin with a thick pencil, brought by an American foreign correspondent who'd come to Paris from Madrid. 'She's in trouble,' he told Castillo. 'I hope you can help her.'

'Where is she?'

The correspondent's mouth tightened as he shook his head slowly – *who knows?* 'On the move when I last saw her, but if she hasn't found a hiding place by now, I'm afraid . . .'

'She could be anywhere,' Castillo said, an edge of despair in his voice.

'She gave me the name of a contact, a Frenchman called Tarbot. He's head of a trade union in Lyons, works with the Spanish unions in Madrid – basically they're buying ambulances in Europe and trying to get them across the French border, then to Madrid. They are very passionate about La Causa – the battle against fascism – in Lyons.'

'Yes, I've seen that in the newspapers.'

'The tramps of Lyons, dozens of them, tried to enlist as a unit in the International Brigade. But the Brigade wouldn't take them on.'

'How would one find this . . . Tarbot, you said?'

'Where you find any of the foreigners, war tourists, journalists, whatever they are. At Chicote's and Molinero's, the great bars on the Gran Vía. That's where you'll find Tarbot. Just ask the barmen.'

Which was exactly what Castillo did when he reached Madrid. They knew right away who he was looking for.

'Oh yes, Tarbot, a big guy with scars on his face, missing a couple of fingers, that's Tarbot. He should be in later.'

'He stopped by yesterday, but only for a few minutes.'

'Somebody said they saw him in Barcelona.'

'Isn't he here? I swear I saw him. No, maybe not.'

'Rumour is he was hit by a sniper.' Secret Franco supporters hiding in Madrid liked to fire a shot or two out of the window when they thought they could get away with it and killed a few people every day.

And then, one afternoon as Castillo read a newspaper at the bar, a man came up behind him and said, in poor Spanish, 'I hear you are looking for me.'

Castillo told Tarbot about the correspondent, used the name Dalia, described her. Tarbot asked him questions, Castillo tried to tell him as little as possible, said Dalia was an old friend, from Paris. He really didn't know what had brought her to Madrid.

'Oh they come here,' Tarbot said, then shrugged. *Who knows why.* 'Anyhow, I'll give you an address. She *was* there but you know the way it is, people move around.'

But she was exactly where Tarbot said she was. Living in the attic of a badly bombed building, once a mansion, half its facade gone, a place where nobody could live. When Castillo saw her he flinched. The Dalia he knew was fashionable, perfectly dressed and groomed, poised, and sure of herself. The Dalia hiding in the attic was filthy, and obviously had not bathed for a long time. She had cut her hand badly and bandaged the wound with a dainty handkerchief.

Castillo waited until dark, then returned to the Hotel Florida and, using a razor blade, cut the lining of his overcoat and removed a set of false documents produced by his Parisian cobbler. Then he bought a dinner – lentils with garlic and a little oil and a small chunk of bread, which was what there was to eat in Madrid – wrapped it in a sheet of newspaper, and returned to the bombed mansion. Dalia ate like a wolf. When she was done Castillo said,

'Here are your new papers. You'll have to transfer your passport photograph, do you know how to do this?'

'Did you bring glue?'

'Yes. A brand that was suggested by the man who forged your papers.'

'Then I can do it.'

'And here is a train ticket, from Barcelona to Perpignan – you'll have to find a way to get from Madrid to Barcelona.'

'There are taxi drivers who will do it – for a price.'

Castillo reached in his pocket and handed Dalia a thick wad of banknotes, pesetas and francs. 'I believe this is enough for the driver – also for the train up to Paris.'

'More than enough,' Dalia said. 'There's a safe apartment I can use to clean up a little – now that I can afford to pay for it.'

'Better for travel,' Castillo said.

She nodded and said, 'Are you coming with me?'

'No, I have a flight from Barcelona to Toulouse on Wednesday – tomorrow night I will find a ride to Barcelona.'

She met his eyes and said, 'I can never thank you enough . . . you didn't have to . . .'

'It needed to be done, Dalia, so I did it.'

'You put yourself in danger.'

'Well, that's over now, all I have to do tonight is get back to the Florida.' He left the attic a few minutes later and took a shortcut through an alley to get to the hotel.

In the sub-basement of the Palace Hotel, Castillo waited at the end of a long line of men and women, shadowy forms in the light of two candles at either end of a table. Seated at the table was a man in civilian clothing and glasses, who the sentry had called *the officer*. The line had moved slowly, but now it sped up – the officer sent the next few men away after a glance at their papers. He'd evidently been doing this kind of work for some time and had thus become good at it, thoroughly efficient. Castillo was now next in line for interrogation. Standing at the table, a handsome young man was explaining something at length, leaning over and speaking confidentially, so Castillo could not hear the words. But the tone, the high pitch of the voice, imploring, whining – that he *could* hear. Then the officer signalled – raised his hand – that he'd heard enough, and the young man cut himself off in mid-sentence and stood straight and silent, as though to receive a judgement.

On the table was a bell, an inverted silver cup with a silver button on top, the sort of bell one saw on the front desk of a hotel, used to summon a porter to take baggage up to a room. The officer extended one hand, hesitated, then tapped on the bell, a single, hollow *clink*. It was apparently an old bell. Or perhaps not so old, maybe just worn out. At the sound of the bell, a giant of a man with a huge beard and small, crafty eyes brushed past Castillo on his way to the table. As he went by, Castillo smelled rotten onions. The giant took the young man by the crook of the elbow, whispered something in his ear, then led him away. He had, Castillo now saw, a large revolver thrust into the waistband of his trousers.

As Castillo waited for the officer's permission to approach the table – this was done palm up, with a *come here* motion of the index finger – the sentry appeared and placed the Cruz passport and permits on the table. The officer was in no hurry, held the passport near one of the candles so he could read the typed print. From somewhere above the sub-basement, perhaps just outside the service entry, came the sound of a single pistol shot. The officer seemed not to notice. When he finished reading, he put the documents aside and looked up at Castillo. 'Comrade Cruz?' he said.

'Yes.' Castillo had caught himself just in time – he'd almost added *sir* to the *yes*. The officer was younger than Castillo had realized, perhaps in his late twenties. His suit was made of cheap material, his spectacles had steel frames.

'You are well dressed, aren't you,' the officer said. Then, 'Where are you staying in Madrid?'

'At the Hotel Florida.'

'And your business here?'

'My mother is ill and cannot get the medicine she needs here in Madrid, so I brought it up from Valencia.'

'Would your mother not be better off in Valencia too?'

'She will not leave. She has lived all her life in Madrid and she is passionate for La Causa. She cannot fight on the battle lines but, by staying here, she fights.'

'And you? Are you also passionate for La Causa?'

'I am, but to earn money I must live in Valencia.'

The officer slid a wooden box in front of him. The box might once have been used by a library – a yellowed card in the brass case on the front of the box said *RIV–STO* – but it now held three-by-five index cards. The officer flipped through the cards until he found the C names, then said, 'You're not Alberto Cruz, are you?'

'No, I am Carlos.'

'Very well, Comrade Carlos, give me your overcoat, then put everything in your pockets on the table.'

Castillo did as he was told. When his things were laid out before him, he saw that the officer had turned his overcoat inside out. 'What a shame,' the officer said. 'You seem to have ripped the lining of your coat. No, no, I am mistaken, the lining has been cut open.' He stared at Castillo, then said, 'Is there something you would like to tell me? To unburden yourself?'

'It was like that when I bought it.'

'Oh, of course it was.'

When the officer tapped the bell, Castillo's legs began to tremble. He feared he might collapse and thought, *God, help me to stand up.* An older woman with white hair in a bun stood next in line behind Castillo and, at the sound of the bell, Castillo heard her gasp. The giant finally appeared and as he took Castillo by the crook of the elbow the smell of rotten onions was overpowering. Leaning over, the giant whispered by Castillo's ear: 'Be a man.'

He led Castillo up the two flights of stairs, then out of the service entry. A few feet away, the handsome young man lay dead. He'd fallen forward, but Castillo could see his face.

The giant said, 'On your knees, comrade.'

Castillo's last thought was the name of a lover from long ago.

Paris, 22 December, 1937. Cristián Ferrar, on his way home from the Coudert Frères law firm, stopped at the *boulangerie* on the tiny rue Grégoire de Tours and picked up a baguette for his dinner. Next, at the grocery store across the street, he bought a thick slice of orange Mimolette cheese, a garlic sausage, a tin of artichoke hearts, and a bottle of grocery-store Bordeaux. As the woman who kept the store wrapped it all in a sheet of newspaper – the right-wing *Le Journal,* he saw – she made a face, a sour mix of anger and disgust. 'Have you heard, monsieur?' she said. 'The Métro workers say they will strike on Christmas Day – for a week.'

'I suspect they'll get a new contract. Just in time, as usual.'

'Imagine, monsieur, *Christmas.*'

'Will you have to close the store?'

'Oh no, I don't live far away. But still . . .'

'Then it won't be so bad.'

'Bad enough. Bonsoir, monsieur. Try to stay warm.'

'Bonsoir, madame.'

He set off towards home, tearing an end off the baguette and eating as he walked. It was cold. Cold and damp with a cutting little wind; a Paris speciality, a diabolical weather that forced its way through your clothing and chilled your very soul. Ferrar shivered and walked faster, entering the Place Saint-Sulpice, heading past the church of Saint-Sulpice towards his apartment. His refuge, where he looked forward to a quiet evening: he had a good chair in the room he used as a study, would settle by the coal-burning fire-place, would read – Robert Byron's *The Road to Oxiana* – drink the bottle of wine, and smoke Gitanes, a blanket pulled tight around his shoulders.

He'd grown up in rooms where you could hear clocks.

The rhythmic ticking created a special silence, a hush, which was the perfect setting for the life of the Ferrar family. His father was a lost soul, an excessively gentle and reticent man dedicated to philately, stamp collecting. In Ferrar's memory of him during the family's time in Barcelona – the first twelve years of Ferrar's life – his father was seated at a desk in his study, bending over a leather album, with some stamp, from Bechuanaland or Fiji, worth three somethings, quivering in a pair of tweezers as he tried to slip his prize into a glassine envelope.

Ferrar's mother was, in a way, not dissimilar. Daily existence was always hard – when she tried to correct the maid, the maid didn't hear her. She loved her children – Ferrar, a pious older sister, and two younger brothers, rascals both – but she couldn't disci-pline them. Faced with disruption of any kind she was meek, and helpless. But Ferrar's mother, like his father, had a singular obses-sion: she believed that her family, named Obrero, was of noble ori-gin, a tiny leaf clinging to a dying branch of the extinct Bourbon-Braganza royal line. Extinct it might be, according to the *Almanach de Gotha,* but there was a sprinkling of Spanish dukes who continued to use the title, and to them she wrote letters.

Not that they were ever answered, but they were meticulously composed – Ferrar's saintly sister helped – so that, perhaps, some day . . . Señora Ferrar's hopes were based on a yellowed packet of letters, tied with a faded ribbon, left to her by a great-aunt. The letters concerned a certain Spanish duchess, descended from Mariana Victoria, Infanta of Portugal, who sometime in the eigh-teenth century had been wed, in an arranged marriage, to an

Italian count. He was three, she was forty-six, and from this marriage there was no issue. *But,* said the great-aunt's letters, the duchess had, in her intemperate youth, been secretly married, and produced a daughter; an ancestor of Señora Ferrar.

Meanwhile, someone had to run this amiably mad family and that someone was Señora Ferrar's mother, Ferrar's grandmother, his beloved Abuela – the Spanish version of *Nana* – who made sure that practical matters were attended to, and kept the family from disaster. She had always lived with them and, now seventy-seven, continued to do so, ruling the house in Louveciennes, just up the Seine from Paris, where Ferrar's parents, sister, and a stray cousin all resided. And it was Abuela who made the great decision of Ferrar's life: 'We must go away,' she said to the family at the dinner table. 'If we stay in Spain, there will be tragedy.' And so they went: night train to Paris, lives as émigrés.

In Barcelona, the last week of July is remembered as the Semana Trágica, the Tragic Week, and commemorates riots, set off by the army's failed adventure in Morocco in 1909, and the subsequent conscription into the army of Catalonian workers. Mobs ruled the city, fifty churches were burned down, and over two hundred people were shot in the repression that followed. Ferrar's father, then a young man, having graduated from Spain's majestic university at Salamanca, had been encouraged by friends to take up a junior position at the Ministry of Justice. When the rioting broke out in 1909, the head of the ministry had fled for his life – the anarchist rioters disliked his politics and meant to kill him. Deprived of this pleasure, they went after his subordinates. On the night of 10 July, with gunfire echoing through the streets, blood was smeared on the door of the Ferrar house. Abuela made her pronouncement over dinner and nobody disagreed. It had become dangerous to live in the city and, Abuela decreed, in Spain: they would leave, or they would die.

Two days later they left for Paris. Ferrar, twelve at the time, would never forget that journey; this rupture in the family's life had frozen them into silence. Nobody said a word, their minds occupied by the refugees' litany: *Where will we live? How shall we survive? What will become of us?* In time, these questions were answered as the family adapted as best they could. After an intensive three-week study of French, Cristián Ferrar was enrolled at the Lycée Charlemagne, near the Saint-Paul Métro station.

Three weeks? This change of existence, brought on by catastrophe, was the first step in Ferrar's future success. The eldest son of the family had always been considered smart: he was a good student – the Jesuit teaching brothers thought well of him, he could answer all sorts of dinner-table questions, he was an avid reader; a smart young man. Meanwhile, Abuela used the word *brilliant*, but she was a grandmother and what grandmother wasn't proud of her grandson? In fact, Ferrar had been born gifted, was exceptionally intelligent, and his teachers at the Lycée Charlemagne took a special interest in him.

Ten years later, by the time he received his degree from the Faculté de Droit, the law school of the Sorbonne, he could read and speak French, Italian, Portuguese – wildly difficult! – English, and German, and could manage in Roumanian and Serbo-Croatian. Among the top five in his graduating class, he was hired as an associate by Coudert Frères, the first interview in his search for a position as a lawyer. By the age of twenty-nine he was made a junior partner and, six years later, a senior partner.

6 January, 1938. The Coudert Frères office was in a handsome old building at 52, Avenue des Champs-Elysées, a prominent address for a prominent clientele. On the list of clients could be found Whitneys, Drexels, Guggenheims, Vanderbilts, Gulbenkians, Wanamakers, and many others. But the interior echoed the style of the New York office: well-aged furniture – simple wooden desks and filing cabinets, battered oak desk-chairs on wheels – and a floor that was no colour beyond *dark* and creaked underfoot. This

absence of pretension spoke well of Coudert: a long-established, honourable firm, it was said that you could sense probity, the legal version of 'integrity', when you walked through the door.

The office of the managing partner, George Barabee, was no exception, its only decoration a group portrait of eight Coudert partners painted in 1889, ten years after the firm was established in Paris. Four seated lawyers, four standing behind them, most be-whiskered in the style of the day – thick muttonchop sideburns; full, well-tailored beards – all the subjects looking terribly stiff and dignified, a portrait genre known waggishly as *a treeful of owls*.

Barabee had tousled fair hair, wore tortoiseshell glasses, his body thick and broad in the way of a former athlete; he'd played football at Princeton. Graduating from the Columbia Law School in 1916, he was admitted to the New York bar, then flew fighter planes over France when the American Expeditionary Force joined the war against Germany. On the inside of his right forearm was a puckered burn scar, the result of being shot down over a cow pas-ture where he'd managed to land the burning Spad. He'd stayed in Paris after the war and gone to work for Coudert, in time becoming managing partner, a position that required social contact with prominent people in the city, a job he described as both his duty and his pleasure. Thus he joined clubs, went to state dinners, played squash once a week with J. J. Wilkinson, the second secretary of the American embassy.

On the evening of the seventh, Barabee leaned back in his chair, hands clasped behind his head. It was quiet in the office – except for taxi drivers honking their horns out on the avenue – the end of the day; he was tired, he wanted to go home, he wanted a drink. But one more problem had to be dealt with and, seated across from him, Cristián Ferrar lit a cigarette and opened a file folder he'd brought to Barabee's office.

'What's our history with these clients?' Barabee said.

'In 1932 we advised the Union of Hungarian Credit Associa-tions on a bond issue. In 1933, when Hitler came to power, one of the members, a small private bank in Budapest called First Danubian Trust, saw trouble coming in central Europe and retained us. They wanted to know if they could transfer their incorporation to France while the physical bank stayed in Budapest. We didn't believe the French would accept that, but what we could do, and ultimately did, was create a French holding company. Thus the bank in Budapest is controlled from Paris; the holding company essentially owns it in every respect and protects it from being taken over, in case things go very wrong in the political future, by the Hungarian government.'

'In fact, things are going wrong all over Europe. So, a small private bank – family owned, I would imagine.'

'It is. Owned by two brothers called Polanyi – nobility, one of them is a count, a diplomat at the Hungarian legation in Paris – and a sister who married a man called Belesz.'

'And then?'

'One of the bank's accounts was a large commercial hotel near the railway station in Budapest. When it became clear that the hotel was failing, First Danubian Trust decided to buy it. This was in October of '37. But then Belesz died suddenly, a hunting accident, shot himself while climbing over a fence. His two children succeeded him, niece and nephew to the brothers, and inherited equally his share of the holding company that controls the bank.'

'Who are the heirs?'

'They are both in their mid-forties, the nephew interests himself in Budapest nightlife, the niece is married to a major in the Hungarian army. When the holding company was founded here, it was the owners' direction that all the shareholders have to agree before they can do anything.'

'Oh Lord,' Barabee said, with the sigh in his voice of *one who sees it all coming.* 'Where is the mother in this?'

'Belesz was divorced ten years ago, at the time of his death he was living with a nightclub dancer. So the mother is not involved, and the nephew and the niece are fighting.'

'Well, of *course* they are . . . inherit wealth and pick a fight. Which is over . . . ?'

'Dogs.'

'Oh Lord, *animals*. The firm's been there before, the New York office represented W. C. Fields when he was charged by the New York Humane Society with the death of a canary, "by torture". The bird flew into a painted flat during the act. Fields was acquitted. So, that said, what sort of dogs?'

'A Hungarian breed called vizsla, they have short-hair coats, like whippets, are coloured brown or rust, with rosy-brown noses. They are excellent hunting dogs and good family dogs as well. In this case there are three, inherited by the niece and nephew. He wants to sell them, she says she loves them and wants to keep them. He refused to vote on the hotel sale until she gave in, and there it sits, the partnership can't do anything and, meanwhile, the hotel has failed and there are many creditors in court.'

'Have Count Polanyi and his brother offered to buy the dogs?'

'They have, but the nephew doesn't want money, he thinks that if he refuses to vote his half-share, he can drive his sister out of the partnership. It was the Count Polanyi who telephoned me this morning, told me the story, and asked if we can do anything under French law.'

'Where are the dogs?'

'They were at the Belesz house in Budapest, being cared for by the servants. But Count Polanyi has a castle in Hungary, and he called his steward and asked him to pick them up. So I expect they're at the castle.'

Barabee brooded for a moment, then rubbed his eyes and glanced at his watch. 'Well . . .' he said. Then, 'We'll have to come up with a list of possible legal moves, Cristián, but not until tomorrow. In here? Ten o'clock?'

Ferrar nodded, they said good night, and Ferrar returned to his office. His secretary, Jeannette, already had her coat on but she'd been waiting for him. 'Monsieur Ferrar? A telephone call came in for you a few minutes ago, a Señor Molina, from the Spanish embassy. There's a note on your desk with the number.'

'Thank you, Jeannette,' Ferrar said. 'And bonsoir.'

Ferrar sat at the desk, staring at the number. He had a bad feeling about this, then chided himself for having the feeling. *Let it be something to do with the émigré community,* he thought, *a funeral, a party, a meeting.* He dialled the number, gave his name, and the receptionist put him through immediately.

'Señor Ferrar, thank you for being prompt. Would it be possible for us to meet, perhaps tomorrow morning?'

'At nine? At the embassy?'

'Thank you, Señor Ferrar. I will see you at nine.'

The embassy was a few minutes' walk from the law firm; Ferrar felt he could just manage the meeting and be at Coudert by ten. He left the office and headed towards the Sixth Arrondissement, thinking he might take the Métro or find a taxi, but he did neither. It was a fine cold night, swirls of powdery snow blew over the cobblestones, Parisians flowed past him in their winter coats and scarves, so Ferrar, in no hurry to reach his silent apartment, crossed the Seine on the Pont Neuf, then stopped at a café and had a coffee, in time reached the Place Saint-Sulpice, and, reluctantly, went home.

Ferrar arrived at the embassy just before nine, gave his name to the receptionist, and the diplomat Molina appeared a moment later. Appeared from the nineteenth century: he wore a high collar, pincenez, a beautifully trimmed Van Dyke beard, and held himself a certain way, his head at an upward angle, as though he were looking down on the world. Molina seemed highly pleased, perhaps relieved, to meet Ferrar, who suspected they'd met before but couldn't remember where. When they'd shaken hands, Molina said, 'Shall we go and have a coffee?' As he said it he raised an interrogatory eyebrow, then held his open hand behind Ferrar's back and pointed his other hand towards the door. At the courteous end of assertive, the gesture meant they were *going* to have coffee.

Once Ferrar was out on the street, the bad feeling returned – what was it that couldn't be said at the embassy? They walked to the luxurious Hotel George V – named for the English king, the *George Cinq* to a Frenchman – and Molina led him to the tea salon called La Galerie. A gallery it was; a long narrow room with tables against the windowed wall and a glossy black piano with top up at the far end. For the rest it was all glowing marble in low light, glittering chandeliers, wall sconces, and tapestries – under foot and on the wall. *Aubussons?* Ferrar wondered. He wouldn't put it past the George V.

Molina ordered coffee, which came with a basket of small brioches. The waiter placed the basket just to the right of Ferrar's hand; he could feel the warmth and the aroma was inspiring. Ferrar wanted one, but waited to see if his appetite survived what Molina was going to say. As the diplomat cleared his throat and polished his pince-nez, Ferrar looked around the room, which was almost deserted. There were two men with briefcases whispering at one table, perhaps Jews, Ferrar thought, of the hard-faced variety; and in the corner, a young, overdressed couple, maybe on honeymoon.

Molina took a sip of coffee, then said, 'Did you ever meet a man called Castillo?'

It took a moment. 'The museum curator?'

'Yes. Did you know him?'

Past tense. 'We were, I believe, at émigré functions now and then, but I didn't really know him.'

'He has met with a great misfortune, I fear. I'm not entirely sure, he could show up tomorrow, but I have to accept the fact that he won't.'

'What happened?'

'Castillo was a good man, too good, really, and he went to Madrid on a kind of private mission, and we have heard he was executed as a spy.'

'And was he? A spy?'

'No. Not really. Perhaps, technically, he was on that sort of business when he was in Madrid, but his work at the embassy was far from espionage. As best we know, this execution was a random event, he was in the wrong place at the wrong time, was arrested, and immediately shot. There was no investigation, it all happened very quickly.'

'You did say he was in Madrid . . .' Ferrar was puzzled. 'So then, executed by the *Republic*?'

'No, no,' Molina said emphatically, putting down his coffee cup and dabbing at his lips with a vast, white linen napkin. 'This was an accident. Castillo would never have worked for the fascists. Never. No, it was just . . . in war, you know, these things happen.'

'I am sorry,' Ferrar said. *What does this have to do with me?* 'Did he have family?'

'No, he was a bachelor.'

Ferrar shook his head in sorrow. He'd heard so many of these stories as Spain tore itself to pieces, so he did what everyone did: reacted, felt sympathy, and waited to hear the next.

'A terrible thing,' Molina said. 'And a grave loss for us, for the embassy here in Paris. Castillo worked in what we call the Oficina Técnica, which tries to buy arms for the Republic on the world market. From the beginning we have lost battles and territory because we lack weapons: rifles, bullets, artillery, aeroplanes, everything.'

'I know,' Ferrar said. 'The world knows and all it does is watch.'

'Stalin helps us, to a point, the Russian pilots in Spain fight the German pilots of the Condor Legion, but this alliance will finish us, in the end.'

Ferrar recalled seeing a headline on the front page of a tabloid in New York. He didn't remember the headline, what he did remember was the phrase *Red Spain*. The American president, Roosevelt, was a determined anti-fascist, but the Spanish anarchists murdered priests and nuns and burned down churches. Which meant that Roosevelt's crucial supporters, Catholic working men and women in the cities, would not tolerate his helping people who did such things.

'Do you really believe we've lost the war?' Ferrar said.

'Not quite yet, not as long as we hold Madrid and Barcelona. We are doomed, however, if England and France and America don't help us. And they won't, politically can't, as long as victory for the Republic is seen as the creation of a Soviet state in Europe. Meanwhile, every day we are more dependent on the USSR. For example, the French and American banks won't process our payments, so we can pay for weapons only through the Banque Commerciale pour l'Europe du Nord, which is the Soviet Union's bank in Paris. Texaco sells oil only to Franco, and Dupont has sold Franco forty thousand bombs and evaded the American embargo by shipping via Germany. The French Popular Front was our great ally, at the beginning, but then the British, and the French right wing, forced France into the Non-Intervention Pact. And they mean it – the Non-Intervention Committee has representatives at the frontiers, making sure no weapons pass through customs. Nonetheless, we persist, the Oficina Técnica continues its work and we have another arms-buying office in New York.'

'Yes, I know, in fact I stopped by there on my last trip to the States and brought some envelopes back to Paris. Envelopes that couldn't be mailed.'

'We are grateful for your help,' Molina said.

'Is there some way the Coudert law firm can help?' Which had to be, Ferrar thought, why he was having coffee at La Galerie.

'I don't believe a law firm can help us now. It's you who can help your country . . . if Spain is still your country.'

'It is. But what would you want me to do?'

'With Castillo's death, our staff at the Oficina is weakened, they work hard but they need guidance, they need ideas, they need someone who can find a path through the swamp. Will you do that for the Republic?'

'In my heart I would like to, señor, but I cannot. I must work as a lawyer because my family depends on me. I support them; my parents, my sister, my grandmother. When the war started in '36 I spoke to friends about going off to fight, but when I suggested to my family that I might join up they were horrified. Nobody *objected*, quite the opposite. They nodded, they exchanged glances, they were silent, they were brave, and it was *that* I couldn't bear, that they would accept terrible poverty in a foreign country.'

From Molina, a subtle dip of the head, eyes for just an instant closed. *Of course I understand.*

'Perhaps now and then, if you face a particular problem, I will gladly help you. But I cannot resign from my firm in order to work at the arms office.'

'We'll take anything we can get, it's what we've done from the beginning.'

'You have my office telephone, and I will give you my number at home.'

'I should add that you might have to be, perhaps not *careful,* a better word is *aware.* Because the Soviets, for their own political reasons, want to be in control of the purchase of whatever arms we can buy. Yes, Stalin sells us armament of Russian manufacture, he likes to see photographs in the newspapers, but most of what the Russians provide is bought on the black market by operatives of the Comintern, the International Communist Party, essentially civilians of strong conviction secretly directed by the NKVD.'

Like the man with slumped shoulders in his blue overcoat. Did the Russians have him followed in New York because they *knew* he was going to be a courier for the arms-buying office? Only people in the embassy would have known what he was going to do. Tell Molina this? No. He couldn't explain why, but no.

'And I must prevail on you,' Molina said, 'to undergo a certain interview with the head of security at the embassy, Colonel Zaguan. Forgive me for this, he can be a difficult fellow, but I must observe protocol.'

'Then I will meet with him.'

'I'll have my secretary arrange the meeting, at your convenience, Señor Ferrar. And I thank you for your offer of assistance. Now, señor, will you not have a single brioche?'

Ferrar walked over to the office only to discover that Barabee had cancelled their meeting; he'd been summoned to a client's chateau in the Loire Valley – an emergency, or what the client thought was an emergency. Ferrar worked through the day, then took a taxi home to the Place Saint-Sulpice. Where he changed to a blazer and flannel trousers and then set out for a little Lyonnais place on the rue du Cherche Midi. He knew what he wanted: winter food – layers of sliced potatoes and onions cooked slowly in creamy milk, and half a roast chicken from Bresse, the best chicken in France.

Hunched over, collar up, the icy, still air burning his face, he told himself he didn't mind yet one more solitary dinner. But it wasn't true. He was lonely, he had no woman friend to take to dinner, he had no woman friend to take to bed. At the moment, anyhow – he'd had his share of love affairs in Paris, some of them exciting. He sometimes thought about Eileen Moore, but he saw her only at long intervals and that wouldn't change. They might be happy together, he believed, but he could not move to New York and Eileen, uprooted from her Manhattan life, would in Paris be lost among strangers. She surely had amours of her own and he sensed that she liked the arrangement they had.

He reached the restaurant, its windows opaque with steam, and was greeted affectionately; they knew him here. Chez Lucette had only twelve tables; the husband and wife cooked, the daughter served. As dinner companion, Ferrar had brought along a copy of *Le Soir,* not that he would read it, he simply found staring at a newspaper preferable to staring at a wall. He had an *oeuf dur mayonnaise* to start, then the *pommes lyonnaise* and *poulet de Bresse* arrived, accompanied by a carafe of red wine. The dinner was, as always, very good, and he ate slowly, taking care to enjoy it. Looking up for a moment, he discovered another solitary diner, a woman at a table across the room. She had light brown hair, almost blonde, falling in soft waves from a tilted black beret, and, he saw, had brought her own reading, a magazine. As Ferrar stared at her she looked up and their eyes met. Then unmet.

The French had a very sensible theory that the office and the dinner table should be kept separate, but Ferrar could not stop himself from going back over his meeting with Molina. He had seemed genial and forthcoming, but he was a diplomat and it was his job to seem so. What was the old joke? Ferrar had to reconstruct the logic but soon enough he had it right. 'When a lady says "no" she means "maybe". When a lady says "maybe" she means "yes". But if a lady says "yes" she's no lady. When a diplomat says "yes" he means "maybe". When a diplomat says "maybe" he means "no". But if a diplomat says "no" he's no diplomat.' Ferrar wondered idly what it would be like to do what Molina did – would he be content with that kind of work? He took the last sip of wine in his glass and reached for the carafe. The woman in the black beret, he saw, was having an apple for dessert. Eyes on her magazine, she cut slices from the apple and ate them with her fingers. What was she, thirty-five? A little older? Small and fine-boned – *petite* was the word people used.

Suddenly she raised her head and caught him looking at her. She met his eyes, then, for a bare instant, an impish smile lit her face and she was gone, back to reading. Was that for him? No, she was just amused, it wasn't flirtation.

What was he doing? Oh yes, pouring wine. The carafe was made of thick, heavy glass, he supposed it would last longer that way, used and washed and used again. Now he tried to be covert, had a brief glance at her, only to discover that she had beckoned the waitress to her table. Was she asking for the bill? Yes, only the apple core was left, she was done with dinner. The waitress acknowledged the request and turned away to get the bill. *Oh well.*

As Ferrar drank from his glass, the waitress stopped, the woman said something, the waitress answered, then hurried off.

Now what? Ferrar ate a bite of potato and waited for developments. And moments later the waitress returned with a coffee. The woman in the black beret had changed her mind, she would linger awhile over coffee. Ferrar didn't want to get caught again and lowered his eyes. Lowered his eyes for a few seconds then looked up. Now he'd caught *her,* peering at him over the cup as she drank. In a small face, large eyes, dark, with long lashes. Like dogs' eyes, he thought. *What a compliment!* Mentally, he laughed at himself. But the silent laugh rose to the surface as a smile.

This time returned.

Ferrar had eaten most of his dinner, did he really want the rest? He signalled to the waitress and, when she came to the table, he looked at his watch, spread his hands in the *nothing to be done* position, and said, *'L'addition, s'il vous plaît.'*

Ferrar paid the bill, then bided his time. When the woman in the beret rose from her chair he could see all of her. She *was* petite – maybe two inches over five feet tall – but well shaped in a chocolate-brown wool dress cinched by a narrow belt. As she headed for the coat tree he followed her, arriving just as she took her overcoat off the peg. Ferrar, reaching for his coat, said, 'Cold tonight, do you have a long way home?'

'Oh, it's not all *that* far.' Her voice, low and resolute, suggested that it *was* far.

'I was thinking, there's a taxi stand a little way up Cherche Midi, I'd be happy to give you a ride home, if you like.'

'Why that is so kind of you. What if I said "yes"?'

'It would be my pleasure. My name is Cristián.'

'And I am Chantal.' She slid her arm into the sleeve of her coat, then said *'Merde!'* and made a face, pulling her arm back out of the sleeve with an oatmeal-coloured wool scarf in her hand. 'I never fail to stuff my scarf in the sleeve so I don't forget it, and I never fail to forget it's there.'

She wound the scarf around her neck, looping it over and under in the style favoured by Parisian women, put on her coat, and led him to the door. Walking towards the taxi stand she said, 'I have always liked Chez Lucette,' and went on for a time about the restaurant, puffs of steam coming from her mouth as she spoke. There *was* a taxi waiting – *thank heaven* – the driver starting the engine as they approached. Ferrar held the door open as Chantal climbed in, then went around and got in the other side. 'I live on the avenue Bourdonnais,' she said. 'Number fourteen, the far end.'

As the taxi wove its way through narrow streets, they were silent; what had gone on between them in the restaurant had been replaced by a certain tension. Outside, Paris was wintry and deserted. As the taxi neared the avenue Bourdonnais, Chantal suddenly looked at her watch, then covered her face with her hands. 'Oh I have been stupid,' she said.

'What did you do?'

'I have loaned my apartment to a friend and her lover; they had nowhere to be alone. But I said I would not be back before midnight and it's a long time until then. Perhaps we could find a café where I can wait.'

'Why not wait at my place?'

'Oh no, I . . .'

'Yes you can, why not? I have some brandy . . . I think.'

'You have already been so thoughtful, I . . .'

'Please, Chantal. I would enjoy the company.'

'Well . . .'

'Driver, a change of plans, we're going to the Place Saint-Sulpice, number five.'

The driver nodded and, as he turned into the next street, kept nodding, as though to himself: *Yes, my dear, why not wait at my place.*

*

When Ferrar had purchased his apartment, the former owner had left a few pieces of furniture and they were still there. One of them, in the room Ferrar used as a study, was a kind of love seat, called a tête-à-tête, and curved in such a way that the seats faced in opposite directions – thus a chaperoned couple could have intimate conversation. A dreadful thing, upholstered in plush velvet of a deep plum colour. Ferrar supposed it was meant to be in the middle of a large room but, having no such room, he had pushed it up against the wall, where one side functioned as a chair, while on the blocked side he'd stacked books that wouldn't fit on his shelves. Chantal sat there, Ferrar slid his reading chair over so he could face her. There *was* a living room, with a proper sofa, but it was underheated; more comfortable to settle in the study.

It turned out that Ferrar did have brandy, even brandy glasses, and as they talked and drank the atmosphere between them warmed nicely. She was a teacher, she said, at a private academy for girls up in the Sixteenth Arrondissement. Her family was from a little village in Burgundy, where her father had worked at one of the vineyards. She loved living in Paris, she went to the cinema whenever she could. Did he like the Marx Brothers? Yes? 'Grou-*sho,*' she said, the French version of Groucho, 'is such a funny man, that silly walk he does.'

His turn. He rattled on for a time, Barcelona, the law office, but the three feet between them began to feel like an abyss. Finally the conversation slowed, and threatened to stop. Ferrar was growing desperate, he wanted to see what lay beneath the wool dress. Then, coming to the rescue, Chantal stretched her arms out and said, 'I am tired of sitting, may I see the rest of your apartment?'

He showed her the tiny kitchen, then the living room where French doors led out to a narrow balcony with a waist-high balustrade of ornamental ironwork. It was meant to decorate the building's exterior but Ferrar liked to have a cigarette out there on warm nights. 'Would you care for a breath of fresh air?' he said.

He opened the French doors, stepped out on the balcony, then took her hand to help her over the three-inch threshold. They stood side by side and, because Ferrar's apartment was on the fifth floor, looked out over the rooftops of the city. 'It is so beautiful,' she said.

'Paris,' he said.

The cold night reached them, Ferrar put his arm around her and she leaned against him and said, 'That's better.' When he pressed gently on her shoulder she turned to face him and they kissed. A formal kiss, nothing fancy, and once again. Her arms circled his waist and she held him tight, her head on his chest. What happened next was unplanned, spontaneous, Ferrar didn't think about it, simply found himself doing it. He slid a hand down the soft wool of her dress, reached under the hem, rested the hand on her leg, and after a few seconds moved it slowly up the back of her thigh, waited at the top, then continued, working his fingers beneath her panties and running his hand over the silky skin of her bare bottom. *'Tiens,'* she said, breathing hard. The word meant *well, well* – mock surprise. And now they kissed again, and this time they meant it.

The poetry of lust describes many inspirations: the moon, a stray wisp of hair; but only now and then cites *haven't done it for a long time*. Thus Chantal and Cristián, heading for the bedroom in a hurry – he barely remembered to close the French doors. Once there, she started to undress, until he said, 'Could I do that? I really like it.' She let her arms hang down, eyes closed, a sweet smile on her face, as he did his awkward best at stripping her naked. That done, she turned slowly in a pirouette so he could look at her. Then she took his clothes off, much better at this game than he was, and they got into bed. Where she asked him, voice tightening with anticipation, to lie on his back.

Greedily she pushed his knees apart, getting him out of her way, and took him in her mouth, thumb on the bottom, two fingers on top. Ferrar felt both a rush of pleasure and a stab of anxiety; if this continued he wouldn't last long. A ten-second lover? Oh no, not that. He believed in foreplay and lots of it, but she had other things in mind. Sensing his predicament, she let him go, lay on top of him, and whispered in his ear, 'Let me have my way.' Well, all right, chivalry took many forms. And, after a Gitane, he had his way with her: low moans that grew louder and longer, then a sharp gasp.

They talked. She had been married for a time, 'but he went away.' He too had been married, a disastrous, fourteen-month marriage when he was twenty-two. She came from another émigré family, was very seductive and sexy until the wedding night, when she froze. And, despite all the patience and tenderness he could muster, stayed frozen. Eventually they divorced, he heard that she had re-married, he wished her nothing but happiness, perhaps he'd just been the wrong man for her.

They were quiet for a bit, then she said, 'There is something I should confess, Cristián, I hope you will forgive me.'

'Oh?'

'I lied to you in the taxi.'

'You did?'

'There was no friend who needed a place to make love. I live with my sister and we share a bedroom. I knew you wanted me, and I surely wanted you, so I made up a story, trying to get you to take me back here.'

'I am glad you did it.'

'Yes? I was afraid you'd tell me I'd been a bad girl.'

In the darkness, their eyes met once again, and the night went on.

At seven in the morning he walked her across the square to the taxi stand by the rue Bonaparte. The January dawn was just arriving, two angry red streaks across black clouds. 'Will you have time to change?' he said.

'Just, if I'm quick about it, I don't teach until nine. Of course, I should have spent last night correcting homework.'

'They won't mind, will they?'

'I think not,' she said. Then gave a single snort of laughter and said, 'Maybe I will tell them exactly how I passed the evening – just to see the looks on their angelic little faces.'

They reached the centre of the square, and a flock of pigeons, which had been feeding on baguette crumbs, took off into the sky.

'Cristián?'

'Yes?'

'You're not involved in that horrible war in Spain, are you?'

He shook his head. 'I'm not. Why do you ask?'

'I don't know why. Since you told me you were Spanish I've been wondering about it.'

'*All* the time?'

'Don't tease me, I am someone who worries. And it's a frightening war . . . those awful scenes in the newsreels.'

'It is very bad. There is nothing worse than a civil war. In time they stop fighting and someone declares victory, but a civil war never ends.'

When they reached the taxi stand he said, 'What is a good time to telephone?'

'These days I don't get home until seven – I'm directing the school play.'

'Then I will call after seven.'

He held the taxi door for her, they kissed goodbye, one cheek then the other, and she climbed into the back seat. As the taxi chugged off he waited until it turned the corner. Heading back to his apartment he thought, *Should I have told her the truth?* Because he was in fact going to involve himself in 'that horrible war', at least on what he put to himself as *the Paris Front*. Surely not dangerous, yet still he had lied, had known it was wiser to lie. This bothered him and ruined his walk across the square.

11 January, 1938. His appointment with the head of security at the embassy, Colonel Zaguan, had been set for six in the evening, after work on a normal day. The Spanish embassy, on the avenue George V, had been the grandest of mansions, all columns and turrets in pale stone, given to Spain as a gift by King Alfonso XIII before his abdication in 1931. An embassy clerk took him upstairs, knocked at a door with no number or title on it, then led him into the office.

Colonel Zaguan, in military uniform, rose from his chair, addressed him as *señor*, and thanked him for coming. The colonel had a narrow face, cheeks lightly pitted, and small, quick eyes – very dark, almost black, which made him look cunning – slicked-down black hair, and a thin moustache above thin lips. After Ferrar was seated, Zaguan held out a silver cigarette case and said, 'Would you care for a Ducado? I get them from Spain.'

Ferrar took one and lit it.

'I will require some information from you,' the colonel said. 'For the records . . . as a lawyer you will understand the importance of records.'

'Of course.'

'May I see your passport, señor?' Ferrar, like all the Paris émigrés, always carried his passport because the police, once they got you to say something in French, demanded to see it. And if you didn't have it with you, deportation could be fast and brutal. Clearly the colonel was aware of this.

Ferrar handed over his Spanish passport, the colonel took a fountain pen from a marble stand and began to write the details in a notebook. When he was done he laid it on his desk for a moment. Ferrar was silent. Zaguan then handed it back to him, saying, 'Sorry, I almost forgot.' After a pause for a smile he said, 'Please tell me the date of your birth, and where, and the names of your parents and other family.' Watching the colonel's eyes, Ferrar realized he was reading from a sheet of paper laid flat on top of an open desk drawer, where the person on the other side of the desk couldn't see it.

When Ferrar had finished answering the questions, Zaguan said, 'Thank you. Now, can you tell me something of your politics?'

'My politics?'

'That's right. For example, would you call yourself a communist? Or, better, would your friends call you that, if they were asked?'

'Certainly not,' Ferrar said.

'Perhaps a socialist? Or a social democrat? A conservative? What would they say, your friends?' His eyebrows rose and he made a soft, interrogatory sound.

'I don't know what my friends would say, Colonel. I believe in parliamentary democracy, as practised in France and Great Britain, and I am an anti-fascist. But I don't spend much time on politics.'

The pen scratched as Zaguan wrote down his answer. 'And are you married?'

'I was, I'm not now.'

The colonel was eager for Ferrar to elaborate, but Ferrar had nothing further to say.

'Are you a Catholic, señor?'

'I am.'

'Observant?'

'Yes, I go to mass with my family on Sunday mornings.'

Zaguan moved on to Ferrar's schooling, then his work. As the questioning went on and on, Ferrar's answers grew shorter and less informative.

Zaguan, a sympathetic lilt to his voice, said, 'I know it's a bother to give out all this information, but we need to know the backgrounds of the people who work with us. In Europe, these days, there are those who, *misrepresent* themselves.'

Ferrar nodded.

'Since you will be working with the Oficina Técnica, you will be learning, ahh, sensitive information. I know I don't have to tell you that you must not talk about what you do. Yes? You agree?'

'I do.'

'And I must warn you that you may be approached, in all sorts of clever ways, by people who wish to learn what they ought not to know. Should something seem not quite right to you, it would be best to report this to me. And only to me.'

'I will keep that in mind,' Ferrar said.

Zaguan didn't like the answer, but could not counter. 'In addition,' he said, 'if you happen to discover information which might be of use to the Republic, please don't hesitate to inform me. Even the smallest detail may turn out to matter a great deal.'

Ferrar nodded. The colonel wrote something in his notebook.

'I'm sure you are tired after a long day, Señor Ferrar, so I will thank you for your patience. And, in the future, we may visit again, from time to time, just to make sure everything is going well.'

They said goodbye. Ferrar, once out on the avenue, took a deep breath. What had Molina called the colonel? *A difficult fellow.* He was certainly that. And he'd been, Ferrar sensed, on his best behaviour.

NATIONALIST FORCES ATTEMPT TO RETAKE TERUEL.

Thus the newspaper headlines on the morning of 17 January. At the beginning of the war, Franco and his generals had chosen to be called *Nationalists,* their war cry *Viva España,* while those who remained faithful to the elected government called themselves *the Republic* and answered their enemies with *Viva la Republica!* Such names were useful for politicians and journalists, such names were an element of the propaganda contest that always accompanies the guns, such names were weapons in what is called *political warfare*. But, in the province of Aragon that day, the warfare was not at all symbolic.

Just before dawn on 17 January, a heavy silence lay over the town of Teruel, the silence of a blizzard. A certain Captain Romar, whose company occupied the basement of the Bank of Spain building, had been ordered on a reconnaissance patrol, so he lit the stubs of a few remaining candles and prepared to distribute the last of his company's ammunition. This company had been fighting since the Army of the Republic's attack on Teruel in mid-December; back then there had been two hundred men in the company, now there were twenty-eight. Still, they had captured the town. Franco's forces had been staging counterattacks for three weeks, and had broken through the Republic's defence lines two miles outside the city. Now, battalion headquarters had told Romar, Franco's forces were about to attack the town itself.

By the flickering light of the candles, fixed in wax puddles to the lid of an ammunition box, Romar sorted bullets by calibre. The Army of the Republic, forced to buy its armaments abroad, had to use ten different calibres for their Mauser rifles, so Romar was fortunate in that his men needed only two: the standard 7mm cartridge for the Spanish-made Mauser 93s, and the 7.7mm for the Mauser 98 manufactured in Germany – the numbers indicated year of design, 1893 and 1898.

Romar separated the bullets only with difficulty, the temperature was eighteen degrees below zero and his fingers did not work well. Still, he persisted, and when he was done each man had forty-one cartridges. If they were engaged by the enemy the fight would not last long; they would have to surrender and then, a long tradition on both sides in this war, they would be shot. But, orders were orders. There were surely supplies headed in their direction, somewhere among the six hundred vehicles snowbound out on the road from Valencia to Teruel. But they would not arrive soon – four feet of snow had fallen, filling the trenches, and it continued to fall, the silence of the blizzard broken now and then by the sighing of the wind.

Romar's company had a few tins of sardines; these he decided would be shared out before they left the basement, and some of the men still had cigarettes. Romar stood, which meant he had something to say, and the men ranged around the walls of the basement turned their faces towards him. 'We will leave in twenty minutes,' he said. 'First we will eat, have a smoke, tend to our rifles. Remember, this is a reconnaissance patrol, so if we see these bastards don't shoot them, stay hidden. After we go out of the door, no talking. Quiet . . . very quiet. Questions?'

One of the men said, 'And which bastards are these?'

'The battalion commanders want to know that. They believe we face the Moors, or possibly legionnaires.' He meant Franco's Moorish mercenaries from Morocco, or members of the Spanish Legion, something like the French Foreign Legion, which Franco had expanded by emptying the prisons. At the mention of the word 'legionnaires' the man who had asked the question turned his head and spat.

Romar was well respected by his men. Two years earlier, when the war started, he'd been an eighteen-year-old mechanic at a textile mill in Barcelona and, when half the army joined up with Franco, the government had armed the trade unions, creating anarchist and socialist militias, who worked out their political differences by shooting each other. Now the government had absorbed the militias into the army, and some of the militiamen, like Romar, turned out to be natural officers who led well.

Outside, the main street of Teruel lay in ruins. A month of artillery fire and bombing had smashed the buildings into piles of bricks. There was no trace of wooden beams or furniture, every scrap of wood in Teruel had been burned in fires as the soldiers attempted to stay warm, to stay alive. On both sides of the street were snow-covered stacks of frozen corpses – four thousand soldiers and civilians had tried to defend the town from the Republic's attack, now they were dead.

Romar led his company towards the western edge of Teruel – his guess was he'd find the enemy about a thousand yards beyond the town. They walked in single file, every few minutes Romar rotated the men at the head of the line, who sank in the snow up to their knees as they broke trail for the company. By the time they reached the end of the street, the company was exhausted, their faces past numbness, burning with cold. Even in the blizzard the darkness had begun to wane as the dawn arrived.

Then, from the southwest, a muffled boom. '*Mierda*,' Romar said under his breath. This was, he suspected, Italian artillery, one of Mussolini's contributions to the fascist cause. There was another report, and another, as the barrage progressed. Which way was it walking? In the distance, the snow exploded and Romar called out 'Down!' The men lay flat for a time, but that was as much as they saw – the barrage continued for twenty minutes, then stopped. The men were, for the moment, safe, but the barrage was likely being used to soften up the defenders for an advance by infantry, so the counterattack was real.

The company walked for another ten minutes and then, as the forest on the edge of town came into view, Romar signalled and again they went flat. That's where the enemy would be hiding. Of course Romar could barely see the forest through the swirling snow, to him it was more like a grey shadow. For a time, he waited to see what might come out of the tree line. Another barrage started up, this one well away to the north. Romar was about to wave his men forward when a soldier came running from the forest. One of Romar's men fired twice but the man kept running, then he was joined by others, struggling through the snow, some falling then getting up, some had thrown away their rifles.

Romar held up a hand, *stop firing*. For this was not an advance by the Moors or the Legion, and this was not an organized retreat

– this was headlong flight in panic. One of the running soldiers saw Romar's company and waved violently, *go back,* then called out, 'Get away! Save yourselves!' Romar's company stayed where it was as the last men in flight disappeared in the direction of the town. Then they saw a group of men in Moroccan caps, rifles ready, move out of the trees. The company fired a salvo of rifle bullets, two of the Moorish soldiers fell, the remainder melted back into the forest.

Romar's company had stayed too long, there was no possibility they could retreat back to Teruel, they moved too slowly in the snow and the Moorish troops would shoot them in the back. So Romar led the company to one side, south of west, then forward into the forest, on the flank – Romar calculated – of the attacking Moors. They could hear gunfire, the Moors shooting at the retreating soldiers, and shouted orders, but they could see nothing. Then they heard the hammering of a heavy machine gun. Romar tried to figure out where it was, then saw a yellow muzzle flash through the trees.

Romar chose two of his men and the three of them, moving from tree to tree, crawled forward towards the machine gun, its position revealed by muzzle flares. Romar moved closer, the machine gun halted briefly as the gunners changed belts, Romar stood, leaned against the side of a tree, and fired four shots. When there was return fire from among the trees, one of his men cried out. Romar, bent double, went towards him at a half-run, the best he could manage. He could hear himself breathing, hoarse and panting with effort. He reached his soldier, wiped snow and blood from his face, and saw that he was still alive, his chest rising and falling as he fought for air. Romar took him by the collar and dragged him through the snow. When he reached his other soldier, the man knelt for a moment and said, 'He is gone, Captain.'

They left him there and made their way back to where they thought the rest of the company was hiding, though there was little chance they would be able to find them. As Romar stumbled forward, the boughs of the pine trees released showers of snow. He was about to give up when he heard a low whistle – one of his soldiers had seen them. He counted the men, a corporal had been shot in the foot and leaned on the shoulder of another man.

Romar led them south for a half-hour, exhausted now, they moved slower and slower but did not stop. By eight in the morning Captain Romar's company had reached the town of Teruel and the Bank of Spain basement. From there he contacted battalion command by field telephone and reported the action. The soldiers took off the wounded man's shoe and bound his foot with strips of rags. That was all they could do.

According to battalion command, the Moorish attack had been stopped. A counterattack was planned for noon. 'We are down to twenty rounds a man,' Romar told the officer on the other end of the field telephone. 'You'll have to do the best you can' was the answer. 'Until the supply trucks can reach us.'

8 February. Ferrar was at work when the diplomat Molina telephoned from the embassy. 'Would you be able to stop by the Oficina Técnica this evening? About seven or so? There's a fellow there I'd like you to meet, he's just recently returned to Paris. The office is at 57, avenue George V, two doors down from the embassy.'

'I'll be there at seven,' Ferrar said.

'He's called Max de Lyon, the fellow you're going to meet.'

A few minutes before seven, Ferrar rang the bell beside a gate in the high iron railing that ran between the pavement and the entry to the building. A porter let him in and told him that the Oficina Técnica was at the end of the corridor on the third floor. Ferrar knocked on the door, the man who answered said, 'Are you Señor Ferrar?' He spoke French with just the bare hint of an accent that Ferrar could not identify. *Slavic, perhaps,* Ferrar thought.

'I am,' Ferrar said.

'Pleased to meet you, I am Max de Lyon.' Something about the way he announced himself suggested *the* Max de Lyon. De Lyon led him to a small office with a desk, a table, wooden filing cabinets, two telephones, and a few chairs, with a window that looked out on a courtyard. The office was dark, illuminated only by lights in windows above the courtyard. De Lyon turned on a small desk lamp, its beam falling on the desk, so that the first time Ferrar was able to study him he was in shadow. 'Do you know who I am?' de Lyon said.

'Forgive me, Monsieur de Lyon, but I have no idea. Should I know?'

De Lyon shrugged and said, 'Well, in my time I have been mentioned in the newspapers. Not in the most flattering way, I regret to add.'

De Lyon reached into his jacket pocket, withdrew a long cigarette in a dark brown wrapper leaf, and lit it with a brass lighter designed to work in the wind. De Lyon had a still face and hooded eyes – narrow and low-lidded with a faint downward slant – that were at once amused and threatening. The world had conspired against him but he had, successfully, fought it off and would again. The gaze in those eyes was conventionally known as *penetrating* – they read deep, they knew who you were. For the rest, he was fifty or so, with a receding line of dark hair, a small, compact body, and had on a very good tweed jacket, casual and loose fitting, a jacket that got better over time. Worn with a broad, black wool tie, it suggested a life among landed gentry. Could he be an aristocrat?

When de Lyon looked up from lighting his cigarette, he said, 'I have been called an arms merchant, and various other things, some of them correct.'

'And are you an arms merchant?'

'I was. A small-time trader who knew some of the right people. It's not a healthy way to earn your living, I don't recommend it. Also, certain righteous people don't care for you.'

'I am a lawyer, monsieur, some people don't like lawyers.'

'True' – that ghost on de Lyon's lips could have been taken for a smile – 'until you need one.'

'People who've been on the wrong end of a lawyer, the business end, don't like them,' Ferrar said. 'On the other hand, it's better than a duel at dawn, which is the way disputes used to be settled. For me, it is the way I make a living, and I am blessed to work for ethical people.'

'I know the firm,' de Lyon said. 'They do good when they can. By the way, may I offer you one of these?' He held the cigarette between the ends of his index and middle fingers, thumb beneath the smoker's end, and now extended his hand so Ferrar could see it. 'I have them made for me at a shop in Istanbul – if you enjoy *very* strong black tobacco you might like them.'

'Thank you,' Ferrar said, in a voice that meant *no, thank you.* 'I'll have a Gitane.'

Ferrar took a cigarette from his packet, de Lyon said, 'Allow me,' flipped up the lid atop the lighter and produced a loud *snick* and a flame. De Lyon then settled back in his chair and said, 'Now, Señor Ferrar, if you don't mind a personal question, can you tell me what you're doing here?' The question was courteous, but there was a jovial, unstated *the hell* after the *what.*

'The basic reason is that I was asked. Señor Molina requested my assistance, so I'm going to do whatever I can to help.'

'To fight Franco?'

'To fight Franco, to fight them all; Hitler, and those who aspire to be Hitlers . . . I don't mean to give a speech but the subject forces you to, doesn't it?'

Slowly, de Lyon nodded. 'We're going to have a Nazi Europe, I fear, which won't be good for either of us. And for a lot of other people.'

'And nothing can be done?'

'Did I say that?'

'You did not, but it's often the next thing that's said.'

From de Lyon, a dry laugh. Then, 'True. And if the time comes when the phrase *to fight* turns into *to fight back,* it will by that time be too late.'

'Are you French, Monsieur de Lyon?'

'By inclination, I am. But I carry a Swiss passport. Useful, these days.'

'And very difficult to get, unless you are born there.'

'That's the reputation, but if you understand the Swiss, maybe not so difficult. Their officials like to be seen as stern and unyielding, chronic rule followers, but, if you can *do* something for them, they will give you whatever they need to.'

'And that's what you did.'

'Made sure to do. I had a taste of life as a "stateless person", not a pleasant way to live, all kinds of civil servants will torment you, not to mention the police, because to be stateless is somehow a crime. For me, I made the mistake of being born in a little ghetto village in what was sometimes Russia, though it isn't now, with no record of my birth.'

'You are Jewish?'

'Some of my ancestry was, some not. My mother died when I was seven, I was then raised on an estate in Poland, not welcomed, tolerated as the result of a youthful indiscretion. I left there when I was fourteen and have been looking after myself ever since.'

'You appear to have survived it.'

De Lyon nodded. 'You grow up quickly, or not at all.' He was quiet for a moment, then said, 'Speaking of "stateless persons", I'm sure you're aware of your own situation.'

'How so?'

'You carry a Spanish passport?'

'I do.'

'If Franco wins this war, some members of the Spanish émigré community will still be considered as enemies. Especially those known to have worked for the Republic and against Franco. They already have a list, of course, with new names added as they are discovered. For example, working with this office is likely to land you on the list, and I doubt a victorious Franco Spain would renew your passport. And *that* will mean your name would appear on a *French* list too. I believe resident-alien status has to be renewed, not so?'

'Yes, it does. How can you be so sure my name will be on their list?'

'There are some people in this embassy who work secretly for the other side. And Franco maintains a considerable spy service in Paris, they may have watched you enter the building.'

'Well, there's not much I can do about their list. As for my legal status, in an emergency my law firm would help me get American citizenship, we already work with clients who have nationality problems and in some cases we do that without charge.'

'Then you will be safe. Still, I tell you all this by way of saying that I won't think badly of you if, on reflection, you wish to make use of the door.'

Ferrar's reply was gentle but firm. 'No, I said I would try to help, and I tend to keep my word.'

'Very well, a trait I admire. Would you like to see what you are getting yourself into?'

'I might as well.' He paused, then said, 'Are you the director of the Oficina Técnica?'

De Lyon was amused. 'I believe they pay me as a technical consultant. But there is a nominal director, a diplomat who has served this embassy for thirty years, he has on his desk an in-tray, and an out-tray, and every day he moves papers from one to the other. He *does* process payment vouchers when I ask him to, you will be shocked to learn the amount of money that flows through this office. Now, to get you into trouble as soon as possible, would you care to join me at eleven this evening? A visit to a nightclub?'

'Where shall we meet?'

'I'll pick you up at eleven, if you'll tell me where you live.'

Ferrar gave de Lyon his address. 'I'll be in front of the building,' he said.

*

Ferrar heard de Lyon coming before he caught sight of him. From one of the streets that ran downhill to the Place Saint-Sulpice came the fierce whine of a small, powerful engine, which paused for a growl as the driver used a gear change instead of the brakes, then whined again, the sound echoing off the church on the square. De Lyon pulled up in a British two-seater, a blue sports car with a soft top and a leather strap across the hood. Ferrar folded himself into the passenger seat, de Lyon said good evening, then put the car into first gear and away they flew. 'Do you like it?' de Lyon shouted over the engine.

'Yes. What is it?'

'What?'

'*What is it?*'

'Oh, a Morgan.'

Ferrar had wanted to ask where they were going but there was no hope of that. Cold as hell on a February night, Ferrar thought, but a fine way to see Paris. Zooming past taxis and street-cleaning tanker trucks, the Morgan wove through the Sixth, crossed the Seine, followed the shabby edge of the First Arrondissement to a neighbourhood of crumbling tenements next to the Les Halles market, then was briefly on the rue Saint-Denis, where the strolling prostitutes just *loved* the sports car and its occupants, waving and calling out to them – juicy sentiments no doubt, but inaudible. De Lyon made a left and, a street or two later, turned into the rue du Cygne, where a giant doorman with gold epaulets on his uniform put two fingers to his cap as de Lyon and Ferrar struggled out of the car. A discreet sign by the door said LE CYGNE, the Swan, a nightclub named for its address.

Inside the door, a maître d' in a tuxedo said, with just a sugges-tion of a bow, 'Good evening, Monsieur de Lyon. Your usual table?' He then led them downstairs, whipped the RÉSERVÉ sign off a table by the wall, and bowed once more, clearly pleased with whatever de Lyon put in his hand. Very chic, Le Cygne; an Art Deco room, the floor in glossy black and white tile, walls painted black, indirect lighting – the lights hidden in a cornice at the edge of the ceiling – and black-lacquered tables. On a bandstand at the far end of the room, a quartet – guitar, violin, bass, and drums – was just getting ready to perform. A waiter appeared, de Lyon ordered champagne. 'They may have something else,' he said, 'but I've never seen it.'

The quartet began to play, a rendition of 'Nuages' in the Django Reinhardt style, as patrons flocked to the cleared area and began to dance. Very highly dressed patrons, some of the women with daring necklines, others in backless gowns. One of the latter was dancing with a man in a tarboosh – the round, red, Middle Eastern hat with a tassel – who wore dark sunglasses. De Lyon saw what Ferrar was looking at and said, 'He's here every night, known as "the Lebanese".' The Lebanese danced beautifully, with clever feet, three fingertips resting low on the bare back of his partner.

As the champagne arrived and the waiter used a linen napkin to open the bottle, Ferrar said, 'Do you know these people, Max?'

'Oh, it's the usual crowd. Parisians of the better class, criminals, swindlers, nouveaux riches from the western suburbs, a spy or two. What you find in a nightclub in this city – at least a nightclub like Le Cygne. Do you see that woman in green, sitting by the bandstand?'

It took some time, then Ferrar said, 'Wearing a kind of oriental tunic, with a high neck? And pearl earrings?'

'That's her.'

Ferrar studied the woman and said, 'An aristocrat, if I had to guess.'

De Lyon nodded and drank some champagne. 'The most perfect bearing, the way she holds herself tells the world she is far above them, and the most perfect manners, she condescends to no one. You should hear her *voice,* low and seductive, and she speaks this educated Parisian French, it's like music.'

'You know her, then.'

'Yes, in a professional way. She is one of the great madams of this city.'

'No! Really? Her? She keeps a brothel?'

De Lyon laughed. 'No, no, my friend, nothing of the kind. But she will arrange, for a breathtaking amount of money, a rendez-vous with a lovely upper-class woman who must pay her dress-maker. The money goes to Angélique over there, and she pays her friend. And then, what happens . . . happens, though one mustn't be too much of a snorting pig, unless the lady wishes it.'

'A service you use?' Ferrar said.

'Not personally, I don't like to pay to make love, but it's one of the, umm, *inducements* I can provide for a business associate.' After a moment he said, 'Would you care to indulge? I will arrange it.'

'No, I like love affairs, a woman's desire is the best aphrodisiac.'

De Lyon raised his glass and they drank to desire.

As midnight approached, a short, swarthy bear of a man came grinning towards the table. He was almost bald, strands of hair oiled to his scalp, wore a baggy, grey silk suit over a black shirt with open collar, and a mist of powerful cologne. He had, on one arm, a blonde in a cloche hat with a feather, on the other, a brunette in a tight, scarlet dress. When de Lyon rose to greet his guests, so did Ferrar. 'Stavros!' de Lyon said.

'Max, my friend!' said the bear.

They shook hands, then the bear put his arms around de Lyon, laughed, and smacked him twice on the shoulder. As introductions were quickly made, both women seemed a little vague, even dazed. Behind the trio came the waiter, carrying three chairs and breathing hard. When the three were seated, de Lyon caught the waiter's eye and raised two fingers and soon enough two new bottles of champagne appeared. 'So, Stavros,' de Lyon said, 'how goes our business?'

'I am close to getting what we want . . . ,' Stavros said, holding his thumb and index finger an inch apart and adding, '. . . this close.' In a deep rumble of a voice he spoke French with what Ferrar took to be a Greek accent. Not wanting to go further in front of his girlfriends, Stavros looked left and right and said, 'Girls, look what Uncle Stavros has for you.' He produced a folded paper square and pressed it into the hand of the blonde. 'Now go off to the ladies' WC and try this out. And we'll miss your pretty faces but don't be in a hurry, take your time.' He rose, pulled their chairs back, and sent them off with a big, evil grin. When they'd gone, he looked pointedly at Ferrar: *who's he?*

'Cristián is working with me,' de Lyon said. 'You can trust him.'

Stavros leaned conspiratorially across the table and said, 'I think I've found the man we want, he owns a company in Brno.'

'A Czech,' de Lyon said.

'Yes, a hungry one.'

'Who is he?'

'He's called Szarny, a big, flabby type with pink cheeks – he looks like a tuba player in an oompah band. Somehow he has got himself into money trouble, though I think he makes plenty. He's one of those solid bourgeois types who's got one big, bad fault, which he hides from everybody, especially his family. I don't know what it is, but someone like me can *smell* it: the guilty conscience. A taste for rare and special sex that's costly to buy? Does he gamble? Does he like to be . . . mistreated? You know what I mean, Max? You, Cristián?'

They knew.

'Szarny has a foundry called Brno Ironworks that's connected to the Skoda arms company. I don't know how, I don't know who owns what, but Szarny says he can deliver what we need.'

De Lyon looked over at Ferrar, meaning *can you find out?* Ferrar nodded, he could discover who owned what. De Lyon said, 'How did you find him, Stavros?'

'I have a man in Brno, where they make the Skoda anti-tank

guns. He's a confidential agent and collects information from chambermaids in hotels, barmen, maybe a cop or two, and when I asked him about Skoda he came up with Szarny.'

As an aside, de Lyon said to Ferrar, 'You know that Czechoslovakia is the leading arms exporter in Europe. They make the Panzer tank the Germans love so much.'

'I do know,' Ferrar said. People who read newspapers knew about Czechoslovakia, so beloved by Hitler. Who had stated rather clearly, if you knew how to read him, that he meant to have it. Thus the propaganda about the poor, much-abused German minority in the Sudetenlands.

'So,' Stavros said, 'Szarny has a bad case of nerves, he's so cautious on the telephone that I sometimes can't understand what the hell he's talking about. He starts calling guns bicycles, "shipping the bicycles", good, I finally figure it out. Then the next time it's lamps. I suppose he's afraid somebody's listening to his telephone, but, I mean, lamps? Skoda makes all kinds of things but lamps is one thing they don't make. If somebody *is* listening to his phone, they're laughing.

'You see, he needs the money but he's scared, goes back and forth, not now, next week. No, not next week, he has to be in Berlin. So I went down there and met him in the bad part of Brno, in a bar by a factory. I was holding a French magazine, so he could identify me, but I don't think he ever saw it, he took one look at me and his eyes got like this.' Stavros opened his eyes wide with horror and de Lyon and Ferrar laughed. Stavros had some actor in him. 'Well, who the fuck did he expect, Shirley Temple?'

'What's he worried about?' Ferrar said. 'Something in particular? Or just scared of getting caught?'

'Everything. The sale has to be approved by various Czech ministries, though he thinks he can get that done. But, because of the Non-Intervention Treaty, there has to be a country other than Spain that's supposedly buying the guns. But what he's really worried about is the bribe.'

'How much does he want?'

'A hundred thousand dollars, in British gold sovereigns.'

'A lot,' de Lyon said, 'but we always bribe when we have to.'

'He's worried about where to keep it – he says he can't keep it at home.'

'Has he heard that there are *banks*?' Ferrar said.

Stavros shrugged.

'*Swiss* banks?' de Lyon said.

Looking past Stavros's shoulder, Ferrar saw that the girlfriends had tired of the ladies' WC and were now seated at a table of eager young men. 'I think you'd better see to your friends,' he said. Stavros turned halfway around, swore in Greek, and went off to retrieve his prizes.

'He's Greek?' Ferrar said.

'Macedonian. He spent his teenage years fighting Bulgarian bandits. After that, being a gangster was easy.' De Lyon paused and said, 'What do you think about this Szarny?'

'Blackmail,' Ferrar said. 'He has to have the money in hand.'

'Yes, that's the way I see it. For what doesn't matter.'

Ferrar thought this over. 'Maybe it doesn't, but you'd be surprised at what sort of jack can jump out of the box when you open the lid. Suddenly, it *does* matter.'

Stavros was standing at the table where the strayed girlfriends had found refuge. But they wouldn't be staying there. Ferrar *really* didn't want to be involved in a nightclub brawl, but relaxed when he saw how Stavros was dealing with the problem. He had a big smile on his face, not quite a pleasant smile, but a big one. He had his arm around the shoulders of one of the eager young men, was now giving him an affectionate squeeze, and laughing. The young man's face was flushed; he was obviously terrified. Stavros then shook the hand of one of the other young men, shook it enthusiastically, couldn't bear to let go. Finally he did, then led his girlfriends back towards the table.

'Probably better,' de Lyon said, 'to stay on Stavros's good side.'

When Stavros returned to the table, he said to the blonde, 'What a funny fellow, that . . . what was his name?'

The blonde was sulking, she'd been having a good time. 'Something like, Clive.'

'Oh, *Clive*. He's English?'

'Yes, he has some sort of title. He's on holiday in Paris.'

'How nice for Clive.'

De Lyon saw that the private part of their conversation was over, and started talking about the weather. Stavros let him go on for a few minutes, then said, 'We're going to a party, let me know what you want to do – I think it's better for you to take over now that I've found our man. If he *is* our man.'

When the trio was gone, de Lyon took a notepad and a stub of pencil from his pocket. He opened the notepad to a page with numbers and letters and used the pencil as a pointer so Ferrar could follow along as he read aloud. In the background, the band was now playing 'September in the Rain'.

'Here's what we have,' de Lyon said. 'We're trying to buy the Skoda A3 thirty-seven-millimeter anti-tank gun. We'll try to get fifty of them, Skoda charges about four thousand dollars apiece. Then we want thirty-six thousand shells, which will be around three hundred thousand dollars. To this we add a hundred thousand for the bribe, and then there's the shipping. What do you think?'

'Very expensive, I had no idea.'

'A seller's market. Since 1933, and German rearmament, the competition has driven up the price. Do you know what an anti-tank gun looks like?'

'I don't think I've ever seen one . . . maybe in a newsreel.'

'It's a small cannon, the barrel is five feet long, half of it extended through an iron shield, and it moves on wheels with wooden spokes. It looks like something from the 1914 war, or earlier. But it works, fires twelve shells a minute and penetrates an inch and a half of plate armour at a thousand yards. Any questions?'

'No.'

'Now, the problem here is the bribe. If we can't use a bank transfer, we'll have to take the money down to Brno ourselves. Are you able to do that, Cristián?'

Ferrar thought about it, and at last answered. 'I'm not sure I can, but I'll try.'

At the Coudert office, the following morning, Ferrar met with George Barabee. They were still working on the Polanyi case, nominally a dispute over three vizsla dogs, but in fact a reach for power by a deceased shareholder's son, who wanted a full share in the holding company that owned a private bank in Budapest. To do that, he would have to force his sister, who he hated, to give up her half share. Ferrar wondered aloud if they could negotiate with the male heir. 'At the moment, we represent all the shareholders, but if the male heir insists on his right to freeze the operation of the company, we will represent the two uncles and the sister. And then, we'll go to court.'

Barabee made notes as Ferrar spoke, nodding in agreement as he wrote. When Ferrar was done, Barabee said, 'A good lawyer will usually counsel a client against litigation, so let's sit down with the nephew and ask him if he will accept a settlement. And we can suggest, just to help him in the direction we want him to go, that being forced to defend himself in court could be a long and expensive ordeal. We can't lean too hard, but there are family lawsuits in France that have gone on for years. Years and years. And then, we should point out to him that we'll try to remove him from the holding company. "You've been a bad boy, junior, so no money for you. You'll have to go to work." Now, Cristián, how do we go about suing him?'

'Under French law, he's entitled to vote as a shareholder, he is *not* entitled to damage the corporation, the holding company. He is, in fact, obligated to act for the *benefit* of the corporation, he cannot simply abstain. And if he holds to his strategy of freezing the corporation, he is then guilty of what in French law is called "waste of corporate assets".'

'You say "under French law". It's my understanding that the nephew lives in Budapest. How do we sue him in France?'

'I'll have to talk to Count Polanyi about that because we'll need his cooperation. Junior, as you call him, will have to be induced to come to France, where he'll be served with process. I don't think we want to be involved with confidential agents – private detectives, that can become a nightmare very quickly. It's the family who will have to do the work, and Polanyi will know how. He's a diplomat at the Hungarian legation here, but there are rumours about his being involved with espionage. So, he's just right for something like this.'

'Good, Cristián. Go ahead and contact Polanyi, tell him what we propose, and, if he agrees, you get in touch with junior, by telephone, and have a talk.'

Barabee was done with the meeting, but Ferrar made no move to leave the office and Barabee said, 'Is there something else?'

'There is,' Ferrar said, lighting a cigarette. He went on to explain about Castillo's disappearance and probable death, Molina's request, and his agreement to work with the Oficina Técnica as an unpaid, and unofficial, consultant. 'What I had in mind,' Ferrar said, 'was the occasional telephone call or meeting, all of it after work or on the weekend.'

'Generous of you, Cristián. They get good legal advice, which has to be helpful – arms purchasing must have substantial grey areas. Very grey, now that I think about it.'

'I will give them legal advice, if they ask for it, but that's not what I'm there for.'

'You're not?'

'I'm there to aid in buying armament.'

Barabee's expression was a veiled, lawyerly version of *you're doing what?*

'I've just begun working with one of the people in the arms office, the man who actually gets the job done. We talked for a long time last night and he wants my help with a particular purchase for the Republic, and that would mean I have to travel to Brno and spend a day or two there.'

Barabee was silent, absorbing what Ferrar had told him. As he did so, a certain look appeared on his face, not horror, but a quizzical expression that sometimes precedes it. At last he said, 'Brno as in Skoda arms?'

'Yes.'

'OK, you're going to Brno to buy guns?'

'I intend to, if the office can spare me for a few days.'

'Official, legal gun buying?'

'Buying the guns will be legal, moving them to Spain is forbidden by the Non-Intervention Pact, which Czechoslovakia has signed, so we have to persuade the Czech administration they're going elsewhere.'

'I had no idea you knew anything about weapons.'

'I don't.'

'Then why you?'

'They need to call on people, professional people like me, to help them in a time of crisis. The previous incumbent was a gynaecologist.'

Barabee shook his head. 'Cristián, lawyers are not supposed to engage in illegal activities. This could blow up in your face.'

'I know. For example, it's illegal to use false documents, just as illegal as helping Jews in flight to cross borders with faked papers.'

From Barabee, a smile. 'You're a good lawyer, Cristián.' Then he picked up a pencil and tapped the eraser on the top of his desk. Finally he said, 'Well, you're lucky in one way. The lawyers in New York, and I mean the senior partners, are active in politics, they take that as a moral obligation. Fred Coudert, who runs the law firm, made great effort – speeches, private dinners, articles in journals, lawyers' committees – to have the US join the League of Nations and the world court in The Hague. As you know, it couldn't be done. Isolationism, especially in Congress, killed any chance of membership. And the firm hasn't changed, most of the partners are active in support of FDR, who would sell guns to Spain if he could. Truth is, ideologues are not popular on Rector Street; Hitler, Stalin, now Franco. So what you want to do, basically on your own time, may not be at all disagreeable to the partners, as long as the firm doesn't get a black eye.'

'Thank you, George.'

'Don't thank me yet, later today I have to call Fred, and then we'll see. But when I talk to him I want to tell him that I have your agreement, your commitment, in one area; under no circumstances can you involve this law firm, or Coudert clients, in what you're doing. Do you agree?'

'I do. You have my word.'

Barabee grew reflective, looked out of the window for a time, then said, 'You know I flew fighter planes for the American Expeditionary Force in 1917. I was a lot younger, but I believe I felt a lot like you do now. If you believe in something, you have to fight for it.'

By four-thirty that afternoon, Ferrar had his answer. Fred Coudert had agreed to let him do what he'd described to Barabee. 'He said you could take time off, and do what you have to do. We'll consider it a form of public service, the 1938 version of public service. He is also concerned, not so much about what you want to do – he knows we have to fight fascism – but about your personal safety. He likes you, Cristián, he always has.'

Now Ferrar could say thank you.

That evening Ferrar was to go out to Louveciennes to have dinner with his family. He had bought them a house there – they all liked the little town on the Seine, which had lively restaurants with dance floors built above the bank of the river. It wasn't far, twenty miles from the city, and Parisians went out there in summer to have a good time. Boating. Picnics. It was a pretty place, the Impressionists had painted the very devil out of it, inspired by the long winding lanes between rows of poplars that led away from the town into the countryside. The house, built in 1830, was two storeys high, with walls of grey stucco, tall shutters weathered grey at every window, and a roof of dark slate shingles. Ferrar liked the slate shingles, but the slate shingles didn't like Ferrar. A cunning, spiteful house it was, constantly needing money for repairs. The shingles cracked, the cellar flooded, Ferrar paid.

He left the apartment at six-thirty. At the foot of the stairway was a miniature lobby where the tenants had their mailboxes; there were four beside Ferrar's, and one for the concierge. As Ferrar came down the last steps, he saw a woman wearing a toggle coat and a soft, peaked cap, a fashionable version of the caps that workers actually wore. She was bent over, using the light of a match to peer at the names on the mailboxes, and when Ferrar appeared she straightened up and blew out the match. Thus Ferrar had only the briefest look at her face in the dark lobby.

'May I help you, madame?' he said.

'I am looking for a Monsieur Leblanc.'

'I'm sorry, madame, there is no one by that name who lives here.'

She blew the little puff of air which served as a sound of frustration for French women. 'I must have the wrong address,' she said. 'Anyhow, thank you, monsieur.' And then she was out the door.

Ferrar caught a taxi for the ride to Louveciennes, and asked the driver to stop at the Spanish pastry shop next to what was known as 'the Spanish church' up on the rue de la Pompe in the Sixteenth, itself fancy, but nothing compared to the luxurious enclave called Passy. At one time, pastries in Spain had been baked and sold at convents, so the names of the little treats came from those days.

Ferrar bought *huesos de santo,* saints' bones; *tetas de novicias,* novice nuns' breasts; and *suspiros de monja,* nuns' sighs. All were soft and thick, and liberally dusted with granulated sugar. Spaniards weren't alone in this. French patisseries offered *la religieuse,* the nun, a large, chocolate-capped puff pastry on the bottom, with a smaller version in the middle, and a little one on top, for the head. Or you could just buy a dozen of the little ones, known as *pets-de-nonne,* nun farts. The young girl behind the counter wrapped the pastries artfully, in pink paper folded into a triangle, then tied with a ribbon which was looped at the end so you could carry the package with one finger.

The family was waiting for him at the house in Louveciennes. His two brothers had long ago emigrated to South America, so the house was occupied by his mother and father, his pious sister Caridad, the spinster cousin who'd been taken in years ago and had been part of the family ever since, and his grandmother, Abuela. She was seventy-seven, stood straight as a rod, wore her ample white hair twisted into a braid, then wound into a bun, and had Ferrar's very own deep green eyes. As they drank a glass of sherry before dinner, Abuela came over and sat next to him on the couch. 'So, Cristián, dear one, what happens with you these days?'

'Life goes on, Abuela. I work hard, and enjoy myself when I can.'

'Nothing new, then, dear one?'

'Not much, I'm afraid.'

'Oh, very well, I simply wondered . . .'

She was, when it came to her grandson, close to psychic, and had sensed he was up to something. She patted his hand, then let her hand rest atop his. 'I worry too much about you,' she said, 'in these bad times.'

Two years earlier, when the war started and Ferrar had considered joining up, she had accepted, seemed to accept, what he wanted to do. Later, when he realized that he couldn't abandon his family to poverty, she'd taken him aside and said, 'Dear one, *listen* to me, do not be tempted by the war, do not give up your life to this bullshit.'

There was plenty to eat; lentil soup, a *céleri rémoulade* – shreds of celeriac root swimming in handmade mayonnaise – pork cutlets, and then pastries. Eating his pastry with caution lest the granulated sugar sprinkle his tie, Ferrar's father said, 'Things are looking up, Cristián. The railroad bonds continue to pay, and I have managed to purchase quite a valuable stamp. From Togo, easily worth four times what I paid for it.' Three days a week, he took the train into Paris and spent hours at the stamp market on the avenue Marigny, hunting for bargains and gossiping with other collectors and the stamp dealers. This was as much of a job as he had and, though he pretended to be content with his life, it hurt him deeply that he could not support his family. Yes, there *were* South American railroad bonds, inherited years earlier from a wealthy relative, which paid a small amount quarterly. Not enough to live on, not nearly, but helpful at the end of the month when funds ran low.

After coffee, Ferrar's sister Caridad, gold cross around her neck, led him upstairs to her tiny room, where a crack ran diagonally across one corner of the ceiling. 'This poor house . . .' she said. 'I love it so but, as you see . . .'

Ferrar smoothed her hair and said, 'Do not worry, Caridad, tell Abuela I said to call someone who can fix it.'

And, it turned out, the spinster cousin, who knitted the family's winter sweaters, needed new glasses.

None of this mattered to Ferrar, the visit had warmed his heart. And he stared out of the taxi window on the way back to Paris and wondered if he'd been foolish to take on his new work.

Max de Lyon called him the following day, could Ferrar meet with him after work?

'I'll come over around six, six-thirty maybe,' Ferrar said.

'Why don't we have a drink? At the big brasserie on the rue

Marbeuf, you know the one? It's just down the boulevard from you.'

Ferrar said he did and at six-twenty he left work and headed down the Champs-Elysées. De Lyon was waiting for him at the bar, drinking a large draft beer. It looked good to Ferrar so he ordered one for himself. 'I have some news,' de Lyon said. 'Our friend in Brno has agreed to a meeting.'

'When will that be?' Ferrar said.

'Perhaps next week. The meeting is in Berlin, he's afraid he'll be seen with us in Brno and that people will wonder about it.'

'Then we'll go to Berlin,' Ferrar said. 'I've been there a few times, on business.'

'We'll have to be careful,' de Lyon said.

'I would say so. Everyone spies on everyone else.'

'Also, I ought to tell you, we're not here because I wanted a drink. We're here because someone has been poking around in my office, in my files.'

'You have a way of knowing that?'

'I do. And I'll show you, if you like.'

'Well . . .' Ferrar had started to say, *why would I need that,* but then he didn't. He said, 'Why not?'

De Lyon looked at his watch. 'Forgive me, but I'm a little pressed this evening.' He reached for a briefcase at his feet, unbuckled the straps, and brought out a manila envelope. 'A present for you,' he said. Ferrar took the envelope, which was unexpectedly heavy and had a bulge at one end. When Ferrar started to unwind the string that held the flap down, de Lyon said, 'Not in here. Later, when you're alone.'

But Ferrar didn't need to open the envelope, the bulge in his hand was a small automatic pistol.

'Have you fired one of these?'

Ferrar shook his head.

'There's a gun dealer at the lower end of the rue Saint-Antoine, by the furniture factories, it's called J. Romault. He has a firing range behind the store, he'll show you what you need to know and he'll sell you ammunition. Then you can practise on the range.' De Lyon waited to see if Ferrar had any questions, then said, 'It's a good weapon, a Walther PPK, and well used.'

'By you?'

De Lyon laughed. 'Nooo, not me. I doubt very much you'll need it but, if you do, you'll be glad to have it.'

'Thank you, Max. Perhaps I should pay . . .'

De Lyon held up a hand. 'As I said, a present.'

THE
ARMS
TRADER

15 FEBRUARY, 1938. THE PARIS/BERLIN NIGHT EXPRESS LEFT THE Gare du Nord at 4:08 in the afternoon and arrived at Friedrichstrasse Station at 10:32 in the morning. Eighteen hours, longer if there were delays – a snowstorm, a cow on the tracks, a fugitive apprehended at a border – but the first-class compartments in the wagon-lit cars were private and comfortable, and when you wanted to sleep you rang for a porter to convert the plush seats to upper and lower berths. Ferrar gazed out of the window as the train chugged northeast, past the local stations of northern France and Belgium, past fields white with snow tinted a cold, pale blue at dusk.

'It would be a lot easier by aeroplane,' de Lyon had explained. 'But the control at Tempelhof Airport is thorough. The Germans are very interested in travellers who have the money to fly. They are polite at Tempelhof, but determined, and if their suspicion is provoked they are known to keep you company during your visit, at a distance, to see where you go and who you meet. For us, the train is safer.'

Ferrar perfectly understood. He didn't, in the event they were searched, want to try to explain the presence of a hundred thousand dollars in one-hundred-dollar denominations. Of these, obtained at the Spanish embassy's Soviet bank in Paris, de Lyon and Ferrar each carried five hundred, in wads of banknotes disbursed in the pockets of jackets and trousers. Szarny, the Czech owner of the ironworks foundry in Brno, had demanded British gold sovereigns, the preferred currency of smugglers and secret agents, but de Lyon had said there was no chance of that. 'Four hundred and sixty-two pounds of gold coins? How? In trunks in a railroad baggage car? In a big Citroën? A big Citroën down on its springs? The German border guards will see that right away. No, we'll put the money on the table and let him walk away if he wants. He won't.' Ferrar had suggested that Szarny could take his money to the Bank of Zurich branch in Berlin and have the bank exchange it into sovereigns as he wished. 'I suspect the gold is the blackmailer's idea,' he'd said.

Ferrar didn't go to sleep, he smoked Gitanes and stared out at the passing countryside, his mind wandering here and there to the beat of the rails. He had once, long ago in his early twenties, made love in a first-class compartment, on a slow train travelling through the night in central France. He had been alone in the compartment when a woman joined him. She was Viennese, was Klara, a solid bourgeois matron returning from the marriage of her daughter in London and 'in no hurry to get home', as she put it. She was much older than he was, with fine skin, a pointy nose, and small eyes, wearing a wedding ring and a green Robin Hood hat with a feather.

She was eager to talk and sat across from him, then next to him. *How people are* was the topic of the evening, *so false* the verdict; they had, she said, desires, but, obsessed with convention, they hid their feelings and feared discovery. Wouldn't it be a better world if people revealed themselves? Did what they secretly wanted? 'I know you want to kiss me,' she said. 'What are you afraid of?' So he locked the door and they went ahead with it, his hands exploring her until he encountered a stiff and unyielding girdle. She stood, removed hat and dress, then took the waistband of the awful thing in her fists and said, suddenly self-conscious, 'Would you look away for a moment?' He did, discovering a perfect image of the dimly lit compartment in the dark window as she wriggled out of the girdle, freeing a cascade of soft, rosy flesh.

They went on from there but it was this particular image that Ferrar would forever remember. He turned it this way and that way in his imagination, then his mind drifted away to the women he'd known in his past; Eileen Moore, others. Eventually he dozed off, but the train would stop, for no apparent reason, then lurch forward, waking him up, coal smoke from the engine flavouring the air of the compartment with the smell of cinders. Ferrar knew where he was: the land of war. A few miles north and south of the tracks were the towns that had given their names to battlefields: Douai, Compiègne, Verdun, Cambrai, Sedan, Waterloo. For a long time, the track wound its way through forest, the Ardennes, the route of the German invasion in 1914. As the train clattered along the bank of the river Meuse, Ferrar could see broken sheets of ice floating on the dark water. Then, after the track curved away from the river, the engine rolled to a halt at a road crossing and two men in hats and overcoats, both carrying briefcases, got out of a Mercedes automobile and boarded the train. At five in the morning, no hint of dawn, farm trucks moved east along the road that ran by the tracks, headed for the markets of Liège.

Thirty minutes later, when Ferrar had at last fallen asleep, he woke to the conductor's rap on the door and the words 'Liège. The last stop in Belgium. Passengers must wait in the corridor for passport control. Liège.'

As they waited in the corridor, a man and a woman hurried towards the head of the line, baggage in hand, murmuring, 'Excuse us, please, we must get off here. Pardon. Pardon.' An anxious couple, Ferrar thought, deciding to end their journey in Liège, the 'last stop in Belgium', rather than enter Germany. The Belgian border guard was barely awake, his eyes heavy with sleep, a cigarette dangling from his lips as he stamped passports without bothering to look at the passengers. The anxious couple, once the guard was done with them, got off the train.

A few minutes later, Aachen Station; they had crossed the frontier into the German Reich and, had some traveller not noticed, there were numerous flags to remind him, the swastikas glowing a powerful red and black under the station lights. Through static, high-volume loudspeakers made announcements in German. Directions to waiting passengers no doubt, but the sound had its effect on Ferrar. There were uniformed officers everywhere, the SS in black, the Wehrmacht in field grey, all of them very conscious of their appearance, standing tall and straight, holstered sidearms on their heavy belts.

Two uniformed border guards, stern and hard-eyed, appeared at the end of the corridor as, passports in hand, the passengers waited to have their documents examined. The officer attending to Ferrar's papers took his time with them, looking up and down to match face and photograph, then again, and once more. His stamp remained unused. 'Herr Ferrar,' he said, 'you are a Spanish citizen, resident in France?' *Thus on the side of the Republic.*

'I am,' Ferrar said. 'I was taken to Paris as a child, in 1909.' *So not on anyone's side.*

'Ah, I see. You gentlemen are travelling together?' he said with a nod at de Lyon. It had, Ferrar realized, been a mistake not to have separated for the border control.

'We are,' de Lyon said.

The officer peered at de Lyon's passport, then looked up and said, 'And you, Herr de Lyon, are of Swiss nationality?'

'I am, sir.'

The officer, holding both passports, flapped them against his palm, did that a few times – which meant he was turning things over in his mind. Then he made his decision and said, 'Please wait here. Do either of you have luggage in the baggage car?'

Ferrar said they didn't, they each carried a small valise and a briefcase. When the officer left the car, Ferrar and de Lyon exchanged a look. As for the other passengers, they had to wait. In some other place at some other time, there might have been complaints, indignation, but not here, here one stood in silence.

Eventually the officer reappeared and, firm but polite, said, 'Will you gentlemen accompany me, please? And bring your baggage.' They did as they were told. Following the officer, Ferrar was relieved that, at de Lyon's direction, he had left the Walther in Paris. As a Spanish émigré, travelling with a Swiss, he had already provoked suspicion, and the discovery of a weapon would have made it worse. 'And,' de Lyon had added, 'pack your bag to be searched.'

Ferrar and de Lyon were led through the busy waiting room – inspiring the occasional furtive glance – to an office with a sign on the door that said GEHEIME STAATSPOLIZEI, abbreviated in common usage to 'Gestapo'. Inside, a bulky man in a suit was sitting behind a desk as the first suspects of the day were brought before him. His colourless hair was shorn on the sides, his thick neck bulged over his collar, he wore steel-framed glasses, and had a gold swastika pin on his lapel. Both passports lay on the desk in front of him, next to a pen, a tearaway pad of official forms, and a cup of coffee. He indicated that they should seat themselves, took a handkerchief from his pocket, blew his nose, then shook his head and said, 'Ach, what weather.' He stared at them for a moment, and then began to work.

Carefully, he tore a form from the pad, looked at his watch, filled in time and date, and slowly copied Ferrar's name. Then, a new form for de Lyon. That done, he said, 'Good morning, I am Major Schwalbe. So then, I will ask what business brings you to Germany? Or are you, perhaps, tourists?'

Following the script de Lyon had laid out for this eventuality, Ferrar said, 'We are magazine publishers, sir.'

Schwalbe wrote this down on the designated line. 'In Paris?'

'Yes, sir,' de Lyon said. 'But our magazines are sold all across Europe.'

'And the name of your company?'

'Editions Renard, sir.'

'And what sort of magazines do you publish?'

'Naturist magazines, sir,' de Lyon said.

'Magazines about nature? Animals and . . . what to say, fish?'

'Forgive me, perhaps I do not have the proper name in German. The word in French means nudism.'

Schwalbe had heavy eyebrows, which flicked upward at the word. 'What then will you do in Germany?'

'We are here to take photographs for a special issue, to be called *Nudism in the Reich*. It is quite popular in Germany, we are told.' It was. In an effort to stimulate the national libido, and thus breed more Germans, public nudity had been officially endorsed. Hitler himself, known to be a great prude in all things, had attended a nude ballet in Munich.

'Yes, it is.' Schwalbe knew the official line and tried to quote what he'd read somewhere but got only as far as 'The human form . . .' before his memory failed him.

'Herr Major?' de Lyon said. 'Would you care to have a look? I've brought along some recent issues.'

'Very well.'

De Lyon unbuckled his briefcase and brought out three copies of a French magazine called *Chez les Nudistes,* which meant nudist colony, and was also the name of a popular nightclub up in Place Pigalle. He handed the magazines to the major, who began to study them, taking his time with each page.

To Ferrar, the pages were upside down, but he could see well enough: grainy black and white photographs of statuesque women with big breasts and big smiles; group scenes of volleyball games

– which was how nudists spent most of their time if you believed the magazines; a picnic in the woods, repose in beach chairs. Wearing lace-up shoes and thin socks, the nudists were enjoying themselves. They were all ages, all shapes, some with tired, saggy backsides, others well formed.

With keen interest, his goaty side ascendant, Major Schwalbe peered at one page after another, while the passengers on the Paris/ Berlin express looked at their watches and fretted.

De Lyon said, 'Would you care to keep those, Herr Major? I have more with me.'

As Ferrar and de Lyon – now officially confirmed visitors to the Reich – settled back in their compartment, the train moved out of the station. 'Well, a taste of what's to come,' de Lyon said, lighting one of his brown cigarettes.

'I was here three years ago,' Ferrar said. 'It wasn't so bad then.'

'It will get worse. A country run by a political party and its security service . . . the newspapers don't really tell the story.'

Ferrar looked out of the window as the train rattled across a railway bridge over a frozen river. The spires of Cologne's cathedral, lit by moonlight, could be seen in the distance.

'We can count on being closely watched in Berlin, followed everywhere,' de Lyon said. 'You go out of your hotel room, they come in. Every foreigner gets the same treatment, the police keep records of who you see, what you do. Of course they could make it difficult to enter the country but they want people to come here, to see what they've accomplished, to admire German progress, the Nazi miracle. Anyhow, for the moment, we're the right kind of foreigners.'

'Thanks to you and your magazines.'

De Lyon shrugged. 'One takes precautions, it becomes a habit.' He stubbed out his cigarette and said, 'And we'll have to play the part in Berlin, those wicked Parisians and their naughty photographs – it's theatre for the police.'

'It seems to have worked with Major Schwalbe.'

'It did. But they're not all like that, believe me.'

After a stop at Cologne, where they waited while a German locomotive was coupled to the carriages, the train crossed the Rhine and entered a new landscape. They were south of Essen now, in what the newspapers called *the industrial heartland of Germany*. All the way to the horizon, in the light of floodlamps, tall chimneys poured smoke into the night sky, huge smelting and refining plants bordered the track – sometimes on both sides, brilliant fires flared in the open hearths of factories, served by workers seen as silhouettes against the firelight, slag heaps climbed far above the roof of the carriage, and the smell of burning coal hung in the compartment. No green thing lived here, only grey concrete, rusted iron, and brown brick blackened by soot.

De Lyon said, 'Did you see the workers? How they hurry?'

'Not running, exactly,' Ferrar said. 'More like a fast trot.'

For a time, de Lyon stared at the spectacle, then shook his head. 'You know,' he said, his expression somewhere between regret and disgust, 'the words "German rearmament" don't really mean much until you've seen all this.'

'The Krupp works.'

'Yes. Cannon, mortars, anti-aircraft guns, and the ammunition they need – millions of shells. And that's what's coming for us, sooner or later.'

'In France? You believe that, Max?'

'As of now, if nothing changes, the fascists will have Spain. Czechoslovakia is next, because Hitler knows that France and England are afraid to fight him. Then he'll want more. And more.'

'For instance, Russia.'

The Russian in de Lyon grinned at that idea. 'Hitler is evil, but he isn't stupid.'

The train slowed, then was shunted into a siding so that a

freight train, having precedence in the German rail system, could pass them by. Two locomotives pulled a long line of flatwagons that carried bulky shapes beneath canvas tarpaulins. Ferrar started to count the wagons, then gave up. Seventy? Eighty?

De Lyon took off his tweed jacket and hung it on a hook by the window, then unbuttoned his collar and loosened his tie. 'We'll ring for the porter later,' de Lyon said. 'I'm not ready to go to sleep.' He reached into his briefcase, took out a newspaper, and, leaning back in the plush seat, began to read, then dozed off. Ferrar stayed awake, fascinated by the dark countryside slipping past as the train got under way.

16 February, Berlin. At 10:30 a.m., in the Friedrichstrasse Station, the pace of the crowd was fast and furious, uniforms everywhere, civilians looking prosperous and well fed as they hurried to make their trains. Passing through the station buffet, Ferrar saw a newspaper kiosk where a headline in thick German lettering announced that Teruel had been retaken by Franco's forces. There were two photographs for this story, important because it told of a victory for a cherished ally: one a stock reproduction of General Franco, index finger raised, making a point during a speech. The other showed a Moorish soldier, holding his rifle above his head in celebration as he stood in front of the Teruel branch of the Bank of Spain. 'This is very bad news,' de Lyon said, his voice low and confidential.

'Teruel was supposed to be the turning point,' Ferrar said.

'Not to be,' de Lyon said.

From a German naval officer, a brusque 'Excuse me' as he pushed past Ferrar, bought a copy of the newspaper, then looked back at Ferrar and de Lyon as he walked away.

On the way to the Kaiserhof, the taxi driver wouldn't shut up, a one-man propaganda machine; the Reich this, the Reich that, things were better every day, everybody had money, the trade unions had been dissolved, so no more trouble from *those* people, they knew who he meant, jah? Next, a sudden stop, as a traffic police-man held up a red paddle. The driver was philosophical, 'They love their parades, so we must wait.' Ranked twelve across, wearing tan uniforms and soft cotton caps with bills, goose-stepping as best they could – throwing the leg high in the air, like the Wehrmacht, was an acquired talent – the zookeepers of Germany were on the march. Up at the head of the column, the zookeepers gave the Nazi salute, raised arm stiff, palm flattened, to a high personage on a reviewing stand.

'They love our Führer,' said the driver, his tone tender and sen-timental. At this, Ferrar and de Lyon would have at least exchanged a glance, or worse, but the driver could see them in his rearview mirror so they stared straight ahead, admiring the strutting zookeepers.

At the Kaiserhof, said to be not quite the equal of the Adlon but luxurious indeed, the performance continued. De Lyon was jo-vial with the desk clerk, a bit of a lout, on the verge of telling a dirty joke. Several guests – likely some of them were in fact guests – seated on elaborate chairs and divans in the lobby, looked over the tops of their lowered newspapers: now who was *this,* with his loud, jocular voice? As the desk clerk tapped the little bell used to sum-mon a bellboy, de Lyon said, 'We are so happy to be back in Berlin.'

'You are always welcome here, sir,' the clerk said mechanically. But he would remember the exchange when a police agent ap-proached the desk after Ferrar and de Lyon had been taken to their rooms.

They didn't stay long. Leaving their valises to be searched – Ferrar had packed a book by a prominent French fascist – they went downstairs, took a taxi to a department store, then used the under-ground train system to reach the Lübecker Strasse. They would officially be guests at the Kaiserhof, de Lyon had explained, but would operate from a pension – a boarding house – kept by one of his old and dear friends, Frau Vaksmann, where the walls didn't have ears.

Lübecker Strasse was in the Tiergarten section of Berlin, a quiet street of five-storey residences built with elaborate stonework, that led to the vast Tiergarten park. The Tiergarten quarter was a genteel place to live, though much fancier neighbourhoods lay to the west. The Pension Vaksmann – there was no sign outside, those who needed to know about it knew about it – was much like its neighbours, old and solidly respectable. De Lyon rang the bell and a maid wearing a pink apron, squinting through the smoke of a cigarette held in her lips, feather duster in one hand, dustpan in the other, opened the door and said, 'Good evening, gents, she's in the kitchen.'

Down a dark hallway that smelled of musty carpets, the kitchen, where, from a chair at the kitchen table, Frau Vaksmann was directing the preparation of a stew by two young girls with their sleeves rolled up. Frau Vaksmann was a great mound of a woman in a floral housedress decorated with stains and cigarette ash, her hair thin and fluffy from a lifetime of shop-bought dyes and cheap beauty parlours. When she saw de Lyon she gave a cry of delight, struggled to her feet, and embraced him, as they both laughed with the pleasure of old friends reunited. 'Dearest Max,' she said, 'where have you been?'

'All over, my love, lately in Paris. And, to tell you the truth, this Berlin you have these days is not my favourite place.'

'Oh, it's Hitler's city now. The other day I bought a mama doll for my grandchild but when you pressed the doll's stomach it didn't say "Mama", it said "Heil Hitler".'

De Lyon shook his head in despair, then said, 'Cristián Ferrar, my old friend Sarah Vaksmann.'

'It's Helga now,' Frau Vaksmann said. 'Has been for a couple of years – no point in letting the world in on your secrets. And, every few weeks when I can stand it, my neighbours see me in church. Being a Jew is not a good idea around here, so . . .'

Ferrar took Frau Vaksmann's hand, which was soft and warm and good to hold. The kitchen was, Ferrar saw, the centre of the house, its walls painted bright yellow, its shelves crowded with all sorts of knickknacks: a ceramic toad, a frog on a lily pad, a shepherdess with a crook and two lambs, and the three little pigs, mouths open with horror as they looked out of three windows of the house that the wolf threatened to huff, puff, and blow down. Above the stove, a cuckoo clock. On the opposite wall, a revolving stand on which a glum fisherman in rainhat and raincoat would appear with foul weather or, when the weather turned fair, his twin came out in overalls, with an oar and a beaming smile.

Now that she was standing up, Frau Vaksmann checked on the stew, tasting from a ladle and saying, 'Throw in some more onions, Greta.' She turned towards de Lyon and said, 'Will you two have dinner with me?'

'We'd love to, but we have to go back to the Kaiserhof – we need to be seen there. I'd prefer your stew, but it's the hotel dining room for us. Maybe tomorrow night.'

'It'll be the same stew, only better. How long are you staying, Max?'

'Three days, no more. You know the rule with this sort of business, in and gone before they think too much about you.'

She grinned and said, with considerable affection, 'Still a rogue, I see.'

'Always,' de Lyon said.

'Is there anything you need? Not much I can't get – cars, drivers, documents.'

'Do you still have a safe in the cellar? We'd like to keep some money there.'

'You're welcome to it.'

'We'll stay here until this evening, so, when you have a minute.' He paused, then said, 'I'm curious, dear, do the police bother you?'

'No more than anyone else. My papers have been fixed, because I have arrangements . . .' She stopped there and pointed her finger at the ceiling, meaning high officialdom. 'They're all gangsters, this crowd, and they're always needing the quiet favour. Some of them use the good bedroom. Oy, such fucking! They like it noisy, the Nazis.'

De Lyon started to answer, but the cuckoo came out of the clock and sounded its call. Frau Vaksmann looked at her watch and swore. 'Time for a Hitler speech. Greta, turn on the radio, good and loud.' To de Lyon and Ferrar she explained, 'It's the law, you must listen to the Führer's speeches. So these little bastards from the Hitler Youth patrol the streets – sneak around and listen at your windows. If they don't hear Adolf, they report you and the Gestapo comes around.'

From the radio, hypnotic raving, a threat in every syllable. During the speech the SS drums never stopped, using, as always, the special SS rhythm: two slow beats, then three faster. Tum, tum, tum-tum-tum. To Ferrar, and not only to Ferrar, it meant *we are coming for you.*

Just before seven, Ferrar and de Lyon took a walk down Unter den Linden, one of the grand avenues of the city, in search of a telephone box. A warmish, foggy evening in Berlin, the usual crowd thinned out at the dinner hour. They talked about Frau Vaksmann, de Lyon told stories. 'I'm fortunate to have such friends,' he said. 'And if something happens to me and you have to do this sort of thing by yourself, they will be *your* friends.'

'Let's hope—' Ferrar said, then stopped. As they walked past a beer cellar, the door was flung open and, for a moment, Ferrar could hear loud voices and drunken singing. Then four or five SS men in black uniforms spilled onto the pavement, unsteady on their feet, faces red from hours of drinking. When they saw de Lyon and Ferrar, they approached them. The leader said, 'What have we here?' and first one, then all the others, threw their arms in the air with a Nazi salute and shouted 'Heil Hitler!' The leader said, 'Now it's your turn.'

Ferrar didn't think long, felt the first twinge of defiance, then understood what had to be done and returned the salute with a rousing 'Heil Hitler' of his own. De Lyon was a second behind him but did the same thing.

'No, not quite right. Try again.'

In unison, Ferrar and de Lyon stretched their arms as far as they could and shouted even louder. The drunken SS men swayed, eyes bleary, and one said, 'Maybe we should teach them to march.'

'Hah, *knee*-march!'

'No, to hell with it, let's go.'

As the group began to stagger away, the leader turned, suddenly not so drunk as he'd seemed, and took a step towards Ferrar. 'Don't let me catch you on this street again,' he said. Then he caught up to his men and they all went weaving and laughing down the street. Half a block away, they began to sing.

'*Merde*,' de Lyon said.

Ferrar's heart stopped pounding, then slowly returned to normal. 'He meant that, you know, about the street.'

'They are going to kill somebody tonight,' de Lyon said. 'You've heard the stories, about some tourist who has no idea where he really is, so refuses to return the salute and gets himself beaten to death right then and there. That's what they had in mind for us, I suspect.' He stopped walking and lit a convalescent cigarette.

'They weren't ready, yet, but they'll find somebody later.'

'You're right, Cristián, as sad as that is for some poor soul. I was *in* gangs, when I was a kid. I know how it works. Nobody *says* anything, they all just sense when the moment is right.'

'That,' Ferrar said, 'plus the fact that there are two of us. They likely prefer five-to-one odds. I wasn't in gangs, but I saw it in the school yard.' He was thoughtful for a time, then said, 'About a month ago I was at a cocktail party in Paris, there were a few people standing in a group, one of them was a young Englishman, of the upper-class type, and when somebody mentioned he was dreading a trip to Germany, the Englishman said he'd just spent a week there, on business, and he'd seen all he wanted of the SS. Then he kind of sighed and said, "What a bore it's going to be to have to kill so many of these people."'

They found a phonebox by an exit from the underground. De Lyon put in a coin and, looking at a slip of paper, dialled the Kaiserhof and asked for Herr Szarny's room. Szarny took three rings to answer, then, a little breathless, said, 'Yes?'

'Herr Szarny, good evening, you'll remember me, we've spoken on the telephone. This is just to tell you we're here and would like to see you.'

'Oh yes, the man from . . .'

'From Prague, let's put it that way.'

'What?'

'Much better to talk in person, Herr Szarny. *Much* better.'

'Do you have—?'

'I do have business in Berlin, so here's an opportunity for us to meet together.'

'I was worried—'

'Don't worry, Herr Szarny, we worry too much these days. I'll be in touch tomorrow morning, can you wait until then?'

'Very well.'

'Good evening,' de Lyon said and hung up the phone.

De Lyon looked up at the sky in exasperation and Ferrar laughed and said, 'Not too quick, is he, that's what it sounded like.'

'He's scared,' de Lyon said. 'He knows perfectly well you can't talk on the telephone here but he was so scared he couldn't stop himself.'

'You headed him off,' Ferrar said.

'Only just. Now, we're going to have a look at the Casanova dance hall.'

*

The following morning, Szarny was in his room when a bellboy knocked at the door and called out, 'Delivery for Herr Szarny.' Szarny opened the door and found the bellboy holding a glorious bouquet of two dozen red roses wrapped in crinkly green paper. 'For you, sir,' the bellboy said. Szarny was still in his dressing gown so went to the wardrobe, took a few coins from his trousers, and tipped the bellboy. When the door was closed, Szarny stared at the roses, what could this mean? Then he saw a small envelope tied to a rose branch, tore it open, and read the gift card. 'We'll see you tonight, about nine, at the Casanova dance hall on the Lutherstrasse.' Signed: 'Your friends.' Szarny's hand began to tremble, the card fluttered to the carpet. Szarny bent over and retrieved it. Then he closed his eyes and said to himself you *must do what you must do*. It was a kind of prayer and he'd said it to himself time and time again since leaving Brno. He went to the dresser and found his wallet, inside there was a business card with a telephone number on the back. Perhaps this could wait, he ought to shave and get dressed, maybe go outside for a walk. A brisk walk, wouldn't that be good for him? Wouldn't that calm him down? Or he could go to the front desk and make arrangements for a flight back to Brno, where he would never, ever, think of this again. No, that wasn't possible, he would never be allowed to do that. Again he closed his eyes and said his prayer.

Then he went to the telephone, asked the switchboard operator to dial the number, and did what he had to do.

Earlier in the day, Ferrar and de Lyon had bought a leather briefcase with handles and at eight-thirty in the evening they retrieved the hundred thousand dollars from Frau Vaksmann's safe, put the bundled notes in the briefcase, and returned to the taxi waiting for them in front of the Pension Vaksmann. If somebody was following them they didn't see him and, the way de Lyon thought, using evasive tactics could provoke confrontation, so they had the taxi drive directly to the Casanova. In his pocket, de Lyon had a photograph of Szarny, taken secretly by the confidential agent in Brno. It showed a plump and supremely confident Herr Szarny arriving at the gate of the Brno Ironworks.

The Casanova ballroom – hot, smoky, and loud – was packed with people of every age and social class dancing beneath the mirrored ceiling. A small orchestra, DER RHYTHMUS MEISTERS according to a sign on the bandstand, was playing 'The Carioca' and the serious dancers took to the Latin beat with a passion. Standing in front of the seated orchestra, a husky man with a grey moustache and thick glasses, wearing a white dinner jacket, was playing the maracas, shaking them left, then right.

De Lyon watched over the briefcase while Ferrar, at his direction – 'we have to look like we belong here' – waited until the tempo slowed, then danced with a woman who said she was a shop assistant. Sweet and soft, she pressed herself against him – he could smell her underarms and face powder – and, likely influenced by some movie, hummed the tune to 'Once in a While' as they circled together. When the music stopped, Ferrar returned to the back wall, where de Lyon said, 'He's here.'

He was. Dressed in business suit and crisp, white shirt, Szarny was making himself evident, threading his way through the crowd as though he were looking for somebody. 'Wait for me,' de Lyon said, tension in his voice. A moment later, de Lyon returned with Szarny in tow. He introduced Ferrar simply as 'my associate', which Szarny acknowledged with a stiff motion somewhere between a nod and a bow. The orchestra was now playing a Latin song and a conga line had formed, snaking around the floor while, with each leg kick, the dancers shouted 'Zo!' on the beat.

De Lyon tried to pitch his voice just above the music. 'Herr Szarny, my name is Max de Lyon and I represent the Spanish Republic. You've agreed to sell us Skoda anti-tank cannon, and you asked for an additional payment of a hundred thousand dollars in gold British sovereigns. That proved to be impossible. Instead, we have the money for you in American dollars, in denominations of five hundred dollars. Thoroughly negotiable, believe me. Do you want it?'

Beads of sweat had formed at Szarny's hairline. 'Yes, very good,' he said. 'May I look at the money, just to make sure?'

'Of course. There's a WC down that stairway, the money is in this briefcase, you can take it into a stall, count it if you like, but it's all there.'

'Very well,' Szarny said.

Quietly, de Lyon said to Ferrar, 'Wait for me where you can see the top of the stairway. If I'm not back in, oh, twenty minutes, return to the Kaiserhof. If I don't contact you, get yourself on a plane to Paris. Right away.'

De Lyon and Szarny headed off, Ferrar found a place for himself by a wall where he could see the stairway. The WC was well attended – beer was available at the bar. A young man emerged, making sure of his pompadour, then two more. Next, two men disappeared down the stairs. Ferrar had a bad feeling about them, he had no idea why, they looked like middle-aged office workers out for a night at the dance hall. He started to follow them, hesitated, then started again, and stopped when a hand was placed gently on his forearm. 'Just a moment, sir,' said a man beside him.

He was short, perhaps five inches over five feet tall, with carefully parted black hair, and wore a well-tailored dark suit. He was a smug fellow, of the sarcastic sort. Not that he said anything derisive, it was in the set of his face, and a heavy upper lip just an instant away from curling into a sneer. Ferrar also had the impression that he was, at this moment, quite pleased with himself, happy. Suddenly he produced a small leather case, flipped it open, and held it up for Ferrar to see. Across the top of a card it said Geheime Staatspolizei Berlin, below that SS-Obersturmführer Jozef Lohr. At the upper corner of the card, a circle enclosed the twin lightning flashes of the SS. There was more, but Lohr flipped the lid back in place.

'Now then,' Lohr said, 'I am going to make sure that all goes well in the WC. You will wait for me here. If you move, there are three of my men watching you and they will . . . intervene.' For Ferrar, it was as though a curtain had been swept aside and something viperous and sickening revealed, and he was instantly ablaze with the desire to pick this little fellow up by the collar and the seat of the pants and dash his head against the wall. Lohr, something of a mind reader, smiled. Then he was gone and down the stairs. Ferrar searched the crowd around him, seeking the Gestapo operatives, but saw nothing. He didn't wait long, decided that a commotion up here, maybe gunshots, would alert de Lyon, and took off running down the stairs. If there were people chasing after him, he couldn't hear them. Midway down, he was blocked by a crowd of men in a panic, climbing the stairs as fast as they could, one of them trying to buckle his belt. Ferrar worked his way past them but it took time. At last he reached the door of the WC, threw it open, and rushed inside, prepared to fight or to be shot.

But the WC was empty. Past the sinks and urinals and toilet stalls was another door, unmarked, with the look of a door that was usually locked, now standing open, which led to a hallway with concrete walls and floor and a ceiling light in a wire cage. Ferrar ran down the hallway, turned a corner, and came upon another door, also open, with a street beyond. Of de Lyon, Szarny and Lohr, there was nothing to be seen.

He emerged on a side street, went around the corner, and discovered a line of taxis waiting outside the dance hall. Where were Lohr's Gestapo pals? Ferrar realized they didn't exist and never had. Lohr had tricked him, had managed an arrest, or a theft, or both, by finesse.

Ferrar looked at his watch and saw that it was almost eleven o'clock. Should he follow de Lyon's instructions and go back to the Kaiserhof? No. He had no idea why Lohr had left him upstairs, perhaps he didn't like the idea of facing two adversaries, or his scheme had involved only de Lyon and Szarny, he hadn't planned on a third man. Still, to go back to the Kaiserhof might leave him vulnerable to arrest, and who he really wanted to see, if there was anything to be done for de Lyon, was Frau Vaksmann. He opened the door of the first taxi in line, climbed in, and gave the driver the address in Lübecker Strasse.

The driver was a bearded man in middle age, something of the artist about him. 'Driver,' Ferrar said. 'I am having problems of the marital sort, a confidential agent is involved, could you make sure we aren't being followed?'

The driver laughed. 'Marital problems my ass,' he said. Then laughed some more. 'If you knew, my friend, how often I have to listen to this sort of thing . . . it's as though half the city is being followed. Anyhow, I will try to help you.'

'Thank you, sir,' Ferrar said.

The driver was true to his word, found a traffic circle, and went around three times, cut across the path of a tram by a whisker, then shot down a side street, stopped dead, and looked in his rearview mirror. 'All is good,' he said. And he did not take Ferrar to the front of the Pension Vaksmann. Better, he told Ferrar, to be out of sight, and drove through an alley where the sides of the taxi almost touched the walls, pulling up in front of a door that he said was the back door of the address Ferrar wanted. Ferrar gave him a tip that was well beyond generous. The driver thanked him and said, 'Perhaps I'll even get to spend it,' and drove off into the night.

Ferrar knocked at the iron door, the neighbourhood silent around him. He waited, then knocked again. And a third time, louder. Three very long minutes later, he heard the rattle of a chain, then the door opened to reveal Frau Vaksmann in a flannel bathrobe over a nightgown, her hair in a hairnet, a Luger pistol held at her side. 'Oh, it's you,' she said. 'Where's Max?'

'Arrested, or something else, but taken by a Gestapo officer.'

She swore, then said, 'Anyhow, come in out of the cold. There's nothing we can do tonight.' She pulled the door shut and relocked the chain. 'You need a couple of brandies, Herr Ferrar, that I can see. And, tomorrow, we'll try to . . .' She was silent, lips compressed, until she said, with a catch in her voice, 'Poor Max.'

It snowed the following morning, light but steady, the air icy and still. Ferrar had slept in one of the guest rooms. He had, at least, tried to sleep, but it was a failure – four stiff brandies having had no effect whatsoever. More than once he'd untangled himself from the bedding, gone to the window, and looked out on the Lübecker Strasse. Not a soul in sight, the empty, silent street oppressive. All night his mind had spun through endless possibilities, none of them of any use.

At seven, Frau Vaksmann knocked at his door and said, 'Come down to the kitchen, I'll make us coffee.' When Ferrar got to the kitchen, Frau Vaksmann was once again in her housedress, standing at the stove. 'We don't have much time,' she said, pouring coffee for Ferrar. 'Or it *may* be too late but, to the Gestapo, you see, someone like Max is a toy, and they'll want to play with him until they grow bored. They'll interrogate him . . . they might do worse, but not right away. What that means is we must use the most powerful connection we have, and we must understand there is only one chance. So, Max will have my best, a Gestapo major-general, an SS-Oberführer, a member of the Nazi party since the 1920s. I've known him a long time, he brings young girls here and makes a great racket and, in return, sometimes he does me a favour. But to him I am no more than a colourful character in his orderly life, he finds me amusing, not to be taken seriously. It is better for you to go, he will listen to you because you are an important person, and may even be of use to him some day. Will you try it, Herr Ferrar?'

'Of course.'

'I'll telephone him in an hour, he is very diligent and comes to work early. He is called Alfred Menke, SS-Oberführer Menke, say it as much as you're able, he never tires of hearing it.'

*

At nine-thirty in the morning it was still snowing as Ferrar walked up the steps of Gestapo headquarters on the Wilhelmstrasse. All along this avenue, that bordered the Tiergarten, Hitler had built monolithic, concrete office buildings, the power centres of the thousand-year Reich. Ferrar was as well prepared as he could be. He had left the pension immediately after Frau Vaksmann made her telephone call, headed for the Kaiserhof. Here he shaved while his suit was being cleaned and pressed by the hotel valet service and his shoes polished to a high gloss by the hall porter. Then he put on a fresh shirt from his valise and chose a midnight-blue tie with three angled gold stripes. At last he put on his overcoat, brown leather gloves, and maroon wool scarf, then picked up his briefcase – a crucial prop in the role he had determined to play – took the elevator to the lobby, and walked down the Wilhelmstrasse. At Gestapo headquarters he was expected, showed his papers at a desk – where the information on his passport was copied down – and was escorted by two SS officers to the top floor, then waited in a reception area where four secretaries were clacking away on typewriters and answering telephones. Finally, an hour later, he was taken in to see SS-Oberführer Menke.

Alfred Menke was a strange-looking man, severe and ice-cold; Ferrar could imagine his ancestors as Prussian civil servants, police officials, or prison wardens. He was tall and thin, with sunken cheeks in a long, narrow face, his hair a grey bristle, his skin dry and papery; he looked like a man who had never been outdoors. On the wall above his desk, the standard colour portrait of Adolf Hitler, the desk itself bare but for a telephone, a pad, and a pen. He directed Ferrar to a chair and said, 'Good morning, Herr Ferrar.' His voice was as dry as his skin.

'Good morning, Herr Oberführer, thank you for granting me an appointment at such short notice. I am here on behalf of my client, whose name is Max de Lyon.'

Menke had Ferrar spell the name and wrote it on his pad. 'You are an attorney, Herr Ferrar?'

'I am, Herr Oberführer.'

'And do you practise here, in Berlin?'

'No, Herr Oberführer, I am a senior partner at the Coudert law firm, in Paris.'

Menke nodded, made a note on his pad, and waited for Ferrar to continue.

'My client, Herr de Lyon, was arrested last night by one of your officers, who identified himself as Obersturmführer Jozef Lohr.'

Menke wrote the name on his pad and said, 'Arrested for . . . ?'

'In fact I don't know. We had gone to the Casanova dance hall, and there Herr de Lyon was taken into custody.'

'This de Lyon, he is a citizen of the Reich?'

'No, Herr Oberführer, he is of Swiss nationality and, like me, is resident in Paris. We travelled to Berlin in order to meet with a gentleman named Szarny, who is the owner of a foundry in Czechoslovakia, and had expressed interest in investing in one of Herr de Lyon's businesses in Paris, the publication of magazines.'

'Very well, your client is a substantial businessman, but, even so, must respect our laws. Tell me, did he perhaps say something that could be taken as a defamation of the Reich, or of our political leaders? A witticism, perhaps?'

'I doubt he would do that, Herr Oberführer. Herr de Lyon has little interest in politics, though I can say he is not unsympathetic to the Reich, he was looking forward to visiting Berlin, "the new Berlin" is how he put it to me. I accompanied him in case Herr Szarny wished to have papers drawn up regarding the investment.'

'I see. And what were you two gentlemen doing at the Casanova?'

Ferrar hesitated, then said, 'We were staying at the Kaiserhof, and wanted to see something of Berlin's nightlife. In truth, being away from home, we hoped to meet young women.'

'Tell me, Herr Ferrar, did the officer make any explanation at the time of the arrest? It would be the usual practice for him to do so.'

'I did not witness the arrest, Herr Oberführer. Accompanied by Herr Szarny, Herr de Lyon had gone downstairs to the WC. The officer approached me, produced his identification, which is how I learned his name, and ordered me to wait where I was. Which I did, for fifteen minutes, then went downstairs to look for my client. Who was not there and had, so it appeared, left the dance hall by means of a service exit that led to the street.'

As Menke thought this over, Ferrar sensed, more than saw, some flicker of irritation in his lifeless expression. Then the Oberführer picked up his telephone, dialled a single digit, and said, 'Have last night's arrest records reached us yet?' He waited for a response, and said, 'Find me a man by the name of de Lyon.' He spelled it, then covered the receiver with his hand and said to Ferrar, 'This might take a minute, it would be typical for us to record two to three hundred arrests a night, we are a busy service here.' Then, responding to an answer, he said, 'Try under *L*.' A minute later he said, 'You're sure?' then hung up the phone.

'It seems,' he said to Ferrar, 'that the arrest was not recorded. We do have a category "brought in for questioning", but these actions are not recorded as arrests.' He paused, once again picked up the telephone, and said, 'I want you to contact an Obersturmführer called Jozef Lohr. Immediately, and have the call put through to me.'

Impatient, Menke tapped his fingers on the desk, then said, 'While we are waiting to reach the officer, I will take down your information. The telephone number at your law office, your home address, and the telephone there.' After a moment, he added, 'If you don't mind, Herr Ferrar.'

'Not in the least, Herr Oberführer.'

When the information was written down, Menke said, 'Sometimes I find myself in situations where it might be of use to contact someone at the Coudert office.'

So he knew what Coudert was – Ferrar had made sure to use the name. 'Naturally I would welcome such a contact. We are mostly involved in international law, and we serve many elite clients.' *Like you.*

When the telephone rang, Menke asked Ferrar to step into the reception area. Ferrar sat there, feeling he had reason to hope. When he was summoned back to Menke's office, he could sense that Menke was, in the way of the powerful, about to bestow a favour on a supplicant. 'In this service, we prize ambition in our officers; however, sometimes . . .' He stopped there, wrote something on his pad, removed the slip of paper, and handed it to Ferrar. 'I have written down an address where your client may be found.'

Ferrar took the piece of paper and said, 'Herr Oberführer, please accept my deepest and most sincere gratitude.'

Menke nodded, which meant it was time for Ferrar to go. As he passed through the reception area, he saw what he took to be Menke's next appointment; a well-dressed woman, taut with nerves, and her beautiful, and very frightened, teenaged daughter.

Ferrar wasted no time. Out on the Wilhelmstrasse, amid the heavy official traffic – gleaming black Grosser Mercedes automobiles with swastika flags mounted above the headlights – he found a taxi. He showed the address to the driver and asked if he knew the street.

The driver squinted at the paper and said, 'I think so, this is in the eastern part of Berlin, down by the Oder-Spree Canal, a port for barges.' Then he added, 'Not a place to go at night, sir, if you don't mind my saying so.'

Once the driver turned away from the major avenues, the taxi passed workers' tenements, women in kerchiefs gossiping in front of grocery stores, finally pulled into a narrow side street, then rolled to a stop in front of a crumbling, soot-stained building with broken windows. To Ferrar, it looked abandoned. '*Here,* sir?' the driver said. 'It is the address you showed me.'

'Then this is where I'm going. Will you wait for me?'

'I will, sir. You won't find another taxi down here.'

The lock on the front door had been broken. As Ferrar climbed the stairs, he heard the sound of scurrying rats and, when he reached the second floor, he saw that the stairway leading up to the third floor had been boarded over. There were two doors on the second floor, Ferrar tried the first, which was locked, then the second, which opened to reveal Max de Lyon sitting in the corner of a couch. There was a kitchen chair in the centre of the room, one side of de Lyon's face was red and swollen.

De Lyon leapt to his feet when he saw Ferrar. 'You did it!' he said. He threw his arms around Ferrar for a moment, then stepped back quickly – he reeked of nervous sweat and he knew it.

'Is there anyone else here?' Ferrar said.

'No, they're gone. A guard, he looked like a local thug, appeared late last night because Lohr had to go somewhere. Then, about a half-hour ago, another one showed up, a messenger. He told me to wait, "your lawyer is coming to pick you up," he said, unlocked the handcuffs, and both of them left.'

Ferrar offered de Lyon a cigarette and took one for himself. As de Lyon inhaled, he closed his eyes. 'Let's get out of here, Max,' Ferrar said. 'I've got a taxi waiting downstairs.' As they walked down the staircase, Ferrar said, 'What did they do to you?'

'Lohr handcuffed me to a chair and slapped me around for a while, just to let me know who was in charge. A vicious little *fakakta momzer*, Herr Lohr.'

'*Fa* . . . what?'

'Fucking bastard, in shtetl Yiddish.'

'Where's Szarny?'

'Lohr counted the money, then let him go. First he said something that made Szarny flinch.'

'What did he want from you?'

'Money. He meant to hold me to ransom.'

'And you said?'

'I said I would try to arrange it . . . pleading, like the snivelling gutter rat he wanted me to be. We're not finished with this, Herr Lohr and I.'

As they approached the taxi, de Lyon said, 'Cristián, how in hell did you manage it?'

'Frau Vaksmann's idea, I went to see a big shot at the Gestapo, where I played the high-priced lawyer.'

'Which you are.'

'Which I am.'

De Lyon wanted to go and thank Frau Vaksmann immediately but Ferrar suggested they stop at the Kaiserhof first – de Lyon could clean up and change clothes and . . . He didn't go on, not wanting to say too much with the driver listening. 'You'll see,' Ferrar said. At the Kaiserhof, de Lyon went off to his room while Ferrar waited for him. When he returned, Ferrar said, 'I have a feeling that Szarny is still here,' then picked up the telephone and asked the operator to connect him to Herr Szarny's room. The phone rang for a long time and Ferrar was about to give up when Szarny answered, apparently out of breath, his 'Yes?' hesitant and fearful.

'Herr Szarny, is everything all right? My name is Ferrar, I'm Max de Lyon's lawyer, and I arranged to have you released.'

'You did?'

'They promised they would let you go, I just wanted to make sure they kept their word.'

'I am very grateful,' Szarny said.

'Herr Szarny, may we drop by your room for a moment? There's more I need to say.'

'Yes, I suppose so, I'm just sitting here.'

Szarny answered the door, then collapsed into a chair, head in hands. Ferrar was horrified at the sight, he'd never seen a man so dominated, it was as though someone had stolen his mind. And, in a way, Lohr had done precisely that, had used his greatest gift, a talent for intimidation – a useful talent in the right time and place: he essentially *owned* this poor man.

They got to work right away. Asked Szarny what he liked to drink, then had a bottle of cherry brandy sent up to the room and began, slowly at first, to administer it. The alcohol helped, so did the conversation. When de Lyon referred to Lohr as 'that pimple on the devil's ass', Szarny smiled, a victory.

'He was blackmailing me,' Szarny said. They nodded, quite overtly not asking why.

'He won't again,' de Lyon said. 'If he tries it, you telephone me in Paris and I'll make sure it's taken care of.'

'I had a mistress,' Szarny said. 'My wife is not well, and her oldest friend was so sympathetic . . .'

'It happens every day,' de Lyon said – *we're all men of the world*.

'He threatened to write my wife a letter, so I gave him money and I gave him money and then, one day, he said that Germany would soon rule Czechoslovakia and he would make sure to have himself stationed there, so he could "take care of me in person". Then he asked for a lot of money.'

De Lyon looked at his watch and said, 'It's almost one o'clock, I think you need something to eat.' He picked up the telephone and asked for the room-service waiter to bring up an extra-large bowl of the famous Kaiserhof speciality: liver dumplings in potato soup, the soup flavoured with bits of sausage and leek.

Szarny ate slowly, with great relish, the soup reminding him that so long as he was alive, things could get better. At one point, as the tension in him waned, he looked like he was close to tears. 'Tell me, Herr Szarny,' de Lyon said, 'what did Lohr say to you as you left the room?'

The deflection worked, tears replaced by anger as Szarny looked up from his liver dumplings and said, 'He told me that if I ever said anything about this he would have my wife and children murdered. What made it worse was that to him this was *comical*, as though he'd played a joke on me. And he somehow let me know that he'd done this before and would do it again.'

'Not to you, he won't,' de Lyon said.

Szarny finished his soup and said, 'Now, if you gentlemen don't mind, I would like to rest for a while, I haven't really slept for days.'

'Then we'll be going,' Ferrar said. 'But first, we would like to ask you for a favour.'

'Yes, of course, for you, after . . .'

'The Spanish Republic has great need for armament, Herr Szarny. And I wonder, even after everything you've gone through, if you are still willing to sell us the anti-tank cannon.'

'I can do that,' Szarny said. 'But certain officials will demand money in exchange for their stamp of approval.'

'We can pay whatever is needed,' de Lyon said. 'We're losing a war, money doesn't matter.'

'In that case, I will sell you whatever you wish. At one time I could have covered these extra costs myself, but over the last year and a half any money I had put aside went into Lohr's pocket.' As de Lyon and Ferrar rose to leave, Szarny said, 'As for losing a war, I pray you don't, my friends, because, if you do, we're next.'

In the elevator, Ferrar was cautious – the uniformed operator could hear everything. 'Did you mean what you said, Max? About a telephone call to Paris and . . . *taking care of* our short friend?'

'Yes.'

Back in Ferrar's room, de Lyon said, 'Now let's get the hell out of this fucking country.'

'Don't you want to visit the museum?' Ferrar said, picking up the phone. He reached the front desk and asked about airline tickets. The clerk said, 'I am sorry, sir, there will not be seats available for days, we have commercial exhibitions in Berlin this time of year. Do you want me to reserve on the first available date?'

'Not at the moment,' Ferrar said. He hung up, then dialled the hotel operator and asked to be connected to Lufthansa, 'not the reservations office, the corporate office.'

When a receptionist answered the phone, Ferrar asked for the law department, and, when they came on the line, he said, 'Herr Bruno von Scheldt, please, and tell him that it's Herr Ferrar, from Coudert.'

Von Scheldt took the call right away. 'Cristián!' he said. 'So good to hear from you, I miss the old firm, I really do. And, as for Paris . . . well, you know.'

'Come for a visit, Bruno. We'll go to the Tour d'Argent, my treat.'

'Maybe some day I will, but they keep me busy here. Is there anything I can do for you?'

'Speaking of Paris, a friend and I are trying to get home, but the planes are booked for days.'

'Can you leave tonight?'

'We can.'

'Where are you, Cristián?'

'At the Kaiserhof.'

'I'll call you back in ten minutes.'

As February turned to March, the spring rains began to blow in from the west, and some of the chestnut trees at Métro entrances started to bud, forced by the warm air drifting up from the stations below. Parisians found themselves restless and vaguely melancholy for no evident reason, an annual malady accompanying the nameless season that fell between winter and spring. The streets were quiet – only dog walkers beneath shiny umbrellas and the occasional couple with nowhere to be alone. In the cafés, newspapers on their wooden dowels went unread, as though the patrons refused to read them until they produced better news. A change of government was in the air, though nobody believed it would change anything but itself.

Ferrar tried to regain his peace of mind but it was slow in coming. What he'd seen in Berlin had affected him. *Evil* was the only word for it, and Ferrar now knew it would not cure itself, as most of the world hoped. He tried to take refuge in work, but work was more and more about what was coming to Europe. Many of Coudert's wealthy clients were converting paper assets into cash, buying paintings of stable value, and shipping them to America for storage. Twice he saw Chantal, the woman he'd met at a restaurant. The first time she spent the night at his apartment, where they tried to find the excitement of their first meeting, but only managed to make love by the book and fall asleep. The second time they went to the movies and he took her home in a taxi. There was to be no third time.

Then, on a drizzling mid-afternoon, he returned from a meeting to find Jeannette, his secretary, waiting impatiently to see him, her expression agitated and concerned. 'You've had a telephone call, Monsieur Ferrar, from a woman friend in America. She has no telephone, so is waiting at a friend's house for you to call her. Here is the number.' She sat there for a time, wanting to say more, and finally added, 'Could you call right away? Even so, there will be a delay for the transatlantic line.'

'Please try it for me, Jeannette,' he said.

Twenty minutes later, he was speaking to Eileen Moore, his sometime lover in an affair carried on during his trips to New York. She had never telephoned before, they wrote back and forth as the time for their meetings approached. She managed to say hello and ask him how he was, determined not to be emotional, then went silent as she started to cry.

'Eileen? Are you there?'

'Yes, I'm here.' Again, she couldn't talk.

'What is it? What's wrong?'

'Cristián, a terrible thing has happened.'

'Eileen?'

'Sorry, I can't help it.' She blew her nose. 'I'm pregnant, Cristián, that's what has happened.'

'Well, we'll just have to . . .'

'No, you don't understand, you're not . . .' This hit him hard – surprised him, how hard it hit. 'Not long after you left,' she went on, 'I met someone. He's a very nice man, we had a fling, I got pregnant. I thought about having it taken care of, but I can't.'

'What are you going to do?'

'He's going to marry me, to do the right thing . . . We aren't in love, Cristián.'

She meant *but you and I are.* His voice tight, he said, 'I'm sorry about this, Eileen, much more than sorry. We . . .' He stopped himself from going further, far worse for her now, because it was too late, to hear a declaration of something that had always been just beneath the surface, and never said out loud. At last, in the transatlantic static, he managed, 'Can I do anything? Do you need anything?'

'No, I'll come through this.'

'I don't want to lose touch with you. If you move, please send me your address.'

'All right, if you want me to, I will. And I do have to move, you can't have a baby at the Iroquois Hotel.'

'I will miss you,' Ferrar said.

'I think we'd better hang up now. Goodbye, Cristián.'

'Goodbye.'

To allow him privacy, Jeannette had stepped into the hallway; now she returned and said, 'I hope everything is all right, Monsieur Ferrar.'

'Maybe it will be,' Ferrar said.

Jeannette went back to work, Ferrar stared at the document he'd been reading, *Marteau v. The Commercial Bank of Aberdeen,* but all he saw were lines of typewritten print. He badly wanted to go home, to be alone, but he couldn't. *I have lost her,* he thought, his turn to realize that sometimes you don't know how much you care for someone until she's gone.

*

De Lyon called the following day. 'I've just had a letter from Sarah Vaksmann, she's living in London, with her nephew, so it seems she took our advice.'

In Berlin, there'd been time, before they left, to go to see Frau Vaksmann and thank her for what she'd done. Then de Lyon had told her in very strong terms that she had to leave Germany, Ferrar adding that her Oberführer would throw her to the wolves without a second thought, she must *not* depend on him. She hadn't been receptive at that moment but with time, evidently, she understood they were right.

De Lyon said, 'We may have saved her. I wish I could feel satisfaction about that, I mean, I'm glad she's safe, but she's lost everything. Told everyone she was taking a vacation, then ran for it. Now she's trying to sell the pension, which is complicated for an owner living abroad.'

'If she needs help with the sale,' Ferrar said, 'have her get in touch with me at the office. It's something we do here.'

On 8 March, after work, Ferrar walked over to the Oficina Técnica. From Max de Lyon's office, the sound of one finger typing. When Ferrar opened the door, he found de Lyon, his face screwed into a scowl of intense concentration, using his index finger to fill out, a letter at a time, a densely printed form of several pages. As de Lyon worked he said, 'May he roast in hell, whoever wrote this fucking thing.'

'There are those who love forms, Max. They think it's clever to make people tell them things. What have you got there?'

'This, my friend, is an end-user certificate, originally dreamed up by the American Congress, in a law known as the Spanish Embargo Act of 1937. Now, of course, the whole world has them. So, if you ship arms from Country X to Country Y, Country Y must swear they are going to keep them, not sell them on to mean old Country Z, otherwise known as Spain.

Without a signed form, Country X can't ship their guns.'

'I know the end-user certificate, Max.'

'Then you also know that everyone cheats, but those who ship to Franco somehow don't get caught at it.' He sat back, shook his stiffening index finger, and said, 'Thanks for coming over, Cristián. This is a new version of the form, maybe you could look it over, then we have an eight-thirty dinner reservation at Lapérouse, have you been there?'

'I have. Very Belle Epoque, as the French put it, and the food is good.'

'An elegant restaurant, expensive and not subtle about it. We want our guest to feel honoured and respected, a man we see as a high personage, because we're going to insult him, by assuming he's the sort of gent who would take a bribe. There's gossip that says he might, but no more than that.'

'And he is?'

'An Estonian military man called General Zoltau. The name is German but no surprise there, the Germans – Teutonic Knights, Baltic Barons, what have you – ran the country for centuries.'

'It sounds like you know him.'

'I don't, but I've seen him in person and heard his voice. I bought his photograph from a French press agency and spent a couple of hours in a car outside the Estonian legation and, hey presto, there he was. As for the voice, a faked-up telephone call works nicely. Once I have a look, and hear a voice, I'm more often right than wrong. So, are you able to join us?'

'I have to go home first, I'll meet you there.' Ferrar was more than pleased, anything to get him out of his apartment and yet one more bachelor supper. He looked over the form, answered a few questions, then, as de Lyon went back to work, said, 'Don't you have a secretary who can type that out for you?'

'Usually I do, but her husband was badly wounded yesterday, by a German tank, as it happens. Anyhow, poor girl, she tried to work but she's better off at home for a few days.'

'The form can't wait?'

'Maybe, but in situations like these, with two bottles of wine and so forth, it's better to have the form ready for signature and in one's pocket. Something to remember if you have to do this by yourself.'

'Just out of curiosity, how did you manage the phone call?'

'I use a woman, so the operator can say, "A Mademoiselle Duval on the line for you." For men, it's good bait. They wonder, Is she young? Is she sexy? I'll just see who she is. Meanwhile, I'm on the extension line.'

From Ferrar, an appreciative laugh, then he said goodbye and left de Lyon to his typing.

At eight-fifteen, Ferrar walked down to the avenue des Grands Augustins, which faced the Seine. He crossed the avenue and spent some time gazing at the river, which was running a heavy swell in the spring flood, the dark surface of the water ruffled by a gusty March wind. Eventually he looked at his watch and set off for the restaurant, sorry to leave the river. But as he entered Lapérouse his heart lifted. Here was a lovely private little world: warm air, fragrant with the aromas of rich food; silverware and china gleaming in the muted light; and the low, civilized music of dinner conversation. Ferrar was led to the table, where de Lyon was laughing, apparently at some clever remark delivered by the general.

General Zoltau appeared to be a man of some vanity, who wore a cavalry moustache with its ends trained to sharp points, of the sort twirled by a villain in a melodrama. He was tall and fair, held himself in a stiff, military posture, his suit likely sewn up by a Bond Street tailor. He rose and shook Ferrar's hand as de Lyon introduced them, then, as Ferrar sat down, de Lyon said, 'General Zoltau has suggested we have *gentiane* as an apéritif, would you like one? Myself, I've never tasted it.'

This was a lead and Ferrar followed it. 'Always good to try something new,' he said.

'It is a liqueur,' Zoltau said, savouring the French pronunciation, 'made from the roots of the gentian plant, little blue flowers picked in the mountains. As for the taste, it cannot be described, so you must try a sip.'

'Then that is what I'll do,' Ferrar said, bowing to the general's sophisticated taste.

'General Zoltau is one of the military attachés at the Estonian legation here in Paris,' de Lyon said.

'Oh yes? And do you enjoy the city, General?'

'Indeed, yes, of course. It's full of Frenchmen, unfortunately, but one can't have everything.' De Lyon and Ferrar laughed at the barb.

'And where do you live?' Ferrar said.

'In the Eighth Arrondissement, on the avenue Montaigne, my wife and I so like that part of the city we've bought an apartment there.'

Ferrar knew the neighbourhood, which was just off the Champs-Elysées, and one of the most expensive areas in the city. What did they pay generals in Estonia? Not enough to live on the avenue Montaigne. *Maybe family money,* Ferrar thought. *Or the wife has money. Or the gossip has it right:* 'Always better to buy, in Paris,' Ferrar said.

'I believe so,' the general said. His eyes wandered over the restaurant's lavish, nineteenth-century decor: the grand style, its crowning glory a magnificent chandelier made of hundreds of perfect crystal pendants. The general's eyes paused there a moment, then he continued, 'We are now engaged, more my wife than I, in redecorating. An impressive apartment, it deserves the best.'

A waiter arrived with the *gentiane,* which Ferrar had always liked, though the general had it right, the exotic flavour was beyond words. As they drank they studied the menu. 'Lapérouse is known for its quenelles of lobster in cream sauce,' de Lyon said, choosing the most expensive dish offered. 'And of course we must begin with the caviar. How does that sound to you, General Zoltau?' From Zoltau, an approving nod. When the sommelier appeared, de Lyon ordered two bottles of Château Mouton Rothschild.

The conversation turned to politics – no French dining rules that night. The general enquired about the progress of the civil war, in the way of a military attaché trolling for information. 'It is not going well,' de Lyon said. 'Now that Franco's Nationalists have recaptured Teruel, they've begun to attack east of the town, heading for the Mediterranean coast. If they reach it, they will cut the Republic in two.'

'And then?' the general said.

'As long as we hold Barcelona and Madrid, there is hope,' de Lyon said.

From the general, a sage nod. He turned to Ferrar and said, 'Your friend has it right, I think, arms merchants are known to have a good nose for war.'

Ferrar said, 'And you, General Zoltau, what is your view?'

'If you can hold out long enough, perhaps a ceasefire, followed by a political solution, especially if the British support the idea.'

'They will not,' de Lyon said. 'They will hem and haw, but in the end they won't. We believe that the British Foreign Office and General Franco have made a secret arrangement. Something on the order of: we will allow you to win, if you will remain neutral when we fight Germany. This would mean the British could keep Gibraltar and thus control the Mediterranean.'

'They are hard people, the British,' Zoltau said, a note of admiration in his voice.

'They are,' de Lyon said. 'And because they, and the French, keep us from buying armaments, we must take what the Russians offer, and then buy the rest wherever we can find it. What that means on the battlefield is that the soldiers of the Republic are armed with forty-nine different types of repeating rifle, forty-one types of automatic weapon, and sixty different kinds of artillery.

Many of the replacement parts can't be found, and we need ammunition of all sorts of calibres. When the war started, we were using hand grenades that were said to be "impartial" – sometimes they killed the man they were thrown at, while just as often they killed the man who threw them.'

'From a military point of view, an impossible situation,' Zoltau said.

A speculative de Lyon said, 'I wonder if Estonia, a small nation bullied by powerful neighbours, Hitler on one side, Stalin on the other, might not be sympathetic to our difficulties.'

'Sympathetic, perhaps, but there's little we can do.'

'There is one possibility, General Zoltau. We have managed to purchase fifty anti-tank cannon in Czechoslovakia, but the Skoda people must have an end-user certificate. Is there some way you could help us with this problem? Because the Non-Intervention Pact does not affect Estonia, only Spain.'

'Ah, the caviar arrives!' Zoltau said. As indeed it had.

The conversation drifted away, to life in Paris and then, as they worked through the second bottle of wine and ordered a third, to *night*life in Paris: nightclubs high and low, and brothels catering to every imaginable inclination. De Lyon's knowledge here was broad and deep, and the general was quite attentive. Finally, after the nude dancing girls and Pierre the Donkey, de Lyon closed with a homily. 'The Parisians are worldly in these matters,' he said. 'They believe that with money, all things are possible. They accept the reality of the human appetite, and the reality of markets. Here, one can have whatever one can pay for. I have always admired their point of view.'

'As do I,' Zoltau said. 'Life is short, one must have all the pleasures it can provide.'

Now matters had proceeded to a certain point, and Ferrar had to let de Lyon know what he meant to do. 'Max,' he said, 'do you recall Monsieur Blanc, one of my clients?'

'A thin fellow? With a limp?'

'Yes. He believed that he'd found the very house he was seeking, but the sale did not go through, and poor Monsieur Blanc had already invested in splendid furniture which – I won't bore you and the general with legal whys and wherefores – now sits in a warehouse and is not really owned by anybody.'

'For splendid furniture, a sad fate,' de Lyon said.

'The best of it is a magnificent chandelier, surely the equal of the one here. And it occurred to me that since General Zoltau is redecorating his apartment, perhaps he has a home for it.'

They both looked at Zoltau, who said, 'Why yes, we have *just* the place for it, in our dining room.'

Back to nightlife in Paris.

After coffee, a cordial good night – if all that Mouton Rothschild didn't make you cordial, nothing would. As they put the swaying Zoltau in a taxi, de Lyon said, 'May I get in touch with you, General, towards the end of the week?'

'I will expect your call,' said the general.

On the following morning, when Ferrar arrived at the Coudert office, he sat down with his secretary and went over what he had to do that day. Reading from a list, she said, 'You are supposed to call Count Polanyi at the Hungarian embassy, he's a principal in the French holding company that controls a Budapest bank. Next you are to call a Monsieur Belesz, in Budapest, he is the heir who refuses to vote in order to force his sister from the holding company. I have a note here that says *vizsla dogs*. Does that make sense to you, Monsieur Ferrar?'

'Yes, Jeannette, it does,' Ferrar said, a sigh in his voice.

Jeannette had the Polanyi file ready for him, Ferrar called the embassy. 'Good morning, Monsieur le Comte,' Ferrar said, following the French protocol for titles. 'This is Cristián Ferrar, from Coudert Frères. Do you have a moment?'

'I do, monsieur, I am fed up with Nephew Belesz and his damned schemes.'

'I will be brief, monsieur. We are preparing your lawsuit against Monsieur Belesz but, in order for us to proceed, he will have to be lured to Paris – we cannot sue him in Budapest. We were hoping that you might suggest a way to induce him to come here.'

'Throw him in the boot of a car,' Polanyi said.

'A last resort,' Ferrar said, with just a hint of lawyer's irony. 'A ruse will cause less fuss and bother.'

'Very well, a ruse. Which means you are asking me what he might find irresistible. Well, what he likes is wine, women, and song, except the song. I can't imagine him coming all the way here for wine, which leaves women. But there are lots of women in Budapest, Monsieur Ferrar.'

'Did he ever live in Paris, monsieur?'

'Years ago, he did, for a time. He pretended to go to the Sorbonne, but mostly he chased girls. He's a lusty little monkey, Nephew Belesz.'

'And did he catch them?'

'Not the smart ones, he didn't.'

'Was there, perhaps, someone special?'

'Not that I . . .'

Polanyi paused, and finally Ferrar said, 'Monsieur?'

'My memory,' Polanyi explained, 'takes its own sweet time . . . I seem to recall one he caught, then lost.'

'And she was?'

'An actress, at the lower depths of the film business. Her name was, oh hell, Albertine? No, that's not it. Why do I think of Babar the elephant?'

'Celeste?'

'Celestine!'

'Do you know what became of her?'

'I have no idea. He was passionate for her, kept her photograph on his dresser, courted her, had her, then lost her.'

'Could she be used as bait?'

'I doubt she would agree to that, even if we could find her.

But it occurs to me that she might be of use even so.'

'How?'

'Perhaps a letter to the nephew from his former sweetheart; she misses him, regrets their amour ended, could they possibly meet again some day. Of course I would write the letter myself. Maybe you would help me do it.'

Ferrar was dubious. 'Do you think a letter would work?'

'I don't know, but why not try? We must do *something*, Ferrar.'

Ferrar saw that Polanyi had become enchanted by the idea of a faked letter and was not to be dissuaded. 'Very well, a letter. Is there any possibility you can remember her last name? For a return address?'

'Surely she had one, but I never knew it.'

'No matter, we'll make up a name, a married name. She'll explain in the letter that her husband is deceased.'

'Do you think this might work, monsieur?'

'It might. If not, we'll try something else. But there is one other possibility,' Ferrar said. 'I could telephone him in Budapest and see if he'll listen to reason. Suggest that a settlement, of the generous variety, might be more to his advantage than being involved in a lawsuit.'

'But you said you can't sue him in Budapest,' Polanyi said.

'I doubt he knows that.'

'Well, I don't think he'll agree, but if you want to try, go ahead. Do you have his telephone number?'

'As a client, soon to be a former client, we do.'

'Then good luck. He's hard to handle and proud of it.'

It took all day to reach Belesz, who was apparently not home. Then, at five-thirty, a woman answered who spoke only Hungarian. After Ferrar tried in three languages, she yelled 'Fabi!' and Belesz came to the phone. Speaking in German, the second language in Hungary, he said, 'Who is this?' He sounded annoyed; either the call had come at an inconvenient moment, or, it occurred to Ferrar,

Belesz was one of those people who are perpetually annoyed.

'Please forgive the intrusion, Herr Belesz, this is Cristián Ferrar, from the Coudert law firm in Paris. We represent the holding company that owns the First Danubian Trust.'

'Yes? And so?'

'I am calling to see if we can help to resolve a problem with your company, Herr Belesz, which cannot function so long as you withhold your vote. Isn't there some way out of this conflict?'

'Oh-*ho*! Now they've set the lawyers on me!'

'There are always alternatives, when people disagree. What would you suggest?'

'I would *suggest* that my sister resign from the company, then she can keep her filthy dogs.'

'I believe your family might be willing to consider a financial settlement. Is that of interest to you?'

'Buy me off, eh? Who put you up to this? My *dear* Uncle Janos?'

'I have spoken with Count Polanyi, as he is the one who would bear the burden of the settlement. You would retain your rights in the holding company, but your vote would have to be cast so that the company can operate in a normal way. Let me point out to you that there are laws obliging you to protect the company and its assets, and if you persist the rest of the family can take legal action against you. And, as your attorney, I must advise you that almost all such lawsuits are resolved in favour of the plaintiff.'

'That's what *you* say.'

'Herr Belesz, you have retained us to offer you our best counsel. Our advice to clients is: avoid litigation if you can. It's expensive, and the outcome is sometimes not what you're seeking. And it can, I'm sure you understand, go on at great length.'

'I don't like to be threatened, Herr whoever-you-are. I happen to belong to a political party called the Arrow Cross, and we are men of honour who despise scheming little lawyers. Understand?'

Ferrar knew of the Arrow Cross, it was the Nazi party of Hungary. 'I don't expect you to make a decision now,' he said. 'Why not think about it for a few days? Decide what's best for you, then let me know.'

'Oh I know what's best for me. Do you know what's best for me?' His voice rose and grew shrill as he screamed, 'I can show you right now!' Then he slammed the phone down on the cradle.

Later in the day, George Barabee, the managing partner, asked Ferrar about the call. 'Well, he threatened me. He and his pals in the Arrow Cross don't like lawyers,' Ferrar said, then shrugged.

'He sounds dreadful.'

'He is. Truly dreadful.'

'What comes next?'

'I talked it over with Polanyi, and we decided to see if we could get him to come to Paris. So Herr Belesz will soon have a letter from an old flame.'

'Give it some time, we don't want him connecting the call with the letter. Do you think it will work?'

'No.'

'Me neither. But you may as well try.'

The first tease of spring may have visited Paris but it hadn't reached Louveciennes. As Ferrar rode the little train on Sunday morning, the countryside was all bare, dripping branches and fields of dead weeds. He would see his family, go to eleven o'clock mass, work his way through the heavy Sunday lunch, then try not to fall asleep on the train ride back to Paris – the usual family visit, its predictability a comfort for Ferrar. But, when he reached the house, all was not as usual, the excitement in the air was palpable. His mother, face flushed, kissed her son hello, then said, 'Oh my dear Cristián, success at last!' Over her shoulder, a quietly amused Abuela met Ferrar's eyes and lifted a meaningful eyebrow.

'That's wonderful, Mama,' Ferrar said, waiting to hear the news.

With some ceremony, his mother showed him an envelope, then

carefully slid the letter out and handed it to him. The letter was from one Alejandro Joaquin Carlos de Montador Abruzzo, Duque de Mérida y Tolosa, and began 'My dear Señora Ferrar Obrero,' adding the maiden name in the formal Spanish custom. The handwriting was exquisite, perfectly slanted script in sepia ink on cream-coloured paper. With a deeply held conviction that her Obrero family had noble blood, was by a secret marriage descended from Mariana Victoria, Infanta of Portugal, she had for years written letters to various duques, condes, and baróns – dukes, counts, and barons – to see if they might support her claim. In the eyes of the family, a harmless folly that kept her busy, but now one of these titled gentlemen had actually *answered* her.

Ferrar read through the letter but found no reference to the Obrero family claim. The duque was writing on behalf of his dear cousin, the Marquesa Maria Cristina de Valois de Bourbon y Braganza, recently widowed, now living in Paris. His cousin, it seemed, once Ferrar got past the flowery style, needed a lawyer. Knowledgeable friends had recommended her son, could his cousin presume to contact him?

'This is wonderful, Mama,' Ferrar said. 'That he answered your letter.'

'May I write back and say she can telephone you at your office?'

'Yes, of course.' This was not generally the way one contacted a lawyer but Ferrar had seen it before, there was a certain breed of individual who believed that special connection led to better treatment, and they weren't always wrong. Still, there was something odd about it.

Abuela said, 'We've talked this over, dear one, and what I believe he wants is you. The Duque Alejandro is matchmaking.'

'But I'm not a noble,' Ferrar said.

'Yes you are,' his mother said.

'He has heard of you,' Abuela said. 'We don't know the marquesa's age, but her husband has died. For her to find an appropriate suitor, noble, wealthy, and available, will not be easy. So the duque settles for wealthy and available, and professional status replaces a title.'

'Well,' Ferrar said, 'an arranged marriage is the last thing I ever considered, especially a marriage into the nobility.' Then he added, tongue in cheek, 'Didn't they used to send a framed portrait of the lady?'

'But you will see her in person,' his mother said. 'You may even like her.'

'Just out of curiosity,' Ferrar said, 'where does the duque live?'

'The letter comes from an address in Brussels.'

They went on for a while, speculating about the duque and the marquesa and having a very good time – it had been years since Ferrar had seen his mother so happy and excited. Eventually, Abuela looked at her watch and said, 'Oh dear, we must set out for church or we shall be late for mass.'

Riding home at dusk, Ferrar wondered about the letter. How could the duque have figured out that some lady in France who wrote him batty letters was the mother of a Parisian lawyer? The duque had mentioned *knowledgeable friends*. Well, they surely were. Or, Ferrar thought, was he being needlessly suspicious? The duque might have done some research on the woman who wrote from Louveciennes. Was she rich? Connected to interesting people? Could she be useful? Ferrar had seen his share of phoney titles – was the duque a real duque? On the other hand, European nobility was a strange and often eccentric breed but they tended to survive, and sometimes flourished. And was he looking forward to meeting the marquesa? Yes, he was, how not.

14 March. The false spring stirred hearts all across the continent and that included the hearts of French politicians. When Ferrar met with de Lyon in his office at the Oficina Técnica, the latter had important news. The French Popular Front had returned to power

and would open the border to arms shipments going into Spain. That meant armaments sent by Moscow, which had been held up at the frontier, would now reach the Republic's forces.

'Which makes life easier for us,' de Lyon said. 'We can ship our cannon up to Poland by rail, then by freighter from Danzig to Bordeaux. Or, what *used* to be Danzig. It's now called the Free City of Danzig, set up by the Versailles treaty to give the Poles a port on the Baltic, and administered by the League of Nations. Or so the diplomats think.'

'I know the history,' Ferrar said.

'Then you know that the Non-Intervention Pact is not enforced in Danzig, and the League of Nations does not control it. There are League of Nations officials in the city but all they can do is complain and nobody listens to them. Who really runs Danzig is the city administration, which is Polish. Now Poland, like every country in Europe, is a battlefield in the political war between the left and the right. And it so happens that, among leftist Poles in Danzig, we have friends. The *Republic* has friends.'

'Friends who will let us ship weapons to Spain.'

De Lyon nodded and said, 'Who will let us do anything we want . . . the twelfth of March scared the hell out of them.' On 12 March, Hitler's troops had marched into Austria.

'Scared me,' Ferrar said. 'Maybe sickened is a better word – those photographs of smiling little girls giving the Nazi salute.'

'It's even worse in the newsreels,' de Lyon said. 'But it's a lie. The Austrians don't want to be ruled by Hitler. Meanwhile, that march had its effect on French politics.'

'Which, as you said, makes life easier for us.'

'It does, up to a point. But Danzig is where criminals go to get rich, and by criminals I mean crooked officials as well as gangs. So we must have somebody in Danzig to make sure the shipment isn't stolen – stolen by sleight-of-hand documents or stolen by force. Which has happened before and more than once. And, just to make things worse, Franco's spy service is active in Danzig – they know what we're doing there and will organize an attack if they can. One way or another, money is going to change hands in Danzig.'

'And the somebody on watch in Danzig, that would be you?'

'That's what I do, Cristián.'

'And you want me to go with you.'

'Well . . .' The telephone on de Lyon's desk had a throaty rasp for a voice, which now sounded twice, then twice again. 'Sorry,' de Lyon said, 'but I must see who is calling me.' After a brief exchange he handed the phone to Ferrar and said, 'It's your secretary.'

After Ferrar said hello, Jeannette said, 'Monsieur Ferrar, you've just had a telephone call from a marquesa, Marquesa Maria Cristina, who's requesting an appointment. I told her I would be in touch with you and call her back.'

'I will see her, Jeannette, I've been expecting the call.'

'You have time tomorrow at three-thirty, I'll make the appointment.'

Ferrar hung up the phone and said to de Lyon, 'We were discussing a trip to Danzig.'

'Of course I'd like to have you with me. I can always ask Stavros to come along, but he has a short fuse, and when things go wrong he explodes. Better to have somebody more . . . even-tempered, but I suspect you must be very busy at the office.'

This was true. The false spring had also stirred the hearts of many Coudert clients, who had decided to marry, divorce, write wills, buy something or sell something, or who were just nervous and needed a good soothing by their lawyer. Ferrar sighed. 'You aren't wrong, Max.'

'We don't have to stay a long time, because the shipment won't be in Danzig for more than two days. I could go early, to talk to people, to see what we're facing, and you could fly in as the shipment arrives. And *that* we can schedule for the weekend.'

'Could we?'

'It's possible. Szarny has confirmed that our bank wire was

received, which included funds to bribe Czech officials. So, this weekend, maybe. If not, the following weekend. And you'll be at work on Monday morning. Can you do it?'

Ferrar didn't hesitate – not after what he'd seen over the last few weeks. 'If you think I can help you, Max, I'll be there.'

The marquesa was prompt, on the following afternoon. Jeannette showed her into the office and, after Ferrar greeted her, she settled on the chair meant for visitors. Was she Spanish? French? She was in her early forties, he guessed, but looked younger, and was not so much beautiful as what was called *striking*. She had strong, finely made features, smooth skin, and hair a dark shade of gold, with the sheen of polished metal, swept back beneath a pillbox hat with a veil. For an afternoon meeting at a lawyer's office, she wore a severe navy-blue suit, a scarf at her throat, and a silver brooch. Now she sat, elegant, composed, and serious, taking a moment before the meeting began. But did she ever sit! The most prim and proper lady in the land: back straight, head up, knees, legs, and shoes not quite pressed together but perfectly met, with hands, in black leather gloves that disappeared up the sleeves of her jacket, folded atop the purse on her lap. 'Monsieur Ferrar,' she said, 'thank you for seeing me at such short notice. It is kind of you, monsieur.' She spoke a very refined French; formal, rhythmic, and beautifully modulated.

'It is my pleasure, Marquesa.' When she did not answer, he said, 'Now, how may I help you?'

In that hypnotic voice, she told him her story. Her dear husband, the marques, had loaned a friend a great deal of money. There was no contract, they were old friends, only a handshake. 'It was a debt of honour,' she said. Was there, perhaps, a letter? The marques rarely wrote letters. Had she been present during a telephone call? 'No, Monsieur Ferrar, my husband saw to his affairs in the privacy of his office.' And did he own a business? 'He did not care for commerce, monsieur, his estates were overseen by a manager.'

This went on for a time, her claim weaker with every question and answer – here was a theft with no witnesses other than the marques, and he had told her of the loan in the last hours of his life. The money, Ferrar thought, was probably gone for good. Still, he would do his best, inspired by . . . by her. He could not stop looking at her: a model of composure, her lips together when she was done speaking, her face as still as ice. Well, prim and proper she might be, but beneath his desk Ferrar was highly aroused. Damn! What had she done to him? A powerful, erotic energy flowed from her like electric current.

'Marquesa, I fear there is considerable work to be done if we are to retrieve your husband's money.'

'I am no stranger to effort, monsieur.'

'Forgive me, but I must ask, does your present financial situation permit you to live as you have in the past?'

'For the time being, it does. But the marques's wealth was traditional, that is to say, the ownership of land.'

Ferrar had seen this before, wealth that was difficult to turn into money, so that the individual was said to be *living in reduced circumstances*. 'And when you spoke with your husband's friend, on the subject of the debt, what was his response?'

'He was rather cruel, if I may put it that way. For he claimed that the marques, in his decline, was not in touch with reality.'

'I dislike asking this, Marquesa, but is there any chance that this was in fact the case?'

'No, monsieur, his mind was clear until the end. He was simply a generous man, often kind to his friends and family.'

Ferrar took a few sheets of Coudert stationery from his drawer and placed them flat on his desk, then, with fountain pen in hand, began to gather details. How much money? The money was in Belgian francs, the equivalent of a hundred and thirty thousand American dollars. Paid – he hoped! – by cheque? No, the marques had a safe in his office and kept large amounts of cash. On and on, worse and worse. And when Ferrar asked about the marques's estates, the answer had to be, as Ferrar anticipated, 'They are in Spain, monsieur.'

When Ferrar had all the information he needed, at least to begin with, he said, 'Can you tell me something of yourself?'

Here she paused, then said, 'My father's family was of mixed French and Spanish blood – I am named Maria Cristina for my father's mother, whose origins were in the Navarre, though she used to say that many generations ago they lived in Portugal. My father's family came from the Norman regions west of Paris, and my maiden name was Palestrin. My mother's people came from Lombardy, northern Italy, and had the title of cavaliere, small nobility, something like a baronet. My mother was born in Padua, and in many ways I favour her – I have, particularly, her eyes.' Using the tips of her gloved fingers, she raised her veil, said, 'Now you can see them,' then lowered it.

He saw. The marquesa's eyes, which had been simply dark when seen through the webby strands of her veil, were prominent, luminous, and coloured a rich, incredibly warm shade of chestnut brown. The combination, of brown eyes and golden hair, had a powerful effect on Ferrar, but a small thing compared to the gesture itself, the raising of the veil. This was seductive, he thought, but meant to be so? The marquesa was all innocence, her expression unchanged, she did not smile. Still . . .

'I was educated at a convent school in Angers,' she continued, 'then at a private academy in Geneva. At the age of twenty-five I married the marques – we met at a spa in Baden-Baden, where young women are often taken by their parents in hope of finding a suitable match. My husband was twenty-two years older than I, but that difference did not affect us, except perhaps in our decision not to have children. We lived, for the fifteen years of our marriage, mostly in hotels. In Lugano, at Saint Moritz in the winter, Biarritz in the summer, sometimes in Carlsbad – my husband always believed himself prone to ailments and often took treatments at spas. We lived, monsieur, the life of the nineteenth-century European aristocracy, coming home to Brussels so that the marques could spend some time at his office, and visiting Madrid when he had to attend to family matters. As for the estates, he never visited them, preferring not to see the condition of the people who worked there. Though they, I should add, now own them.' After a moment of reflection, she said, 'It was in fact a quiet life and we were in many ways a happy and well-suited couple.'

When she went no further, Ferrar said, 'And where are you staying in Paris, if I may ask?'

'I was for a time at the Bristol, but have recently taken rooms at a small hotel in the Seventh Arrondissement called the Windsor. Do you know it?'

'I have heard of it,' Ferrar said. More a residence than a hotel, the Windsor was expensive, private, and discreet, known to be a preference of foreign artists from wealthy families, eccentric older women with small dogs, and disgraced aristocracy. Ferrar sensed that the marquesa had told him all she wanted him to know, so said, 'You have been very generous with your time, Marquesa, I shall be in touch with you once we determine how to proceed.'

She rose effortlessly to her feet, and Ferrar also stood. 'Monsieur Ferrar,' she said, 'thank you for your gracious interest,' then extended her hand, palm down. Ferrar held the hand lightly, and even though he kissed it with the merest brush of his lips, he could feel the warmth of her skin through the thin leather of her glove.

Ferrar went to his office window and looked out on the Champs-Elysées. It was dusk, and it was raining, so that the light of the streetlamps was reflected on the wet pavement. A few minutes later, a driver in a suit emerged from a large automobile, closed umbrella in hand. When he reappeared, the umbrella was up and held above the marquesa's head as the two walked to the car. The driver held the door, the marquesa slid inside, and that was the last he saw of her. But, he thought, he would see her again.

*

Early Friday morning, three-thirty, the phone rang in Ferrar's apartment. He woke with heart pounding, rolled out of bed, and, with a blanket over his shoulders – he did not wear pyjamas – stumbled into his office. 'Yes? Who is it?'

'It's Max, I'm calling from Karviná, the railway border station between Czechoslovakia and Poland. They're giving me trouble here. They've told me our freight wagons can't go directly to Danzig, they have to wait in Warsaw for a day, then they'll be added to another train that will be made up in the Praga freight yards. The delay isn't serious, we just have to make sure that it works as they say it will. And you have to fly into Warsaw anyhow, so I'll meet you there and we'll check on the shipment.'

'Freight shipping, you think it's all set, but then . . .'

'If I want to talk to you later will you be at your office?'

'Until about three in the afternoon, then I'm leaving for Le Bourget and taking the five o'clock LOT flight to Warsaw. I'll be there about nine-thirty on Saturday morning.'

It was freezing in the apartment, Ferrar held the blanket together with one hand and with the other searched through his desk drawer looking for a Gitane. There were three, very stale and dry in an old packet. Ferrar lit one and said, 'Have you been in Poland?'

'Yes, for a week or so.'

'How was it?'

De Lyon was careful on the telephone. 'Not bad, not good . . . you could feel the tension. After what happened in Austria they figure that their appointment with Hitler has been moved up . . . It's all over the newspapers, but they're being tough and brave about the whole thing. As for us, our arrangements, I believe we'll be all right. The Germans in Danzig are in the street, but so far they're only marching. Listen, Cristián, you're going to be met at the Warsaw airfield by a friend of mine called Nestor. Don't be put off by the way he looks, he does . . . some necessary work for me and he's good at it. He might be late but don't worry, he'll be there.

He speaks some French . . . you don't speak Polish, do you?'

'Not a word.'

'You'll manage. You have your visa?'

'Yes, Max, I have my visa. One of the associates in my office is assigned to take care of travel documents; he knows all the consular officials at the Paris embassies.'

'Good. Then, if all goes well, I'll see you in Warsaw on Saturday morning. Nestor will know which hotel, probably the Europejski. Oh yes, can you get a thousand dollars from your bank? If you can, bring it with you, and also the . . . present I gave you. Do you know what I mean?' Ferrar had to think about it, finally realized that de Lyon was talking about the Walther PPK automatic.

'I do.'

'Then I'll see you Saturday.'

'Be careful, Max.' Ferrar hung up the telephone and returned to his bedroom. Should he try to go back to sleep? He went into the kitchen, poured himself half a glass of brandy, brought it into the bedroom, and sat on the edge of the bed. Outside, seen through a glaze of frost on the window, the Place Saint-Sulpice was lit by a single streetlamp. When he finished the cigarette and the brandy, he went over to his armoire, took the Walther from the drawer that held his socks, and put it on a table where he kept his wallet and keys, so he wouldn't forget it when he went to work in the morning.

The LOT flight wasn't crowded, Ferrar had two seats to himself. Across the aisle, a round woman with red cheeks was praying – lips moving, eyes closed – certain that this devilish contraption would fall from the sky. Ferrar had bought a *Le Soir* at the waiting-room news-stand; there was a front-page news from Spain – Barcelona had been bombed by Italian pilots flying German Heinkel aircraft. The bombing, seventeen raids over two days, had been unopposed – the Republic didn't have the fighter planes to protect the city. The

Italian pilots flew just above the buildings, moving from neighbourhood to neighbourhood, killing one thousand three hundred residents and wounding over two thousand. According to the *Le Soir* correspondent, the injured lay on stretchers in the street and gave the clenched-fist salute when people stopped to see if they could help. Afterwards, from around the world, there was angry protest over the barbaric assault.

In Warsaw, at ten-twenty in the morning, Ferrar waited in the doorway of the corrugated-iron building that served as airline terminal. The wind was blowing hard from the northeast, from the Russian steppe, the cloudless sky a powerful shade of deep blue. Ferrar looked at his watch, the other passengers from the LOT flight had long ago departed so he stood alone, and feeling as though he had grit under his eyelids. Had he been abandoned? At last he was approached by a short, thin man, maybe thirty years old, hurrying towards him with hands in pockets, who said in French – at first Ferrar didn't know what it was – 'Sorry late, you are Ferrar? Yes? I am Nestor.' He grinned, eyes sparkling, mouth wide to reveal terribly crooked brown teeth, and shook Ferrar's hand up and down. He was a strange-looking fellow, in a tan suit that sagged at the knees and a shirt of green and lavender checks buttoned at the neck. Ferrar had never seen such a shirt, perhaps, he thought, an eastern European shirt. Nestor pointed to the other end of the terminal and said, with another dreadful grin, 'Come with me, sir.'

Ferrar walked the length of the building, following Nestor to a heavy Buick automobile which he knew to be the favoured transportation of those with both money and experience of Polish roads. It wasn't an old car but had been hard used, the front end was covered with dried mud, the windshield, starred with pebble hits, had a zigzag crack from top to bottom on the passenger side and bore semicircular streaks of mud above the windshield wiper.

Settling himself behind the wheel, Nestor said, 'To Europejski!

Hang on!' He meant it – the car sped off, big and well powered, bucking over ridges in the dirt road, throwing up great splashes of brown water as it bounced through potholes. To Nestor, a car was meant to go as fast as it could and Ferrar wondered, seriously wondered, if this was the end for him. As they sped around a curve, the back end began to slide, but Nestor stepped on the gas and the Buick straightened out of the skid. Swinging into the next curve, still speeding, they came upon a horse-drawn cart headed the other way. Ferrar stiffened, prepared for impact, then Nestor swore and threw the wheel over hard, the tyres chewed up clumps of dirt from a field, the driver of the cart made an obscene gesture, and his horse whinnied with fright as the Buick flew past.

Eventually, they rolled to a stop in front of the Europejski, where the giant uniformed doorman never blinked an eye – he'd seen worse in his time – and held the door as Ferrar emerged, grateful to be in one piece. 'I wait,' Nestor said. The Europejski lobby was luxurious, all plush furniture and potted palms. At the desk, Ferrar was told that Monsieur de Lyon was in Room 412, then was taken up to his own room by a bellboy, no more than thirteen years old. Ferrar called de Lyon's room. 'Hello, Cristián,' de Lyon said. Then, with a laugh in his voice, 'You enjoyed the ride?'

'*Merde*,' Ferrar said. 'Does he always drive like that?'

'Always. He hits only small things, and never animals. Nestor is good to animals, especially chickens, though I'm not sure how he does it.'

'Do we have to go somewhere right away?' Ferrar said. 'I'm in need of a hot bath.'

'Help yourself. You have twenty minutes for a bath, then we're going to look at our shipment.'

Ferrar had his bath, looked longingly at the bed, then called de Lyon and they met in the lobby. 'Now it's off to the railyard,' de Lyon said. 'We've got six freight wagons all to ourselves.'

The railyards were in Praga, Warsaw's industrial zone across the Vistula from the city. Here the Buick bounced over rough cobbled streets, past miles of factories and workshops which flavoured the air with the smells of burned metal and coal smoke. At last they came to the railyards, below street level in a kind of valley enclosed by weedy hillsides, where some thirty or so tracks, steel rails glinting in the sunlight, ran off into the distance, then disappeared into a tunnel. On the street above the tracks, the yard supervisor's office was in an ancient wooden shack. De Lyon knocked on the door, the supervisor answered. He was a weathered old man wearing a cardigan and a railway uniform cap from another time. De Lyon, speaking native, idiomatic Polish – he would later tell Ferrar what had been said – was courteous and spent a moment being amiable. The yard supervisor peered up at a blackboard and said, 'You're looking for the Karviná/Warsaw train, originating in Brno.' He squinted at the chalk writing, then said, 'It's in, come with me.'

They descended to the tracks on a rickety stairway, then walked, their shoes crunching on cinders, beside the rails as the supervisor searched for the Karviná/Warsaw freight train. At last he found it, a line of old covered wagons that rode high above exposed iron wheels. From his briefcase, de Lyon produced the carbon of a waybill, and the three moved along the track as the supervisor checked each wagon, looking for the corresponding numbers. Forty wagons later, they came to the locomotive, where a mechanic was using an oilcan to lubricate the wheel bearings.

The supervisor was puzzled, shook his head, and said, 'How did we miss them? Can I have another look at the waybill?' De Lyon handed it over, the supervisor studied the numbers, then said, 'This *is* the right train, unless the waybill is wrong.'

'Does that happen?' de Lyon said.

'It *can*, I suppose. Mostly it doesn't. Let's go back to the other end.'

They turned and walked the length of the train, the supervisor was careful, checking the numbers on every car. When they reached the last car, the supervisor took off his cap, smoothed his hair, put the cap back on, then reached into the pocket of his cardigan, brought out a half-smoked cigar and lit it. 'Something's not right,' he said. 'Your freight has to be here. Are you sure it was Karviná/ Warsaw?'

De Lyon nodded.

'Did you see it loaded?'

'I saw the wagons, at Karviná. The railway people there checked them through to Warsaw.'

The supervisor was stumped. 'Well . . .' he said.

From his pocket, de Lyon took a wad of hundred-dollar bills. 'We really need your . . .'

'Put that away,' the supervisor said.

The money disappeared. 'I didn't mean to . . . sometimes people . . .'

'Not me,' the supervisor said. 'It's my job to help you, so let me do it.'

Finally, Ferrar could stand it no longer and said to de Lyon, 'What the hell is going on?'

'Our wagons seem to have vanished.'

'Let's go back to the office,' the supervisor said. 'I have to use the telephone. What were you shipping?'

'Armaments, anti-tank cannon that are going to the Army of the Republic in Spain, and crates of anti-tank shells.'

The supervisor's cigar had almost gone out, he blew on the lit end, then inhaled, produced a cloud of fragrant smoke and said, 'To fight the German tanks, is that it?'

'Yes,' de Lyon said. 'We work for the Spanish embassy in Paris.'

'The Germans weren't so bad in 1916, we had them in Warsaw and they were decent enough – they chased the Russians out of here so we were happy to have them. But they're different now, they've changed, so better if they stay in Germany.'

'For your sake, I hope they do,' de Lyon said.

'Let's get back to the office,' the supervisor said, and they climbed up the long stairway to the street. In the office, the

supervisor started to telephone stations down the line from Warsaw, taking a few minutes to say hello, then asking questions. Ferrar
stood there, listening to the stream of Polish, his heart sinking each
time the supervisor hung up. 'Not in Radom,' he said to de Lyon.
'You're shipping through here to the port of Gdansk?' he said,
using the Polish name for Danzig.

'We are,' de Lyon said. 'The shipment was supposed to leave
tonight, we wanted to make sure everything was all right before it
left Warsaw.'

'Well, it's good you did, otherwise you'd be sitting up in Gdansk
wondering what happened. Let's try Kielce,' he said. Another chat,
a few questions, then the supervisor said, 'Not in Kielce.'

'Could a shipment like this somehow be rerouted?'

'It *could* be, if somebody altered the waybill, but why would
anybody do that?'

'Our freight is worth a lot of money,' de Lyon said, 'and there
are people who don't want these weapons in Spain.'

'Then it could be anywhere,' the supervisor said. 'There's
miles and miles of railway track between Brno and Gdansk.' He
paused for a moment, then said, 'Did you have trouble in Karviná?
Some of the railwaymen down there have their own ideas about
politics.'

De Lyon was hesitant. 'No, I didn't think so, they told me the
shipment had to have a layover in Warsaw, I thought it was just a
change of schedule.'

'Maybe more than that,' the supervisor said.

He tried Karviná, asked a question, then said, 'Is Vladek there?'
He waited, hand over the mouthpiece of the telephone, and said to
de Lyon, 'Old friend, down in Karviná, at least he'll tell me the
truth.' When Vladek picked up the phone, the supervisor talked for
a while, then once again waited. Finally, Vladek returned, but
didn't stay on for long. The supervisor turned to de Lyon and said,
'The waybill was altered in Karviná, your shipment went right
through Warsaw last night.'

Now there was desperation in de Lyon's voice. 'Does he know where it is?'

'Bydgoszcz,' the supervisor said, dialling the phone. 'Let's make sure.'

He spoke briefly with someone in Bydgoszcz, then hung up and said, 'Your wagons are sitting in the Bydgoszcz railyard, waiting to be offloaded. I think you'd better get up there and see about it.'

'Is it far?' de Lyon said.

'A hundred and eighty-eight miles,' the supervisor said. Then, '*Bastards*.'

De Lyon put out his hand and as the supervisor took it said, 'Thank you, sir. Thank you.'

'I'd hurry, if I were you,' the supervisor said.

De Lyon and Ferrar crossed the street, Nestor was asleep in the front seat of the Buick.

Ferrar would remember the drive to Bydgoszcz. Nestor did his best, or his worst, depending on how you saw it. For most of the way to the town, the road surface was frozen mud, sometimes thawed. Ferrar was in the back seat, using both hands to brace himself on the smooth leather seat-covering. When the car bounced, his head hit the roof of the car, so he clamped his jaws together in order not to crack a tooth. In the car, nobody spoke, Nestor was all concentration, squinting at the road ahead of them, trying to see through the muddy windshield, hands white on the steering wheel. At one point, when he took a curve too fast, they spun in a circle and the Buick stalled as a farm truck managed to swing around them with a hoarse bleat of its horn. Nestor swore at the truck, then, after a few tries, the ignition worked and the engine coughed to life. A mile later the car skidded off the road, Nestor had time for a twist of the wheel, which meant the car hit the tree with the edge of the wheel well, not the radiator. Again, the Buick stalled. The three climbed out and gathered at the side of the car, where they saw that the bottom of the bumper had wedged against the front tyre. Now they weren't going anywhere. But they were. De Lyon and Ferrar grabbed either side of the bottom of the bumper next to the wheel and, slowly, straining as hard as they could, forced the metal away from the tyre. This effort cost them; Ferrar bent over with hands on knees, de Lyon leaning on the car, trying to catch his breath. Finally de Lyon said, 'We'd better get moving,' and they climbed back into the Buick. Nestor revved the engine, engaged the clutch, and away they went. When they saw the cow, Nestor slammed on the brakes and the car stopped a few feet from the animal, which stared at them. Nestor rolled his window down, stuck his head out, and shouted. The cow didn't move, why should it? De Lyon got out of the car, walked towards the cow, and clapped his hands as hard as he could. This didn't work. So he circled the animal and smacked it on the rump. Puzzled, the cow looked over its shoulder and swished its tail. With the second slap the cow, taking its own sweet time, put its head down and moved out of the way.

By the time they found the Bydgoszcz railyards it was after four. De Lyon, holding a handkerchief on his palm where he'd cut himself freeing the tyre, entered the railyard office. Ferrar followed. A railway clerk was in the process of filling out a form, typing carefully, making sure he got it right. 'Excuse me,' de Lyon said, 'Can you—'

'Can't you see I'm busy?' the clerk said.

'Sorry,' de Lyon said. 'We'll wait.'

Like the cow, the clerk didn't care to be hurried and made a show of taking his time. De Lyon did not do to him what he'd done to the cow but he surely thought about it. At last, the clerk felt that he'd shown who was boss here and, turning in his swivel chair, said, 'Now, how can I help you?'

De Lyon explained that there had been an unfortunate error in the waybill prepared in Karviná, and was seeking to have his shipment, in six wagons, sent up to Danzig.

'That's a shame,' the clerk said. 'People ought to be more careful. But, don't worry. No, calm down, we'll take care of it.'

De Lyon visibly relaxed. The clerk reached into a drawer and
took out a printed form. 'All you have to do is fill this out and post
it to the central freight office in Warsaw. A few days, you'll be on
your way. There's a nice hotel on Pilsudski Street, I'm sure they'll
have a room.'

De Lyon took a deep breath. 'Sir,' he said, 'our shipment is
scheduled to be loaded onto a freighter in Gdansk. Tonight.'

The clerk shrugged. 'I expect you will have to reschedule. Now,
just fill out that form, you can get an envelope at the post office.'

Ferrar stepped closer to de Lyon and said, in French, 'Ask to see
the stationmaster.' When de Lyon did this there was, just for the
barest instant, a spark of hatred in the clerk's eyes, then it was gone.
He picked up the phone and spoke a few words, then said to de
Lyon, 'The stationmaster's office is at the central station, but he
won't be there long. On Saturday he goes home early.'

'Thank you,' de Lyon said. 'Can you direct us to the central
station?'

'Oh, just ask somebody on the street how to get there, I'm sure
you'll find it.'

They sat in the Buick for a time and talked it over. 'What if the
shipment were delayed for a week?' Ferrar said. 'Would that
be . . . ?' But he never reached the *so bad,* de Lyon cut him off.

'But it won't leave in a week,' de Lyon said. 'It will be unloaded
and sold off, and the people who organized this will take the money.
We are not facing the annoying difficulties of life, we are under attack, an attack designed to draw us into accepting our loss, and
pretending that it was simply misfortune.'

'Who is it?' Ferrar said.

'We'll never know. If this is being done professionally – and it
is – these bastards will remain in the dark. Where they live. It could
be Franco's operatives, it could be the Germans, it could be the
Russians – the Comintern. Spain should be flattered to have so

many enemies. But it doesn't matter. Now, what to do with the stationmaster?'

Ferrar thought it over. 'If he's in on it, the clerk has telephoned him, and he's sitting in his office, rubbing his hands, waiting to play his part. Still, we have to play *our* part, which means we must ask him for help.'

'Should we try to scare him?'

'That will lead to jail, Max.'

De Lyon nodded and said, 'Let's go, Nestor.'

They found the station easily enough. It had been built to be a symbol of the town's progress, two storeys of grey brick with elaborate stonework over the entry, but an upper corner had been blown off during the fighting in 1914 and the roof had been repaired with heavy planks. Nestor waited in the car, de Lyon and Ferrar found the stationmaster's office down a hallway from the waiting room. The stationmaster himself was on the telephone when Ferrar and de Lyon entered.

He was a big, handsome, square-jawed fellow with a thick moustache, and very much at ease – feet up on the desk, railway uniform jacket hung over the back of the chair revealing braces and a carefully ironed shirt. Waving them to sit down, he continued his conversation, speaking in Polish. But Ferrar caught a word he recognized, *zhid,* which meant Yid. It happened that Ferrar could see de Lyon's face when the word was spoken, but de Lyon barely reacted – a single, involuntary blink, that was it. The stationmaster hung up and, still leaning back in his swivel chair, folded his hands behind his head. 'Gentlemen,' he said, genial as could be, 'how may I help you?'

De Lyon was nervous, upset, not exactly *pleading* for help but close enough. Poor them. What could they do? They'd been told their wagons were in Bydgoszcz, but earlier they'd been told they were in *Warsaw.* Was there anything they could do? Anything at all? If not, de Lyon continued, they would fill out the form as they'd been instructed by the clerk in the railyard office. Gloom.

Submission. It was, Ferrar thought, a fine performance.

The stationmaster was sympathetic, and reassuring. 'Oh your shipment is here, gentlemen, that I can promise. This is just one of those damn breakdowns you get in a railway system. I spend my life trying to straighten things out when somebody fills in the wrong name, that's all it takes.'

'Well, so we just submit the form? How long will they keep it?' de Lyon asked, a whine in his voice.

Not long. In fact, the stationmaster would save them the cost of a stamp, they could fill in the form right here, in his office, and he'd send it with other paperwork that had to go to the central freight office in Warsaw.

Grimly, de Lyon nodded, taking his medicine. If that was the best that could be done, then that was what they would do. 'Monsieur de Lyon,' Ferrar said in French – French was the second language of Poland and Ferrar suspected the stationmaster understood it. 'Would it be possible for us to make sure that the wagons are in the Bydgoszcz railyard?'

Ferrar had guessed right, the stationmaster switched to French, saying, 'And you are, monsieur?'

'My name is Ferrar, I'm with an American law firm in Paris, I'm Monsieur de Lyon's attorney.' *American* was a good choice here, Ferrar saw it hit home.

'It would be a great favour to us if we could at least be sure the shipment isn't lost,' de Lyon said.

The stationmaster had a big, gold watch. He looked at it, then said, 'I don't see why not, I just have time.'

'Oh, that would be . . .' De Lyon was almost overcome with gratitude, causing Ferrar to think: *Easy, Max, don't overdo it.*

'I'm happy to help,' the stationmaster said. 'May I see your copy of the waybill?'

De Lyon took the waybill carbon from his briefcase and handed it over, the stationmaster put it in the inside pocket of his uniform jacket and said, *'Merci bien.'*

Ferrar read the stationmaster's mind: *And you'll never see* that *again.*

'Our friend is waiting in the car,' Ferrar said. 'I'll just go get him, he must be wondering what's become of us.'

Daylight was fading when they, now accompanied by Nestor, reached the railway tracks. Fortunately, the numbers on the wagons were painted white – thus visible in contrast to the dark wood. De Lyon and the stationmaster chatted as they walked, trudging along the tracks until they reached a line of freight wagons still coupled to a locomotive. Just to make sure, the stationmaster retrieved the waybill from his pocket and was struggling to see the print when he was aided by the light on the engine of a train that had just arrived on a neighbouring track. With a series of clanks and bangs, the train came to a halt, the locomotive venting a plume of white steam into the dusk. 'The wagons should be here somewhere,' the stationmaster said. 'This is the train from Karviná.' They moved from one wagon to the next, then the stationmaster said, 'Ah, here they are! Just as I said. You see? 605 and 606 and the rest.'

'Excuse me, sir,' de Lyon said. 'Could we perhaps have a look at the freight? If it's not too much trouble. To make sure the shipment is . . . as it should be?'

The stationmaster wasn't pleased. Still, he'd come this far, why not take the next step in the little play? But, when he went to raise the iron bar that locked the door of 605, a surprise. 'What's this?' he said. There was a yellow cardboard ticket, covered with print, wired to the bar. 'How on earth . . .' he said, theatrically shocked.

'What is it?' de Lyon said.

'My regrets, gentlemen, but your shipment appears to have been impounded.'

'Impounded?'

'I had no idea, but the central freight office has directed that your shipment be held until an administrative procedure determines its disposition.'

'How long will *that* take?' de Lyon said.

'Who can say? A few weeks perhaps, unless there's some problem.'

De Lyon, tired of the game, took out one of his brown cigarettes and lit it with his steel lighter. When he snapped the lighter closed he said, 'Monsieur stationmaster, it's time we had a real discussion, I think, because this is all horseshit, I think.'

'What did you say?'

'You heard me. Now, these wagons contain armaments, for which we have all the proper documents. So, you will kindly tell me how we are going to move them up to Gdansk. Tonight.'

'It can't be done. We have our regulations, they must be observed.'

'Not this evening.'

Defiance? The stationmaster would not stand for it. His face knotted with anger, his voice raised, he said, 'Don't you dare contradict me, Monsieur Cohen or Levy or whatever your name is. I say what goes on here, so don't you try any of your sneaky little tricks on *me*! We've had more than enough of your kind in Poland.'

Crack. The speed of the blow was astonishing. De Lyon's hand, as though on a coiled spring, swept backhand across the stationmaster's face. Shocked, his mouth open with surprise, the stationmaster put his hand to his cheek.

'How's that for a little trick?' de Lyon said.

'You won't get away with this,' the stationmaster said, rubbing his cheek. 'I'll have you in jail.'

'Maybe. But tonight we're going to Gdansk.'

Ferrar had been absorbed by the exchange between the stationmaster and de Lyon, now he noticed that Nestor had disappeared. He'd been there when the ticket of impound was discovered, but had slipped away.

'Here is what we will do,' de Lyon said. 'It will be your job to drive this train up to Gdansk.'

The stationmaster wilted; arrogance deserted him, now he was frightened. 'No, I can't,' he said, pleading. 'I don't know how, I worked for years as a conductor, punching tickets.' This was credible – de Lyon believed it and the stationmaster, sensing that he did, pressed his advantage. 'The train will *crash*,' he said.

For some seconds they all stood there, de Lyon trying to decide what to do next, but Nestor was ahead of him: he'd foreseen what would happen and had done something about it. They could barely see him as he came along the track, almost hidden by the large man in front of him. What they *could* see of Nestor was his hand, which, as he marched the man forward, was pressing the snout of a revolver into the soft flesh beneath the man's chin.

'I thought we might need him,' Nestor explained. 'He was driving the train that just arrived.'

'What about the stoker?' de Lyon said.

'I told him to wait.' After a moment, he added, 'Do you want me to tie him up?'

'Yes, Nestor, if he hasn't already run away, make sure he doesn't.'

Nestor headed back down the track. The terrified engineer said, 'Please don't kill me, I have a wife and a child.'

'What's your name?' de Lyon said.

'Kowalski.'

'Tell me, Kowalski, can you drive this train up to Gdansk?'

The engineer nodded.

'Then,' de Lyon said, 'that's what you'll do.'

It took time, but eventually they got under way. Nestor, having tied up the stoker, was sent back to the car and told to drive it up to Gdansk – they would meet at the Bernhof Hotel. 'We'll wait for you,' de Lyon said. 'It's dark. Drive slowly, you're no use to me dead.' After a moment he said, in a different voice, 'Thank you, Nestor.'

They had removed the impound tags, opened the wagons, found crates of anti-tank shells with Skoda identification markings stencilled on the raw wood, and the anti-tank guns themselves, smelling strongly of preservative grease. They put the stationmaster in there as well, telling him he would be released in Gdansk, then barring the door.

'Can we let him go in Gdansk?' Ferrar said. 'He'll run straight to the police.'

'Hostages are a real nuisance,' de Lyon said. 'We'll just have to keep him until the last moment.'

After the freight rolled out of the yard, Ferrar and de Lyon took turns shovelling coal into the locomotive's firebox, and soon enough their hands and faces were powdered with coal dust. When it was de Lyon's turn, Ferrar stood next to the engineer and stared out over the night-time countryside. Not much to see, beneath a quarter moon low on the horizon; now and then the distant light of a farmhouse, occasionally a local station, dark and deserted. At Chelmno, there was a crowd of passengers on the platform, waiting for a night train headed north to the Baltic coast, idly watching the freight as it clattered past. A few miles later they slowed for a railway bridge, where the sound of the train deepened as it crossed the river. 'We're coming up on Terespol station,' the engineer said. 'There's a switch that has to be thrown, so we move to another track.'

As the train stopped, a railwayman with a lantern came out of the station house and approached the locomotive. 'What's this?' he called out to the engineer. 'It can't be the eleven fifty-six.'

'It's a Special,' the engineer replied. 'Freight going to the port.'

The railwayman walked up the track and, using both hands, moved a lever from one side to the other. Then he raised the lantern twice and the locomotive was shunted onto the track to Gdansk.

*

11:25, Gdansk. The bar stood at the foot of a wharf in Gdansk port, where the lights of the quayside buildings were reflected in the still, black water. Inside, in clouds of cigarette smoke, off-duty stevedores were drinking vodka or beer or both until it was time to load another freighter. Ferrar and de Lyon – Nestor was still battling the Polish roads – had cleaned up at the Bernhof, then found the bar where they were to meet de Lyon's friend, called Bolek, who ran the Polish dockworkers union in the city. They took an empty table, then were joined by two young stevedores, Zigi and Ivo, blond, snub-nosed, and hard to tell apart; both wore brimmed caps down over their eyes and had unlit stubs of cigarettes pasted to their lower lips. 'Bolek said to tell you he's been held up,' Zigi explained. 'He'll be here as soon as he can.' He took a sip of his vodka and said, 'You got here right on time, any trouble on the way?'

'Some,' de Lyon said. 'Our wagons are ready to be unloaded, do you know when that will be?'

Zigi shrugged. 'What ship?'

'The *Sabina,* out of Valencia.'

'Maybe after midnight . . . they'll let us know when they need us.'

Ferrar was drinking beer. He would have preferred a vodka, but in his present state of exhaustion that might have knocked him out cold. He lit a Gitane and offered one to Ivo, sitting next to him. Ivo, who spoke a bit of French, thanked him and said, 'So, you're in Max de Lyon's gang.'

Ferrar nodded. 'I am,' he said.

'You must be busy, with the war going on.'

'We are,' Ferrar said.

'Fucking fascists,' Ivo said. 'The union gave a big party last week, proceeds to Aid for Spain. We made plenty, believe me.' Something across the room caught his attention and he said, 'What's *he* doing here?' Then tapped Zigi on the shoulder and with his eyes pointed out a man having a drink at the bar.

'Somebody you know?' Ferrar said.

'German crane operator. Germans don't come in here, this is the Polish bar.' Gdansk was a German city, ten percent Polish.

'He's just having a drink,' Ferrar said.

'For now. You know Bolek?'

'I don't, he's Max's friend.'

'He's the boss of our union, and he'll make sure your shipment gets into the hold . . . the Germans don't like to load freight that's going to Spain.'

Zigi said, 'Now look at this.' Two men entered the bar and stood next to the crane operator. 'What do they think they're doing?'

Ivo shook his head. 'Making trouble, maybe.'

'They better not,' Zigi said.

A minute later, de Lyon went over to the bar and bought a bottle of vodka. As he turned to go back to the table, the crane operator bumped against him. De Lyon stared at the man, who said, 'You made me spill my drink,' and poured some beer on the bar. The bartender said, 'Hey, take it easy.' The man sneered. De Lyon returned to the table.

'He push you?' Zigi said.

'Forget it,' de Lyon said. 'He's drunk.'

'Looking for a fight,' Ivo said.

'He'll find it,' Zigi said. 'I haven't hit a German for days.'

'Ignore him,' de Lyon said.

From Zigi, a certain laugh, *as though I could*. Two more men came into the bar, some of the stevedores stopped talking. Outside, a ship's foghorn cut through the sound of the engines that ran the loading machinery.

De Lyon unscrewed the cap of the vodka bottle and said, 'Who's ready?'

Zigi and Ivo drank off their vodka and de Lyon refilled their glasses. 'Cristián?'

'I better stay with beer.'

De Lyon grinned. 'It's been a long day.'

Zigi stood up and walked to another table where a man, a little older than the other stevedores, was talking to his friends. He had a tough face, scars by his eyes, his nose broken, maybe more than once. Zigi stood by his shoulder and said something, the man looked around the room. He didn't like what he saw.

De Lyon said to Ivo, 'Tell Zigi not to start anything. We're going to need you to load our freight on the ship, we don't want you locked up.'

Ivo said, 'We won't start it. But if they do . . .'

Another man came into the bar. He had a beard that traced his jawline and wore a loden jacket and a green hat. 'Hessler,' Ivo said.

'Who is Hessler?' de Lyon said.

'German politician, Nazi party leader.'

Hessler spoke briefly to the man next to the crane operator, then left the bar. 'I guess he's not staying for the fun,' Zigi said.

From the bar: 'Hey! What the hell?' The front of the man's shirt was wet. 'Watch what you're doing.'

'You watch,' the crane operator said.

The man swung and connected, the crane operator hit him back. The bartender vaulted over the bar, the bottom half of a pool cue in his hand. A table went over with a crash of broken glass. Somebody swore, another fight started, this time close to de Lyon and Ferrar. Zigi came on the run and said to Ivo, 'Tomasz says to get them out of here.' Then he grabbed Ferrar by the shoulder, hauled him to his feet, and started to shove him towards the door, as Ivo did the same thing with de Lyon. But two big men came running through the door, and a group of stevedores went for them, hitting hard, Ferrar could hear the meaty thuds of body punches amid snarled curses. One of the Germans had blood running from his nose, another one swung at de Lyon, who blocked his hand with his forearm, then Zigi grabbed him by the head. The two struggled for a few seconds, then another man broke a vodka bottle over the

German's head and he said, 'Ach,' and went down to one knee. He started to rise and Zigi kicked him in the stomach. He folded in half and something fell from his hand. Ferrar saw that it was a knife and tried to reach for it but there was somebody in his way so he kicked it across the floor.

Then Ferrar and de Lyon were pushed out into the street.

It was after two in the morning when de Lyon and Ferrar stood with Bolek and watched crates of anti-tank shells in cargo nets being lowered into the hold of the *Sabina*. Towards the bow of the ship, the stevedores were using a winch to roll the anti-tank cannon up a gangplank. Ferrar should have felt satisfaction but he was too tired to feel much of anything. The first wisps of a night-time fog drifted through the glare of the dock's floodlights.

'What happened in the bar?' Bolek said. He was a balding man with a paunch and an educated voice.

'A fight . . .' de Lyon said.

'It was certainly a fight,' Ferrar said. 'A fistfight, a bar fight, but one of them had a knife and went after Max. So maybe the whole thing was staged, to get rid of my friend here.'

'In Gdansk? Here it's usually in the back, down an alley,' Bolek said.

'Your stevedores saved us,' de Lyon said. 'Ivo's at the hospital getting sewed up.'

'They're tough kids,' Bolek said. 'I had a feeling you might be better off with a little protection. You never know, right? And, any day now, this city is going to explode, and we'll be fighting them with guns. Hitler has started screaming "Danzig! Danzig!" and his propaganda machine has been turned on. You see it in the British press: "To die for Danzig?" As in, who would be so stupid to go to war over some Polish city nobody has ever heard of? And it's work-ing; the party has technicians who study public opinion and they're usually right.' For a time they watched the loading, then Bolek said,

'By the way, we've got the Bydgoszcz stationmaster at the union office, he'll be on a train in the morning.'

'Did he ask for the police?'

'Not that I know of. He had a bad experience and now he just wants to go home.'

'How long until our shipment is loaded?' de Lyon said.

'Six wagons? Maybe another half-hour.' Bolek looked at his watch. 'The *Sabina* sails at five-thirty, are you going to stay here until then?'

'I might,' de Lyon said. 'I'd at least like to see the loading done, then we have to go back to the hotel and make sure Nestor got there. He drove up from Bydgoszcz last night.'

'At night?' Bolek laughed. 'Good old crazy Nestor.'

'There when you need him,' de Lyon said.

Bolek looked at his watch again and said, 'I have to be somewhere, so . . .' He shook hands with Ferrar, then with de Lyon. 'Coming back any time soon, Max?'

'Maybe not for a while.'

'Then I'll say goodbye, because if this war starts you won't see me again, likely never again.' He shrugged and said, 'But we did some good work together, and that's what matters.' They shook hands once more, then Bolek turned and walked away down the dock.

The *Sabina* left the dock at six-thirty, working through a heavy sea in light fog. Her original destination was the port of Valencia, which meant sailing through the Straits of Gibraltar and into the Mediterranean. And that would have been the end of her – an Italian submarine was waiting at the Nationalist port of Palma de Majorca, with orders to torpedo the *Sabina* as she approached the Spanish coast. But now, because the French had opened the border, she would make for the port of Bordeaux, 938 nautical miles from Gdansk, where the shipment would come under the control of the

Army of the Republic, then be sent south by rail. The *Sabina* was an old ship, for years a tramp steamer, and nine knots per hour was the best she could do. So, five days to Bordeaux, then on to Salou, the base of the Republic's Fifth Army Corps, now rearming for a stand at the river Ebro.

If it failed, the war was lost.

THE
MARQUESA

A PLEASANT DAY IN PARIS, THE NINTH OF APRIL, THE SUN IN AND OUT of the billowy white clouds that blew across the city from the North Sea. Cristián Ferrar was in the walled garden of the Hungarian legation: gravel paths, well-barbered shrubs, and a fountain where a green-stained face of Pan produced a trickle of water that formed a puddle in the marble basin. He had come to the legation to work with the Count Polanyi on a nefarious love letter to the nephew in Budapest, which they started to write in Polanyi's office – portraits of fierce Magyar kings staring down at them from the walls – but Polanyi said, 'It's been too long of a winter, I can't stay indoors any more, I'm tired of it,' so they moved to the garden.

Ferrar liked Polanyi, a diplomat/spy now in his sixties, and a gentleman from another time. He was a large, heavy man with thick, white hair, who wore suits cut by London tailors and smelled like bay rum, cigar smoke and the excellent Burgundy he drank with lunch. Once they were settled in garden chairs, Polanyi said, 'So, are we really going to do this?'

'It's a long shot, Count Polanyi, but unless we can get the Belesz nephew into court, the future of your bank is . . . questionable. He intends, I think, to destroy it.'

'Tell me *why*, for heaven's sake! It does him no good that I can see.'

Ferrar agreed. 'All I could sense in Belesz was malice, a kind of pure hatred with God knows what cause. But then, when I was trying to reason with him on the telephone, he said that he belonged to the Arrow Cross.'

'Yes, you told me. We too, in Hungary, have our Nazi party. In fact, last week, my steward only just got away from them.'

'There is a good possibility that his malice is political. Fascism is a revolutionary force, it wants to destroy the established order and take its place – take its money, its businesses, everything it has because, to these people, the governing class in Europe is hesitant, ineffective, effete. So, destroy it. That's what they've done in Germany and Italy and what they will do in Spain, with the excuse that they're fighting Bolshevism.'

The count looked grim, with the insights of a diplomat and a spy, he believed Ferrar was right. 'Very well then,' he said. 'Let's write the damn letter.'

Ferrar stared at the pad of lined paper on his lap, tapped it speculatively with the eraser of his pencil, and said, 'We'll need an address, so that he can write back to her. Should we use *poste restante*?' It meant general delivery.

'Like a spy novel from the twenties?' Polanyi was amused. 'No, he'll surely smell a rat.'

'Well, not American Express.'

'Hardly – she's no tourist. Actually, this comes up in my work from time to time, and I use a little hotel on the rue Chemin Vert, not far from Place Bastille. Hotel Victoria, it's called, we give the manager the names we're looking for and he brings the letters over here.'

'Then it should be on hotel stationery.'

'I wonder if they have such a thing? But, a nice touch. I'll have some made up.'

'Cheap paper, poorly printed.'

'I know, Monsieur Ferrar,' Polanyi said gently.

'So, from Celestine, umm . . . her married name? Perhaps Duval, something common, not foreign. Then, to start out, "My dear Fabi"?'

' "Dearest".'

Ferrar nodded and made the change. 'I wonder if she had a pet name for him?'

'Maybe, you never know, with love affairs. Shall we say, "I hope you will remember me, and the times we had together"? No, "*Perhaps* you will remember me, I hope you do." And "sweet times" – meaning times in bed.'

' "Intimate times?" '

'Rather elevated, for her.'

'I have it! We say "our nights together".'

'Ahh.'

' "Our nights together" and she often thinks of him now and wishes, no, *dreams,* that they could once again have such pleasure.' Ferrar wrote that down, then inspiration struck and he looked up from the paper and said, 'Perfume!'

'Yes, of course, good idea. A perfumed letter. Nice perfume, not cheap, and plenty of it.'

'Cheap perfume can be seductive.'

The count laughed; a deep, bass rumble. 'What a pair of scoundrels we are. You're right, she hasn't any money, so it's what she uses now. Cheap perfume, filthy nights of lovemaking, all modesty abandoned. White Ginger, something like that. He'll like it, my nephew will, a poor girl at his mercy.'

Ferrar was impressed, the count remembered the name of a perfume. He smiled and said, 'I suspect you've been down this road before.'

Polanyi nodded. 'Haven't we all?'

'Those of us who love women, and how they go about things, yes.'

'White Ginger,' the count mused. 'I wish she'd write to *me*.' Then he sighed and looked at his watch. 'There is something I must do, I'll be back in a minute.'

Ferrar was content to wait in the garden. *For the marquesa, what perfume?* He tried to recall if she'd worn scent, and rather doubted she had. He'd been close to her, kissed her hand as they parted – wouldn't she have worn it on her wrist? On her pulse? Of course, in the excitement of the moment . . .

This wistful thought was suddenly interrupted by three vizsla dogs, who came bounding through the French doors into the garden, quivering with outdoor freedom, the two males seeking the right shrub to water while the bitch squatted on the gravel. 'Yes, here they are, the dogs my nephew meant to sell,' Polanyi said.

'How did they get *here*?'

'Nephew Fabi organized a kind of raid on my castle in Hungary. The steward grabbed the dogs and escaped through an old tunnel, eventually he got them to Paris, where they'll be safe.' Polanyi watched as the males marked the shrubs and said, 'The legation gardener is not happy about this but I'll be damned if I'll take them out to the street and stand there while they do their business.'

One of the males, done with business, galloped up to Ferrar and, wanting to play, smacked his forepaws on the ground. The vizsla was a hairless breed, all muscle and sinew in visible motion beneath a reddish-brown coat, but the irresistible features of the vizsla were its soft, floppy ears, velvet to the touch. Ferrar couldn't resist, playing with the dog's ears, rumpling them gently, and saying, 'What a handsome fellow you are, yes you are,' in a talking-to-a-dog voice. The dog sprinted away, leapt easily into the fountain, and began to lap up the puddled water. The other two followed. The bitch, who was quicker than her brothers, stood on her hind legs and licked at the water coming from Pan's mouth.

Polanyi took a grey tennis ball from his pocket and tossed it to one side of the fountain. The vizslas were immediately in hot pursuit, one of the males skidded on the gravel but snatched up the ball in his mouth, then brought it back to Polanyi and waited for the next throw.

'Did you see, Ferrar? The finest breed there is, a pointer/retriever, finds the game, waits for you to shoot it, then brings it to you with a soft mouth. A great hunter's dog.' He flipped the ball to Ferrar, who threw it high in the air. All three jumped, ears flying.

'Now I'll have to find an excuse to hold talks with you here,' Ferrar said as the bitch dropped the ball at his feet.

'You are welcome, any time. They love to play,' Polanyi said. Then, 'Now, where were we?'

'We have most of it, she has to explain that her marriage wasn't so good, implying that her husband was never the lover that Fabi was and now he has died, leaving her in a cheap hotel and dreaming of lost love.'

'How do we close?'

' "Please write to me, dearest, at least I will know I am not forgotten." This will take an exchange of letters, and *he* has to be the one who writes, "Guess what, I'm coming to Paris on business, would you care to have a cocktail?" '

'True. And she signs . . . ?'

' "Your Celestine", best to keep it simple.'

'Then let's do that,' Polanyi said.

The vizsla got Ferrar's attention with a little whine and he reached for the tennis ball.

The following day found Ferrar working on a letter of his own, a letter to the marquesa. He wasn't really supposed to do such a thing, court one of the firm's clients, but Coudert left such matters to its attorneys' discretion. The general rule, not said aloud, was that serious affection, so long as it was kept separate from legal business, might be pursued, but making passes at female clients was frowned on. Ferrar would use his personal stationery, with the Place Saint-Sulpice address, and write briefly. 'Dear Marquesa Maria Cristina . . .' He hoped she was well, and likely looking forward to the spring season. Would she care to join him, next Wednesday at five o'clock, for hot chocolate at Angelina's? He looked forward to hearing from her, then closed respectfully with one of the French formulas. He licked the envelope and sealed it, then went off to the Bureau de Poste.

Angelina's, beneath the arcades on the rue de Rivoli, was a Paris institution, in business as an elegant tearoom since the turn of the century, and famous for its Mont Blanc pastry and hot chocolate. Here Ferrar preferred the French version, the warm, soothing sounds of *chocolat chaud:* 'shawco-la-show'. As for the Mont Blanc – noodle-shaped strands of cream of chestnut over whipped cream – watching the marquesa go to work on it was, for Ferrar, beyond appetizing. She scooped up a tiny spoonful and closed her lips on the spoon, resulting in the daintiest smear of *crème de marrons* on her upper lip, a sight which she allowed him to enjoy for an instant before raising her napkin.

'And do you travel for your work, Monsieur Ferrar?'

'At times I do, to meet with clients.'

'And have you travelled lately?'

'Last week I was in Poland, in Warsaw and Danzig, or Gdansk if you prefer the Polish version.'

'A troubled place, one reads in the newspapers.' With delicate fingers, she raised her cup of chocolate and took a sip. She was dressed for afternoon tea in a pale lilac blouse, with a strand of pearls at her throat, and a suit coloured dove grey which, he suspected, came from one of the better fashion houses. She wore her hair back, twisted into a chignon, and in the low light of Angelina's it glowed like metal. She had been wearing fitted suede gloves when she entered the tearoom, these now rested in her lap.

'Have you been in Poland, Marquesa?'

'I was there years ago, at the Krynica spa in the Tatra mountains, where the marques went for treatment.'

'They are uneasy now, the Poles, they fear the ambitions of their neighbours.'

'And so they should. Do you not agree, Monsieur Ferrar?'

'I'm afraid so, Marquesa.'

'I do try to keep up with European matters,' she said. 'I was raised in France, at an old house on the edge of Angers. But then, at the age of fourteen I was sent to a Swiss boarding school for young women. There were girls from England, and Italy, and Spain, and I came to realize that the world was a much bigger and more varied place than I had imagined.'

'And did you learn to like it there?'

She smiled and said, 'I do not believe one was supposed to *like* it, but I don't recall being miserable; oh perhaps now and again, in the way of young girls. The school was run by a religious order and the sisters could be severe.' She paused, remembering, and said, 'We had to work very hard, and write with perfect penmanship. If not, we could expect . . . punishment. I mean of the physical sort.' Again she smiled.

A smile, just shy of naughty, which implied she had a good idea of what his imagination might make of that. *Would you care to describe it?* Ferrar thought. *Oh if only I were so daring.* He settled, instead, on 'Still, a good education is crucial these days, do you agree?'

'Certainly. And some of my schoolmates were good companions, I still have two or three friendships from those days.'

Ferrar had a sip of his chocolate, first dipping up a spoon of

Angelina's exquisite whipped cream from the little pot that accompanied the cup and saucer.

The marquesa said, 'And are you still in touch with friends from Spain, Monsieur Ferrar?'

'I am not,' he said. 'And I expect that the boys and girls I knew in Barcelona are scattered far and wide by the war. And I fear that some of them are no longer alive.'

'What terrible things war does to us,' she said, with sorrow in her voice.

He nodded. Wanting to move away from this subject he said, 'One has to escape it, however one can. For example, having hot chocolate at Angelina's.' Then he said, 'With a friend.'

She nodded her head to one side, eyes briefly closed – thus she accepted his compliment. 'You don't sound as though you have much desire to return there.'

'That's true, sad to say.'

'And is that because your sympathies lie with the Republic?'

'Yes,' Ferrar said.

'I would imagine,' she said, 'that you have been tempted to act on those sympathies.'

'Of course I have . . . most of the Spanish émigrés here do what they can . . . in the way of donations, meetings, whatever support is possible. But you don't have to do much; if General Franco wins, and it is beginning to look like he will, it would be unwise for me to go back to Spain. And then, I've become a lover of this city and will stay here. If I can.'

'Oh I'm sure you can, Monsieur Ferrar. One would hate to lose you.' At this, she looked very directly into his eyes.

They went on for a while longer, leaving the border of intimacy and settling on the pleasures of the city for their conversation. When he sensed that she was ready to leave, he asked if he might accompany her to her car and, after she had worked her hands into her gloves, they left the tearoom. Outside, the day had turned cloudy and chilly at the end of the afternoon, he said he hoped they could meet again, she said she would look forward to it and offered him her hand, palm down.

When Ferrar reached the office the following day, Jeanette said, 'Mr. Barabee asks if you'll please stop by his office.' He waited an instant, wondering if she might let him know more, but she returned to her work. Barabee was affable enough to begin with. Still, Ferrar felt something was troubling him. At last Barabee said, 'Of all the strange questions I've ever had to ask anybody, this may well be the strangest.'

From Ferrar, a non-committal 'Oh?'

'Cristián, is it somehow possible that you stole a Polish train?'

Ferrar took a moment, then said, 'Perhaps "borrowed" is a better word, the train is still there. But we were having difficulties with the Polish railway authority – an attempt to block our shipment – and my associate, a fellow who does not easily accept failure, found an engineer who would drive the train up to Danzig.'

Barabee was tight-lipped, then shook his head in a way that meant, *what times we live in.* 'The reason I ask is that I'm in touch with an official at the Sûreté Nationale, the French security service, and received from him an unofficial telephone call. Someone in the Polish government called him and said they were contemplating legal action against you. The French security official said he would see to it, informally, and the Pole said in that case they would not proceed. So, now I've *spoken to you* about it. But, Cristián, please, try not to draw fire, and, if you're contemplating another visit to Poland, you might put that off for a time.'

'Thank you, George. And, I promise, no more stealing Polish trains.'

'The truth is, we're being drawn into European conflict, more every day. The French have sent an arms-purchasing commission to New York and they have retained Coudert to advise them. What's happened is that they are attempting to purchase five thousand warplanes and have fallen foul of the Embargo Act. Now, we may be able to help, France may well *need* those warplanes, but I'm told they don't exist, they will have to be built, and it will take a while to build them. This is a new industry – most of the men who own aircraft manufacturing companies built their first aircraft with their own hands.'

'This isn't such good news, about the French.'

'No, it isn't. We're safe enough here, for the moment, but that may change in a hurry. The French are *scared*.'

Barabee's secretary knocked at his door, then opened it and said, 'Mr. Barabee, Mr. and Mrs. Blaustein are here for their ten o'clock meeting.'

'We'll talk later,' Ferrar said, and left the office.

That evening Ferrar went to Chez Lucette for *poulet de Bresse,* then returned home, settled a blanket around his shoulders, poured himself some brandy, lit a Gitane, and found his place in the Robert Byron book he'd been reading, *The Road to Oxiana.* Byron was one of the truly great English travellers and Ferrar read him in order to become lost in another time and place – in this case 1933 and Persia.

> *The day's journey had a wild exhilaration. Up and down the mountains, over the endless flats, we bumped and swooped. The sun flayed us. Great spirals of dust, dancing like demons over the desert, stopped our dashing Chevrolet and choked us. Suddenly, from far across a valley, came the flash of a turquoise jar, bobbing along on a donkey. Its owner walked beside it, clad in a duller blue. And seeing the two lost in that gigantic stony waste, I understood why blue is the Persian colour, and why the Persian word for it means water as well.*

Rising to have some more brandy, Ferrar felt as though he was at least beginning to calm down. The conversation with Barabee – who had his ear very close indeed to the political ground – had unsettled him. What if the Germans attacked France? What would he do with his family? Take them to New York? And just when should he start to make such arrangements? Then, too, working with de Lyon had stirred a certain part of him, and he found himself wondering if it wouldn't be better to stay and fight, if they would let him.

He poured the brandy in his kitchen, then, on the way back to his study, he opened the shutter over the single window that faced directly away from the Place Saint-Sulpice, and through which he could see a few treetops in the Jardin du Luxembourg. The night sky was clear, the trees visible in moonlight.

3 May. In mid-afternoon, a sudden thunderstorm: lightning bolts flashed over the Champs-Elysées, rain poured down, and Ferrar watched through his window as people ran to shelter in doorways, covering their heads with newspapers. As he forced himself back to work, his telephone rang. The call was from a young woman who worked for the diplomat Molina, the second secretary at the Spanish embassy and the man who had recruited Ferrar to work at the Oficina Técnica. Could he, she asked, come to a meeting that evening? Ferrar agreed. The young woman said he would be telephoned later in the day and given the time and place for the meeting.

'Is it not at the embassy?' Ferrar said.

'We will call you later,' she said and hung up.

By five-thirty Ferrar was beginning to wonder what was going on, then, just before six, the young woman telephoned and said the meeting would be at six-fifteen and gave him an address on the rue de Berri.

Strange, he thought. The rue de Berri was not far from the embassy, but hardly the place for an official meeting; it was a thoroughly commercial street, always busy, home to press agencies, small shops, and a few cafés. Ferrar left the office, then put up his umbrella as he crossed the boulevard. On the other side, he noticed two men sitting in a car, their eyes following him. What was this? Probably nothing. But at the address he'd been given, a man, somehow kin to the men in the car, was waiting just inside the door. He asked Ferrar who he was, politely enough, then directed him to another building, just up the street. Where, in the lobby, yet one more man who happened to be there said, 'Can you tell me your name?' Ferrar told him, then was given the number of an apartment on the fourth floor. He was ushered into the apartment by two men, bigger and tougher than their colleagues, who stared at him a moment longer than necessary, then stepped aside.

'Ah, it's you,' Molina said, rising from a sofa. The parlour had the feel of a living room at the end of a long social evening; full ashtrays, empty wineglasses and coffee cups, stale air. Even Molina, as always in pince-nez and Van Dyke beard, appeared slightly rumpled. This was not, Ferrar thought, the first meeting held in the apartment that day. 'Señor Ferrar,' Molina said, some drama in his voice, 'allow me to introduce General Juan Quebral.'

A young man, surely not yet thirty years old, rose from the couch. He was tall and fair-haired, wore glasses with steel frames, had his jacket off, tie loosened, and shirtsleeves rolled up. 'Pleased to meet you,' Quebral said and took Ferrar's hand in a powerful grip. His presence was that of a man well known and well respected. And he was, Ferrar knew, all of that and more. General Quebral was one of a small group of young communists who had joined the Army of the Republic, fought well, been promoted through the ranks, led brilliantly, and become senior officers. Formerly an electrician at the Gijon shipyards, he had risen to be the military hope of the Spanish Republic – if their troops were to be led to victory, it was Quebral who would lead them. 'Julio,' Quebral said to one of the men guarding the door, 'please get a glass of wine for Señor Ferrar.' Turning to Ferrar he said, 'Unless you would prefer coffee.'

Ferrar, sitting in a wing chair, said, 'A glass of wine, please.'

'I thought so,' Quebral said.

'It is an honour to meet you, General Quebral,' Ferrar said.

'*My* honour, Señor Ferrar. We are grateful to you and the Oficina Técnica. The Skoda cannon have reached our base in Salou, thanks to your determination.'

There was a knock at the door, everyone in the room tensed, then the door opened to admit Max de Lyon. Again Molina rose and, as he began his introduction, de Lyon glanced over his left shoulder, then his right, spoofing the man unnerved by excessive security.

Molina was amused. 'You're a comedian, Max. But you understand precaution. General Quebral has come secretly to Paris, he is in danger here, so we shall keep his visit a secret.'

De Lyon took an armchair and lit one of his brown cigarettes. Molina said, 'We've been at this all of yesterday and today. Talking to a number of our arms buyers, some of whom had to travel a considerable distance.'

'People we need more than ever,' Quebral said. 'Because we are going to make our most important effort of the war. For this we are forming a new army, to be known as the Army of the Ebro. This too should remain secret, of course, although anybody with a map and some knowledge of the terrain will have a good idea of where this campaign will take place.'

Molina said, 'Of course we will be fighting, like any army, to gain territory, but I should remind you that we are this time fighting to prove to the world, and particularly to the politicians of Europe, that the Republic is still a powerful force that is nowhere near surrender.'

'We'll do our best,' de Lyon said.

'Of course you will,' Quebral said. 'We expect that. But the reason you are here is that we will now concentrate our efforts in one area, and I thought it would be a good idea if you heard it from me, personally. Now, if I were a fancy journalist, I might call it "the future of warfare". Our soldiers are digging trenches as I speak, our navy is fighting the submarines, but what we've learned in this war, and spilled blood to learn it, is that the outcome of any battle, now and in the future, will be determined in the sky.' He paused, then said, 'I didn't mean to make a speech, but in a political life I've made a lot of them, it becomes a habit.'

'It's true,' de Lyon said. 'We've watched it happen. The troops advance, then the Messerschmitts show up and destroy them.' He inhaled on his cigarette, sat forward in his chair, and said, 'So then, General, what do you need? And how much time do we have?'

'As for time, that depends on when we begin the campaign,' Quebral said. 'Which I know but I can't tell you.'

De Lyon nodded that he understood. He too had been brought a glass of wine, now he took a sip and said, 'I ask because it used to be that we needed everything, and right away. This is different.'

'I know it is,' Quebral said.

'I imagine you have a list,' Ferrar said.

'I do. A short one. It starts with warplanes, which are impossible to find, there's too much competition – Turks, Greeks, Poles, Yugoslavs, the *French*. Suddenly the world woke up.'

'Didn't it though?' de Lyon said, with a bitter smile. 'The prices of replacement parts for aeroplanes are hard to believe. And then, even if you're willing to pay whatever anybody asks, you can't find them.'

'There is also oil; we still have refineries and can produce aviation fuel.'

'Better for someone who knows that business,' de Lyon said.

'Next, anti-aircraft ammunition. The USSR shipped us anti-aircraft weapons, the seventy-six-millimeter Model F-22, and they are effective, but we lack ammunition. If we can't fight the Messerschmitts from the air, we will have to fight them from the ground.'

'We may be able to find it,' de Lyon said. 'Should we take that as our responsibility?'

'Yes,' Quebral said. 'If you think you can do it, it's yours.'

In time, Ferrar and de Lyon left together. Outside, the rain had stopped and the air smelled fresh and clean.

'What are you doing this evening?' de Lyon said.

'I'm waiting to hear,' Ferrar said.

'Come over to Le Cygne, I'll be there at eleven-thirty.'

Le Cygne was as Ferrar remembered it; a glossy, black and white Art Deco room in the cellar of a crumbling tenement, not far from the Les Halles market. As always, Max de Lyon's personal table awaited him, the maître d' whipped the RÉSERVÉ sign off the black lacquer tabletop and pocketed his tip, then beckoned imperiously to a waiter, who hurried over to take de Lyon's order for champagne. Just about the time it arrived, so did Stavros. With a new girlfriend – he'd had one on either arm the last time they'd met – this one a pale brunette with waves of black hair falling around her face. She wore a black dress that showed a bare shoulder and, Ferrar suspected from her myopic stare, carried a pair of glasses in her bag. He was able to diagnose her myopia because she was staring at him while he, recalling Stavros's inclination towards Balkan jealousy, looked everywhere but at her.

Stavros, a swarthy bear of a man in a grey silk suit and a black shirt with an open collar, was pleased that de Lyon had called him. They bantered for a few minutes, then Stavros said, 'So Max, tell me, what are we looking for?'

'Anti-aircraft ammunition, seventy-six millimeter. All we can find, price doesn't matter.'

'Who makes it? Skoda? Do we call on our old pal Szarny?'

'The Russians make it for their AA guns. Maybe they also sell it, I don't know. But they won't sell any to Spain . . . because of Stalin's devious machinations, or because they're keeping it for themselves.'

'I can ask around,' Stavros said, not sounding confident about what he would find. 'But, as we say, if you can't buy it you have to steal it. That's hard when you're dealing with the Russians, and then, if you do manage to steal it, you can't get it out of the country.'

'Sounds like you've tried, Stavros.'

'No, but I have a friend who did. He knew a guy, a gangster in Kiev, and this guy had a lot of tyres in a warehouse.'

'And . . . ?'

'Who knows. The gangster disappeared, maybe the police caught him, maybe somebody killed him.'

'Did your friend tell you anything else? How the tyres got to Kiev?'

Stavros shook his head. 'He told me what he wanted to tell me.'

'Can you get in touch with him?'

'That's easy, he's in prison, in the Santé, right here in Paris.'

De Lyon grimaced. 'If you visit someone in the Santé, the guards listen to everything. We have to work as quietly as we can.'

Stavros laughed. 'Ahh, Max, you always say that. And then . . .' Stavros threw his fingers into the air and made the *ka-boom* sound of an explosion.

'But we have to *try*, Stavros, really.'

'Sure, Max, I know.'

The brunette, watching a small combo setting up on the bandstand, said, 'Oh, there's music, who wants to dance with me?'

'Sorry, dear, we're busy,' Stavros said.

'You're no fun,' she said, teasing him.

'What's your friend in prison for?' de Lyon said.

'Murder. He's a murderer. That's his job.'

The band began to play 'Begin the Beguine' and the brunette pinched Stavros's earlobe between thumb and forefinger and said, 'Let's go, Monsieur le Bear, out on the dance floor.'

Stavros made a what-can-I-do gesture and took his brunette off to dance.

Ferrar said, 'There are munitions companies everywhere,

somebody should be willing to sell us what we need, the difficulty is figuring out who that is.'

'This business is always difficult, one way or another. I have a collection of ring binders at the Oficina Técnica, a sort of library, newspaper clippings, military journals, whatever I can find, and I had a look after the meeting with Quebral. Only a few countries make anti-aircraft guns; Britain, France, Germany, Italy, America. Sweden makes one called the Bofors, and the Swiss make the light version of the weapon, called the Oerlikon. And, of course, all the calibres are different. So, what we have is the heavy Soviet weapon.' He shrugged, *our bad luck*. Then he said, 'We'll find a way.'

'Can't we have the ammunition manufactured?'

'You know, we did some of that – had weapons and ammunition manufactured – in the first year of the war. We found a factory up in Belgium, you gave them a sample and they'd make whatever you wanted, but the government shut it down.'

'These shells, where are they stored?'

'Armouries, military bases. All closely guarded. Sometimes the guns are mounted on ships.'

'Steal ammunition from a Russian ship?'

'Even if you found a way to steal, there wouldn't be enough. One thing my library made clear – you want to shoot down an aeroplane, you need a lot of shells. The aiming method is complicated, mostly you miss.'

Stavros, beads of sweat on his face, held his girlfriend tight and stomped around the dance floor, doing his very own version of the beguine. But the Le Cygne crowd, slumming nouveaux riches, swindlers, spies, prostitutes of the higher order, didn't laugh or stare, not at Stavros they didn't. The scene struck Ferrar as a kind of undersea world. Beneath a placid sea, exotic creatures mated and fed on each other and, as you sank deeper, the world turned darker and the creatures grew strange indeed.

Stavros returned from the dance floor, brunette in tow. Dancing was hard work, the nightclub was warm, so the smell of his cologne was stronger than usual. He drank off his champagne and de Lyon refilled his glass. 'Not the dance for me,' Stavros said. When he sat down, de Lyon said, 'Tell me, Stavros, do you think there's a way you can speak privately with your friend?'

'I'll find a way. Maybe a bribe. You want me to try it?'

'Might as well. We have to talk to people, if you talk to people they turn out to know more than you thought. Sometimes more than *they* thought.'

'I'll do it,' Stavros said. 'He's an old friend and I'm sure he'd like a visitor.'

'As soon as you can,' de Lyon said.

The following day, de Lyon made contact with one S. Kolb, a meagre little man nobody ever noticed and a spy. De Lyon's customary spy, in his business a necessary acquaintance. To reach Kolb you called a certain number, a woman answered, you gave her a name, some name, maybe your name, and, in time, Kolb would find you. He did travel for his work, you never knew where he was, but he always knew where you were. In this case, Kolb was apparently in Paris, because he turned up at the café where de Lyon went for lunch. De Lyon was eating veal stew, took a bite, went to take another, and S. Kolb was sitting at the table. De Lyon said the spring weather was fine and how did one go about buying Soviet anti-aircraft ammunition.

Kolb looked at the handwritten menu, summoned a waiter, and ordered the veal stew. 'Might as well have lunch, right?' he said.

'You're my guest,' de Lyon said. 'Have a glass of wine.'

'What a question you ask,' Kolb said. His French was fluent, but not native. Surely he'd grown up somewhere and spoke the language, but where that was nobody knew, although there were plenty of theories. It was also said of Kolb that he was a *British* spy, but there were plenty of theories about that as well. 'And what if,' Kolb continued, 'I said "I don't know"?'

'You often say it.'

'Yes, but what if, this time, I were telling the truth?'

'Then I'd ask how you might go about finding out.'

'Here's the problem, Max. To find out – about anything – you have to ask questions and, with what you need, you would be asking questions about Soviet military matters, which are secret, like everything else in the USSR. And when the Russians discover that somebody is asking such questions, they will want to know what's going on . . . they are *extremely* ticklish in this area, and they don't like to be tickled. *F'shtai*, Max?' Which meant *you understand?* in Yiddish. Not that Kolb was Jewish, he wasn't, but he knew a few phrases and used them for emphasis.

'I do.'

'Now I appreciate your asking me, I like to be asked questions, just as I appreciate hearing about any tidbit you happen to turn up in your work. So my first answer has to be: don't go poking your nose into Soviet secrets, because it will produce the NKVD on your doorstep. No, I tell a lie . . .' he laughed – 'it will produce the GRU, the military service, which is just as mean but twice as smart.'

'Then what? Give it up? Stay safe?'

'You?'

'I've done it before.'

'Really? Often?'

'No, not often.'

'All right, Max, you're a friend, as far as it goes, so I'll let you talk to a certain man, a man who . . . a man who knows everything? No, no such man exists. But this one has now and then surprised me. I say now and then because I don't often use him, only once in a while, since I don't know much about him and that makes *me* ticklish. Also, he is the oddest human being I've ever encountered, which is saying a lot, believe me.'

'And his name?'

'I've named him Professor Z' – he pronounced it 'zed' – 'as I have no idea of his real name, it's not what he calls himself. He reminds me of a professor, though, a professor from a foreign land who is no longer a professor. He *knows* things, all sorts of things, and he hates the fascists. But, you must be careful.'

'Why is that?'

'Better these days, when someone knows what you're doing, that they don't know who you are.'

'Very well, I'm warned.'

Kolb's veal stew arrived and he ordered a carafe of red wine.

'So, how do I find Professor Z?'

Kolb chewed on the tough veal, then said, 'I will have to set it up. Someone will contact you with a time and a place. And you go alone.'

'I am grateful for your help, Monsieur Kolb.'

'Are you?'

'I am.'

'Well then, where have you been lately? Any place interesting?'

The meeting with Professor Z was scheduled for noon on the ninth of May, on the Square Récamier, which was perhaps the most private park in Paris. Private, de Lyon soon learned, because it was hard to find. He walked past the entry, off the rue de Sèvres, twice. Then, getting anxious, he had to ask the girl behind the counter of a *boulangerie*.

Finding Professor Z was not hard; he was sitting on a bench at the foot of a staircase beneath an ivy-covered pergola, reading a French novel. When he looked up and saw de Lyon, he kept his place in the book with his finger, and there it stayed for the length of their conversation. The professor was wearing a battered old chalk-stripe suit and had the sort of beard worn by men who don't like to shave but don't like beards either; a scraggly growth, brown and grey, chopped back when it grew too long. He was smoking a cigarette in a cigarette holder and was, apparently, a chain-smoker

– there were more than a few squashed-out butts on the cobblestones by his feet.

'Good morning,' de Lyon said. 'A friend told me I would meet
you here.'

'At your service,' the professor said. De Lyon heard the trace of
an accent but couldn't say where it came from.

'I am here on behalf of some friends who are working to help
the Spanish Republic.'

The professor sighed and said, 'Spain.'

'A sorry time for us, if that's what you mean.'

'Europe is a nice neighbourhood with a mad dog. Just now the
dog is biting Spain, and nobody else in the neighbourhood wants to
get bitten, so they look away.'

'That's true, but we do what we can. At the moment we're trying to buy ammunition for a Soviet anti-aircraft gun.'

'Don't have any, myself.'

'No? Then who does?'

Silence, as the wheels turned in the professor's mind. 'The Red
Army. Have you asked them?'

'We have, they won't sell.'

'Understandable, with Hitler chewing on his carpet.' He
paused, then said, 'In the old days, the way to deal with the USSR
was the bribe, you could buy a Soviet general, back then. But, with
the Stalin purges, that's changed, they're all terrified now, they will
think you are an agent provocateur. Of course you *could* take a
chance, as long as you got it right on the first try, otherwise . . .
well, you know what I mean.'

'Yes, you would have to be sure of your target, if you don't care
to be arrested.'

'Mmm, Siberia.'

'Not my preference.'

'Nor mine.' The professor was briefly absent – lost in the memory of another time and place. When he returned he said, 'Still,
there might be a way. Perhaps diversion, a shipment of arms leaves

the factory and is never seen again. It sounds unlikely but in Russia it actually happens – whole trains have been known to disappear. Where are they? Nobody knows, and they are never found.'

'How would you go about diversion?'

'Perhaps on the clerical level, where, say, an office worker believes himself to be a fish so small that no one will catch him. He will be wrong, but you will have what you want, so he will have to be sacrificed. People are, you know, they are . . . sacrificed every day.'

'Do you suppose it would be possible to steal the ammunition? Not by diversion, by force.'

'Spill blood? Yes, I suppose you could. Are you prepared to die for this ammunition, monsieur?'

'I'd rather not.'

'Or do you plan not to be there when it happens? Now there you have an entire class of people in the modern world, the class that arranges not to be there when it happens. Criminals, among others, think that way. Are you a criminal?'

'Mostly not. Though I have done things.'

'I would guess you are not prepared to kill for your ammunition, or to be killed. But then, we've only just met.'

De Lyon sensed that the discussion was over and said, 'Thank you, sir, for your help. Would you allow me to offer you something for your time?'

The professor laughed; a dry, rattling laugh that sounded like a cough. 'No, no,' he said. 'That is not what I do.'

De Lyon went back up the staircase. Birds were singing in the park; beneath the ivy, sunlight cast leaf shadows on the steps. When he reached the street, he found a busy afternoon in Paris, it was as though the conversation in the park had taken place in another world.

Stavros prepared carefully for his visit to the Santé prison. He bought a Panama hat, made of yellow straw, which was too big for him so rested on the tops of his ears and made him look silly, not dangerous. He next prepared a parcel for his friend in prison and wrapped it in brown paper. Then he took the Métro up to the Fourteenth Arrondissement and walked over to the prison on the rue de la Santé. Built long ago, the prison looked like an old factory, its low buildings darkened with time.

At the entry he was asked for his passport and produced one of his better forgeries, standing quietly while a clerk copied out the information into a huge register book with blue lines that, like the prison, belonged to an earlier century which, perhaps, it did. 'I am here to see prisoner Videau, Albert,' he said. A guard was summoned and Stavros was taken through a door of iron bars, down a hallway, and into a room where visitors could meet with prisoners. A guard was always present, and prisoner and visitor sat across from each other at a wide table.

Stavros handed the parcel to the guard and said, 'I have brought some things for Prisoner Videau.' The guard opened the parcel, then found what Stavros had put there for him to find: canned sausages, canned spinach, canned sardines, canned soup, and a thick wad of francs, the equivalent of five hundred dollars.

The guard shook his head at such naiveté. 'You can't bring money to a prisoner, don't you know the rules?'

'I'm sorry but I don't, I've never been here before.'

'Well, this money has to be forfeited, that's the rule here and I didn't make it.'

'Oh, I thought my friend could use it to buy a few luxuries. What about the food?'

'That is permitted. Eight cans. You've brought four. We will keep those until Wednesday, which is the day when prisoners may receive gifts. You will sit on that side of the table, I will stand at the end, and your conversation must be at a normal level. No whispering allowed. And you may not touch the prisoner.' Stavros did as he was told and Videau was brought in a few minutes later. He was much as Stavros remembered him: bald, with a hard, round, bony head and glasses – these had broken at the bridge and he'd stuck the halves back together with a piece of tape. When he saw Stavros his face lit up and he said, 'Stavros!' The *what are you doing here* was unspoken.

Forbidden to shake hands, Stavros waved and said, 'Hello, Albert, I thought you might like a visit from an old friend.'

'Thank you for coming, Stavros, it's good to see you.'

'Honorine sends her best.' There was no such person.

'How is she?'

'She misses you, Albert. Does she write you letters?'

'Not often, she isn't much for writing, Honorine.'

The guard, bribed with a wad of francs, now did what he'd been paid to do – left his standing position at the end of the table, found himself a chair by the door, and began to read a newspaper. Stavros didn't exactly whisper, but a lifetime of conspiracy had taught him to use a low voice that didn't carry. 'How's it going, Albert?' he said.

'It's prison, I make the best of it.'

'Any chance of getting out?'

'My lawyer tells me I have to do another year before they'll think about it. But he's a good lawyer, and so far he's kept me from being guillotined and stopped them from transporting me to Guyana. Technicality after technicality, petition following petition, bless his heart.' He paused, then said, 'So then, Stavros, what brings you here?'

'Albert, about two years ago you told me about some guy in Kiev who had a warehouse full of tyres.'

'Sure, I remember. He wanted help selling the tyres in France but nothing came of it.'

'Who was he?'

'A Russian gangster, what was his name? Bratya, something like that.'

'What happened to him?'

'I don't know. We met a few times and were supposed to meet

again but he never showed up, never telephoned, so . . . gone.'

'This was in Kiev?'

'What? No, this was in Marseilles.'

Stavros was incredulous. 'The Corsicans let him work in Marseilles?'

'He just used Marseilles as a meeting place. Maybe the Corsicans knew about it, maybe they didn't. As I remember, he was in some gang, a very rough gang, but all the Russian gangs are like that, it's another world.'

'So, a gang in Kiev, one of them called Bratya, now vanished. Do I have that right?'

Videau thought it over, then said, 'It wasn't easy, talking to this guy. He spoke some French, a little English, but what I understood was that they weren't *from* Kiev, that's just where they'd hidden the tyres, they were from someplace else.'

'Where, Albert? Can you remember?'

'Not Moscow. Maybe . . . Odessa? You know, Stavros, I think that's right. Odessa. I thought the gangs in Odessa were Jews, but this Bratya said they were from Greek families who'd been there forever. Is that possible?'

'I don't know, maybe it will mean something to Max, he's the one who sent me up here.'

'Well, I think that's about all I remember.'

'Albert, how can we help you?'

'Lawyers cost a lot of money, you know. So far I've managed to pay the bills – people like us have to put some money aside, here and there, and have the kind of friends we can trust to deliver it, but I can't work now so . . .'

'How do we find him?'

'His name is LaMotte, he's got an office by the Notre-Dame church in the Ninth.'

'Notre-Dame-de-Lorette?'

'That's the one.'

They talked for a time after that – friends they knew, good

times they'd had, then the guard rattled his newspaper and stood up, so Stavros said goodbye and told the guard he was ready to leave.

That night de Lyon and Ferrar were back at Le Cygne to meet a pair of Turkish brothers who bought and sold weapons on the black market and regularly visited Paris in search of trade. Before the meeting, de Lyon mentioned, without making too much of it, that he was armed, and once they arrived Ferrar saw why. They were the sort of men, suspicious and violent, who threatened by instinct – everybody was out to get the better of them and that included de Lyon and Ferrar. Their speech was civil enough but the way they held themselves, the way their eyes worked, said that they would kill you if you crossed them. And they knew you would try. De Lyon wasn't going to tell them the truth – because they might well sell it – but in his business he had to find a way to talk to sinister people who could find what he needed. De Lyon said he was interested in buying Polish armament. Sure, what did he want? Artillery, field pieces. That was easy, what was he ready to pay? De Lyon was vague – that depended on age and condition. Then he mentioned Soviet weapons, did they have anything available right away? Well, maybe, if he could pay before delivery. Though de Lyon kept refilling their champagne glasses, they never got drunk and talkative, only closer to the edge. Finally de Lyon grew tired of it, stood up, wished them well, and said they would meet again soon.

'What a waste of time,' de Lyon said when they were gone. 'Still, you have to try.'

'At least it didn't come to shooting,' Ferrar said.

'No, it didn't, not that it hasn't happened in here.'

An hour later, Stavros showed up, this time alone. De Lyon had made sure that Stavros and the Turkish brothers didn't meet, which might have led to a real confrontation. Stavros had a piece of paper with notes he'd made in blunt pencil – he'd written down what

Videau had told him so he wouldn't forget anything. He didn't stay long, left the notes with de Lyon and went off to see his brunette, who had a room up in Clichy. After he left, Ferrar said, 'Does Videau's story help us?'

De Lyon laid Stavros's page of notes flat on the table and kept smoothing the rumpled paper with his hands, as though that helped him to concentrate. Finally he said, 'It's like working on a jigsaw puzzle, but if I put together what I've learned in the last few days, then add what Videau said at the Santé, I can see how some of the pieces fit.'

'Tell me then, what goes where?'

'Do you recall saying something about stealing ammunition from a Russian ship?'

'You said it wouldn't work – not enough shells.'

'And it wouldn't. But Soviet ships get their supplies from Soviet armouries. Cristián, do you know what's in Odessa?'

'Not really. When I think about Odessa, I see the famous steps in the film, and I know you don't mean that.'

'What is in Odessa is a very large Soviet naval base, one of their warm-water ports on the Black Sea.'

'Of course,' Ferrar said. 'At least we know where the ammunition is stored. And do you think an Odessa gang could steal it?'

De Lyon nodded. 'We'd have to be careful with them – if they become suspicious they don't ask questions. But it's a place to start.'

'How would we find a gang in Odessa?'

De Lyon shrugged. 'I have no idea, tonight, but, tomorrow . . .'

'One thing I should point out,' Ferrar said. 'The Republic has only two national allies, one is Mexico, the other is the USSR. We are considering an attack on an ally, and the Russians will soon figure out where their shells went – there is only one country that has weapons which take such ammunition. What then?'

'Stalin will be quite angry. But he isn't helping us now and he won't in the future, because war is coming and he must conserve what he has. And, beyond that, the USSR has never really been our ally. For example: the Republic shipped the national gold reserve to the USSR because they were afraid Franco would get hold of it, and the Russians have been using that gold as payment for the arms they sent us – Stalin doesn't *give* anybody anything. And they have been stealing it, by fiddling with the exchange rate for gold and the rouble. Is that what an ally does?'

'All right, but we have another problem. We will have to tell Molina what we're doing, and he will say no.'

'I would remind you that General Quebral said yes. The Republic is desperate now, which means the general is far more powerful than the diplomat.'

The Le Cygne crowd was getting louder as they drank and danced the night away. Ferrar had the last of his champagne and said, 'So then, Max, what next?'

'We work on finding a Russian gang that operates in Odessa – maybe we find the gang that Videau discovered, maybe a different group. Then we figure out how to approach them and, then, how to use them without getting robbed or stabbed in the process. The difficulty here is that we don't have much time, I suspect the Ebro offensive will start in the summer. It is now May.'

'And how do we work on finding a Russian gang?'

'Contacts, Cristián. Always and forever, contacts.'

Working at a law firm in Paris, with many clients from America and Great Britain, Ferrar had encountered one aspect of the profession that had nothing whatsoever to do with legal matters. Certain clients saw their lawyer, discreet and helpful, as an advisor on the darker pleasures of the city. After some hemming and hawing he would be asked, in a certain voice, where sexual excitements, of this or that sort, were to be found. Ferrar had consulted the native Parisian lawyers and drawn up a list. Far easier were requests such as *you know Paris, Mr. Ferrar, where shall we eat?* So, another list, kept in a different drawer to avoid mortal error, perhaps by a secretary. *But Mr. Ferrar, can the bistro really be called domination and whipping? Do they have onion soup?*

As Ferrar had worked on his restaurant list he had come upon the Brasserie Heininger. He had tried it out and discovered a particularly Parisian setting: the Heininger was exciting; smoky, noisy, crowded, the place to go for an evening of good times, and the food was excellent. If Ferrar found that his clients had tired of solemn gastronomy, he encouraged them to try the Heininger. The brasserie was not only riotous – many Parisian brasseries were easily its equal – but it had a story, a story to tell the folks back home. In the spring of 1937, the maître d' at the Heininger was a Bulgarian émigré called Omaraeff with an unfortunate passion for émigré politics. He surely angered the wrong people because one night young men with tommy guns arrived at the brasserie and gave the dining room a good spraying. Meanwhile, poor Omaraeff had hidden in a stall in the ladies' WC and, badly frightened, had made the mistake of taking his trousers down to his ankles – a dead giveaway to an assassin peering below the door, which resulted in a dead maître d'. Miraculously, not a single person in the dining room had been shot. As the patrons cowered beneath their tables, the tommy gunners had concentrated on the gold-rimmed mirrors above the banquettes and had shattered every one of them except for the mirror above Table 14, which had only a single bullet hole. Papa Heininger was a sentimental man and, when all the mirrors were replaced, he left the Table 14 mirror as it was, a memorial to Omaraeff.

This became a popular table, for those who knew about it, but Ferrar had found that with sufficient time a reservation was possible so that Mr. Pinkston, of the Pinkston flour mill family, had an intriguing tale to tell when he returned to Ohio. Now Ferrar had an inspiration: after time spent with the marquesa at the Coudert office and Angelina's tearoom, he would try something different, something that would suggest they ought to acknowledge their more beastly selves by having fun together, by drinking a little too much at a brasserie and who-knew-what later. Thus he wrote to her at the Hotel Windsor and asked permission to telephone. She sent him the number, he called, praised the Heininger, and asked her if she knew it. She didn't, and four days later he picked her up at her hotel in a taxi.

Once they were settled in the back seat and making small talk as the taxi sped through night-time Paris, the marquesa said, 'Your gracious formality is much appreciated, Monsieur Ferrar, but I wonder if, from now on, you might wish to call me Maria Cristina?'

'I would very much like that. And I hope you will call me Cristián.'

A promising start to the evening.

Even more so, the first impression of the Brasserie Heininger. On the border of a neighbourhood that was home to dance halls and cheap restaurants, down the street from the Place Bastille, a waiter in fisherman's oilskin sou'wester coat and hat prepared shellfish from a bed of crushed ice. Opening the nearby door led to an enchanted world: under bright lights, the Parisian national colours red and gold glittered in the grand mirrors. The waiters, in fin de siècle whiskers – thick sideburns curving up to moustaches – hurried between the tables at a waiter's run, balancing huge trays of *choucroute garnie royale* – sauerkraut with pork cooked in champagne – shellfish, sausages, and skewered meats. Standing at the maître d' station was Papa Heininger himself, who led Ferrar and Maria Cristina to a table with a polished brass plate on a stand: TABLE 14, as Ferrar had requested. Gesturing towards the red plush banquette, Papa Heininger said, 'And how shall we sit tonight, *mes enfants?*'

Ferrar and Maria Cristina looked at each other for a moment, then Ferrar said, '*Côte-à-côte*, I think.' Side by side on the banquette. A waiter appeared and took the chairs away, Ferrar ordered apéritifs, then grand menus, two-handed menus, were whipped open for them. Maria Cristina said, 'Cristián, may I look at your menu? I have the ladies' version, no prices, and I always like to know what things cost.' She wore black that evening, a bias-cut dress in a finely woven material that suggested rather than revealed her figure, and thin enough so that when she slid over to study his menu a soft hip pressed against him. 'What shall we have, Cristián?' Now that she was close to him he realized that she was wearing perfume, more spice than sugar.

'Anything you like.'

'Hmm, that fisherman in front of the restaurant was preparing a *langouste*.' Spiny lobster or crayfish, succulent and sweet. 'I see they serve it cold, cut in pieces, with a mayonnaise.'

'Let's start with that,' he said. 'Do you suppose it goes well with champagne?'

'I would think so.'

'And then?'

'Maybe, *boudins blancs?*' White sausages; pork ground with cream and butter.

'Sounds good, I will have that also.'

The champagne arrived in a silver bucket, the sommelier poured a thin, pale stream into each glass. Ferrar raised his and said, '*Salut, Maria Cristina.*' The commonplace toast – he found the other possibilities too intimate or just plain silly. Maria Cristina raised her glass, met his eyes, and said, '*Salut.*' They drank, then she said, 'Cristián?'

'Yes?'

'There is a hole in this mirror. Everything else here is so perfect, I wonder they don't see to it.'

With some relish, he told her what had happened and she watched him as he spoke – interested by the man telling a story more than the story itself. The *langouste* arrived, Maria Cristina took a forkful, tasted it, closed her eyes, and made a low sound of pleasure.

Ferrar said, 'Oh this is very good.'

As the night wore on, the spirit of the brasserie rose to a high pitch, the conversation louder now and occasionally punctuated by a woman's peal of laughter; somebody had said something irresistibly droll. Ferrar and Maria Cristina finished the bottle of champagne and Ferrar ordered another as they worked on their *boudins blancs*. The new bottle was uncorked and they each had more than a sip – Ferrar was beginning to feel a certain hazy elation.

'What a place this is!' Maria Cristina said. 'And what a crowd, so . . . carefree, it's like going to a party.'

'I hoped you would enjoy it.'

'Thank you,' she said, and briefly rested her hand on his forearm. 'Just the thing for me, I spent the day brooding about a friend of mine, and this evening has made me feel better.'

'Brooding? What's wrong?'

She sighed. 'An old friend in trouble, I knew her at school in Switzerland, Benita.' When she spoke the name she smiled, a triste smile, as she remembered her friend. 'I had a letter from her this morning, she is in difficulty and doesn't know what to do.'

'And the difficulty is?'

'Benita grew up in Madrid, her father was Spanish, her mother English. She has been living in Geneva but she cannot remain there, her residence permit will expire soon and cannot be extended. A few months ago her father died and, some time later, she went to the Spanish consulate to have her passport renewed, but her application was, after a few weeks, denied. The consul said something about a change in regulations that called for a search of records in Madrid, which is now impossible.'

'Sad. This does happen though, I've seen it before.'

'The consul in Geneva suggested she make application for what he called a compassionate exception, but her letter never arrived in Valencia, and now the time period for the request has expired.'

Ferrar shook his head. 'Governments are often not compassionate, Maria Cristina. They make rules and enforce them.'

'Yes, I know, I know how they are. Now the only chance she has is to make a personal plea to the Spanish Republic, to, for example, the Spanish embassy in Paris. But, how to do this? She knows nobody in the government, and fears her application will be rejected by a clerk.'

'I'm afraid she isn't wrong.'

'Then I wondered, what if I went myself, on her behalf, to plead her case?'

'You would have to see one of the senior diplomats,' Ferrar said.

'So I thought – the most senior diplomat who would agree to a meeting, but I don't know a soul at the embassy.'

After a moment, Ferrar said, 'I might be able to help you, I'll look into it.'

'You will? I would be very grateful . . .'

'Now, my dear Maria Cristina, is that an empty glass I see?'

Again she touched his forearm and said, her voice emotional, 'You are sweet, Cristián, you are a kind man.'

They had a *tarte tatin* for dessert; soft, golden slices of apple in a flaky crust. And left the brasserie at midnight.

In the taxi back to the Windsor, Maria Cristina was pensive, sat close to Ferrar, and rested her head on his shoulder. When they reached the hotel, Ferrar, his courage greatly buoyed by champagne, took a chance. 'Maria Cristina?' he said. 'May I see you to your room?'

A subtle nod and, almost inaudible, a whispered yes.

He followed her up the two flights of stairs to her room, which was in fact a suite, virtually a private apartment. It was not at all luxurious – floral-print wallpaper that had seen better days, overstuffed furniture with forest-green slipcovers – but quite comfortable. He sat at one end of a sofa, she at the other.

'May I smoke?' he said.

She went off to another room and returned with an ashtray and a packet of Gauloises. 'I will have one as well,' she said.

'I didn't know you smoked.'

'*So* old-fashioned,' she said, 'but I was raised to believe that it was not genteel to smoke in front of people.'

Ferrar said, 'Times change, thank God.'

Now a silence that would grow awkward if allowed to continue. Finally he said, 'I've been wondering all day . . .'

'Oh? Tell me then, what is it that you have been wondering about?'

'If we would kiss.'

They stubbed their cigarettes out in the ashtray, he moved to her side, she raised her face, their lips met. A chaste kiss that stirred him deeply. When the kiss ended Ferrar stayed close to her so that his voice was low as he said, 'I was about to say goodnight but . . .'

'But . . . ?'

'I wondered also what would happen if I asked you to take off your dress.'

'Well, now you will find out,' she said, her voice not entirely steady. She stood, worked at the back of her dress, then took it off, looked around, and laid it atop an easy chair. She remained standing, in a black silk slip with lace at the top and bottom.

'And then . . .' he said.

She took a breath, raised the hem of her slip up and over her head, then folded it beside her dress. She had on a one-piece undergarment of glossy silver satin that went from the top of the breast to mid-thigh, where garters held up her stockings. His eyes moved up and down her profile, finding small breasts, the beginning of a tummy, and a derriere rather more splendid than he had imagined.

Now he stood, placed his hands on her bare shoulders, and was about to kiss her when he saw two tears rolling slowly down her cheeks, her mouth compressed in the manner of a woman who is about to weep but doesn't want to. 'I'm sorry,' she said, so quietly he could barely hear her. 'I can't. Not now . . .'

He took her hand and led her back to the sofa. She said, 'I wanted to, I imagined we would . . .'

'Don't worry, the first time doesn't always go easily.'

She wiped at her eyes, he gave her his handkerchief and said, 'Here.'

'Oh dear,' she said. 'What have I done?'

'In time we'll get around to it, there's no rush, let's just sit here, talk a little, be friends . . .'

'Thank you,' she said.

On 16 May, Ferrar took a train down to Lisbon, boarded the Pan Am flying boat, and was in Manhattan on the evening of the following day. The desk clerk welcomed him back to the Gotham and, not nearly ready to sleep, he took a walk down Fifth Avenue. On a warm night in May, New Yorkers strolled along the avenue, looking at the displays of spring fashion in the windows of the department stores. To Ferrar they seemed confident and relaxed, and the phrase *taking it easy* came to mind. Yes, among the crowd were faces taut with worry – New Yorkers were good at worrying – but what was missing here was the undercurrent of tension that he'd grown used to in Paris. When Ferrar reached Thirty-Seventh Street he paused, for a moment wanted to turn east, towards Delaney's Bar and Grill in the Murray Hill neighbourhood. In fact, being in Manhattan reminded him too much of Eileen Moore and he didn't want to make it worse, so he walked back to the Gotham. That part of his life was over.

In the morning he was at Coudert for meetings, which lasted all day. He sat at conference tables and contributed what he could, much of the legal work concerned the coming war, especially so now that the law firm represented the French arms-buying commission. At six-thirty he took a taxi up to Park Avenue – one of the senior partners, Hugh Courtney, had kindly invited him to 'a home-cooked dinner'. They had chicken and string beans and mashed potatoes, then angel cake and coffee for dessert. After dinner he sat with Courtney, now in shirt and loosened tie, his wife, Faye, and Courtney's oldest son, who was at Princeton. The host poured scotch for everybody and they settled down to talk.

'We look for Hitler to start it in 'forty-one or, at the latest, 'forty-two,' Courtney said. 'He'll have all his planes and tanks by then. One thing about Coudert, you are in touch with people from industry and government who have a real grasp of the future.' Courtney sat forward in an easy chair, elbows on knees, both hands holding his highball glass. 'Meanwhile, the newspapers are filled with local scandals and baseball.'

He was going to continue, but Faye Courtney said, 'Tell me, Cristián, do you have family in Paris?'

'I'm not married, but my parents and grandmother, a sister and a cousin, all live a few miles away, in a town called Louveciennes.'

Courtney Junior spoke up and said, 'There's a really good Pissarro painting of Louveciennes.'

'I know the road he painted,' Ferrar said. 'It's on the way to the house.'

'What will your family do if there's a war?' Faye Courtney said. 'Have you made provision for them?'

'I've thought about it,' Ferrar said, guilt in his voice. 'But the idea that they'd have to go somewhere new . . .'

'Paris will be bombed,' Courtney Junior said. 'Just like Spain was, *Life* magazine had photographs.'

'Yes, I suppose it will,' Ferrar said.

'Then you must do something about that,' Mrs. Courtney said. 'Really, Cristián, you must.'

'What do you suggest?' Ferrar said, meaning it.

Thus Ferrar left the office early the next day and, accompanied by the Courtneys, found himself at a tall apartment house on West End Avenue.

'Of course you have a choice,' Faye Courtney said, 'but the people coming out of Europe now are taking apartments up here.

So your family would be with other refugees.'

'Yes, you're right, Faye. They are isolated in Louveciennes.'

Led by the owner of the building, who spoke English with a thick German accent, they looked at several vacant apartments – big apartments with plenty of room, the Ferrar clan would need at least four bedrooms. On the third try he found one he liked, airy, with high ceilings, that looked out on a courtyard formed by three sides of the building. The owner said, 'Is this one right for you, Mr. Ferrar?'

'Yes, I think so.'

'There's a doorman and an elevator man,' the owner said. 'The rent is sixty-eight dollars a month.'

'You can afford it,' Hugh Courtney said. 'Money well spent.'

'Then I'll take it,' Ferrar said. 'They might never come here, perhaps the future will turn out differently in Europe.'

'A future to hope for,' Faye Courtney said. 'But, better safe than sorry.'

As Ferrar was renting an apartment, Max de Lyon was in a brothel in Istanbul. Not the worst he'd seen – two floors in a lime-green building that looked out over the Golden Horn, with the Bosphorus in the distance. De Lyon had taken a girl, and her room, for the night. The girl had the stomach of a belly dancer, round and firm, and sat naked on the bed, content and peaceful, repairing a ripped stocking with a needle and thread, awaiting the pleasure of her customer.

De Lyon had worked hard on his contacts in Paris, a city rich in Russian émigrés; some had fled the revolution in 1917, others had reached Paris in 1920, as the White Army was beaten by the Bolsheviks. Eighteen years had passed, yet certain of the émigrés, using clandestine methods, had managed to stay in touch with family and friends in the USSR. De Lyon had handed out a lot of money to various taxi drivers and nightclub doormen and dishwashers, some of them terribly poor, all of them eager to help de Lyon, who always paid generously for information. But, in the end, the man with the information wasn't poor at all; he owned a garage in the Paris suburb of Saint-Denis, he was rich, and deeply interested in politics. That interest was not comfortable for de Lyon – politically active émigrés drew secret police like flies – but the garage owner's contacts were up-to-date and he himself was from Odessa which meant, as he pointed out to de Lyon with some vigour, that he was not Russian, but Ukrainian. Still, he knew the gangs and claimed his information was current. 'Bratya?' he said. 'That's not a man's name, it means "cousins", the name of a gang, and they are all, every one of them, in Siberia or in the ground.'

The best of the gangs, whatever that meant – fiercest? richest? – had no name for the NKVD to file and was led by a man named Vadik, short for Vadim. Could the garage owner arrange a meeting? Anywhere outside the USSR? He could. De Lyon tried to pay him but he held up a stiffened hand. 'If it works, a favour some day when I need it.' Which made de Lyon even less comfortable, he didn't like owing favours, returning a favour could be dangerous, whereas money was money, but the garage owner was emphatic.

So then, Vadik. The belly dancer looked up now and then to see if her customer might be ready to have what he'd paid for, but de Lyon just smiled and the belly dancer smiled back; they had not a word of any language in common. From the garage owner, de Lyon knew that Vadik would have to spend a good day and a half on a freighter steaming down the Black Sea coast to Istanbul, so he had offered to pay for the meeting. But he would have to pay Vadik directly. When he'd suggested a payment in advance, the garage owner had wagged his index finger, *naughty boy,* and said, 'No, no, can't send money.'

At three-thirty in the morning, two light raps on the door. De Lyon was relieved, he'd begun to think that Vadik wouldn't show up and, at that time of night, the belly dancer was looking better and better. She woke from a doze and opened the door to reveal two individuals; one thin and dark with watchful eyes who remained in the hall, a guard; the other, entering the room, was a broad-chested man in the shapeless suit favoured by Soviet apparatchiks. His grey hair was cut short, he had a bullet head, high, Slavic cheekbones, and the stocky, round-shouldered build found in exceptionally strong men. He was in fact handsome, with a face made to smile.

'You are de Lyon?' he said.

'Yes, and you must be Vadik.'

'None other. Let's send the girl away.'

Vadik said a few words in Turkish and, as the girl left the room, bottom wobbling as she walked, he gave her some Turkish lira as a going-away present.

Both men watched her leave and, when he'd closed the door, Vadik said, 'Not so bad.'

De Lyon agreed.

'You speak good Russian,' Vadik said.

'I was born there and left as a kid, but it stays with me.' He reached into the inner pocket of his tweed jacket and handed Vadik a thick envelope containing five thousand dollars in roubles. Vadik put the envelope in his pocket; he didn't open it, didn't count it, anyone who did business with Vadik knew better than to steal from him.

Vadik sat on the rumpled bed and leaned against the headboard, de Lyon remained in his chair. Vadik said, 'Care for a cigarette? I could offer you the Russian kind, makhorka, black tobacco. I carry it with me, just in case, but I expect you'd prefer one of these.' He offered de Lyon a pack of Chesterfields, de Lyon lit one with his steel lighter. Vadik said, 'All right, Max, you paid to talk, so let's talk.'

'I'm working for the Spanish Republic, and we're looking for Soviet anti-aircraft ammunition. Some of these guns are mounted on ships, so, we thought, Odessa . . .'

'The naval base?'

'There must be an armoury at the base where the ammunition is stored.'

From Vadik, a single bark of a laugh. 'You're serious, aren't you?'

'I am.'

Vadik looked dubious. 'I don't know . . . damn . . . what haven't I stolen; furs, jewels, trucks, horses, caviar, machinery, money . . . *eggs,* when I was a kid robber, but never anything like that.'

'Always something new,' de Lyon said.

Vadik thought for a time, then scratched his head. 'And how do you come to have this job?'

'I worked for an arms merchant, when I was in my twenties, then I ran the business for a time. I never liked it – selling to both sides, making money from slaughter – but when Franco started his war I volunteered to help the Republic.'

'For money?'

'No, they pay me a little, but no. I'd seen the fascists at work, it did something to me.'

'You want to be a hero? Heroes die, Max.'

De Lyon shrugged. 'Everybody dies, eventually.' He paused, then said, 'What's your feeling about this job? Do you think you might take it on?'

'I don't know . . . yes, no, maybe. I have about forty men, most of them are brave and determined, and skilled at what they do. Still . . . this is no bank robbery, walk in, shoot your way out, you can't do that on a naval base.' He thought for a moment, then said, 'Tell me about the money.'

'On the munitions market, seventy-six-millimeter shells cost about nine dollars and forty-seven cents apiece. We need fifty thousand, which is four hundred and seventy-three thousand dollars, so let's call it five hundred thousand.'

'Let's call it six hundred thousand, Max.'

'Agreed. Half to start with, the rest when we receive the ammunition.'

'Fair enough. If all goes well, you'll receive it in Odessa. After that, it's up to you.'

'How do you want to be paid?'

From Vadik, a faint scowl. 'Now that is forever the fucking problem – even if you could buy all those roubles, the NKVD would hear about it.'

'Do you have a bank account? A foreign bank account?'

Vadik laughed. 'I don't make deposits in banks, only withdrawals. And, as for a *foreign* bank account, I can't do anything like that.'

'We can. A bank account in Switzerland, anonymous, just a number.'

'I'll have to think about it,' Vadik said. He stifled a yawn and looked at his watch – a cheap watch made of steel, likely USSR manufactured. 'It's four-thirty, can we get some air?'

'There's a kind of balcony on this floor, down the hall.'

Vadik nodded and rose from the bed. Outside the door, the guard was leaning against the wall, and de Lyon saw that he held a sawn-off shotgun beneath his jacket. Vadik spoke with him for a moment, in a language de Lyon didn't recognize. 'That was Armenian, in case you wondered. Joe is Armenian.'

'Joe? An Armenian name?'

'He got it from the cowboy movies.'

Heading for the porch they heard, as they passed one of the rooms, the rhythmic creak of bedsprings and, from the floor below them, somebody said goodnight in German. 'It's quiet for a brothel,' de Lyon said.

'This place is for foreigners – a real Turkish whorehouse is a lot noisier.'

Down the hall, an open door led to a narrow balcony with an intricate wooden balustrade. From here, they could see a docked freighter with hamals – Turkish stevedores – bent under the weight of huge, burlap-covered bales as they climbed a gangplank. A few trucks, headed to the open markets, rattled along the rough road past the dock. Vadik gave de Lyon another Chesterfield and, as de Lyon lit it, said, 'I've never seen a lighter like that.'

De Lyon snapped it shut, said, 'It works in the wind,' and handed it to Vadik. 'This is for you, Vadik, a gift.'

Vadik said thank you and put the lighter in his pocket. De Lyon said, 'When will you know whether or not you can do this?'

'I'll have to figure out the details, which means watching the armoury, talking to the sailors who work there, then I can tell you yes or no. It won't be right away, maybe two weeks, maybe more.'

'Once you're back in Russia, is there some way we can communicate?'

'I have a contact in Paris, a confidential agent called Morand – he used to have a Russian name but he changed it. He's dependable, a tough guy, though he doesn't look it – he looks like Hardy, in the Laurel and Hardy movies. Also, he's clever, he found a safe way to get messages in and out of the USSR. So, when you return to Paris, look him up.'

'I found you through a man who owns a garage north of the city.'

'No, no, he just contacts Morand. A big talker, better you don't see him again, he can't be trusted.'

'Is a telephone call possible?'

'Yes, but we'll have to use fake names, you know? Say things like "the machinery" and "the delivery". And if we take the job we'll have one more meeting here.'

They leaned on the balustrade and watched the lights on ships making their way through the Bosphorus channel. 'I'm getting hungry,' Vadik said. 'There's an all-night kebab place near the dock, you can get a plate of soup, good soup.'

They left the brothel, the Armenian guard a few paces behind them. On the way to the dock they passed a parked Opel, and the young woman behind the wheel exchanged glances with Vadik.

*

When Ferrar returned to Paris from New York, he found that Count Polanyi had telephoned him and was expecting to be called back as soon as possible. Perhaps the love letter had done its job, Ferrar hoped it had, because he wasn't really sure what to do if it hadn't. Reached at the Hungarian embassy, Polanyi asked if they could speak in person. 'Of course,' Ferrar said.

'Tomorrow is Saturday, do you go into the office on Saturdays?'

'From time to time, when it's necessary. Usually I go riding on Saturday morning, I could stop by the embassy on my way there.'

'Riding? In the Bois, I suppose.'

'Yes.'

'Would you mind company?'

'Not at all. We can rent you a horse at the stable by the Long-champ racetrack. Do you ride often?'

'Not now, I'm too old and fat for it, but I did my military service as a cavalry officer, so I think I can manage a bridle path.'

It rained at dawn on Saturday, then cleared to a sunny, windy May morning. Ferrar wore a sport coat with scarf and gloves, jodhpurs, and boots. Polanyi's outfit was tight on him but he rode easily and, since both men were mounted on the Selle Français, the muscular and responsive breed preferred by almost all French riders, they moved along at a slow trot and, side by side, were able to talk. The Bois de Boulogne forest was at its spring best; birdsong everywhere, the chestnut and oak trees in new leaf, light green, that danced prettily in the breeze.

'Lovely day,' Polanyi said. 'I wish I had good news to go with it.'

'Well, we tried,' Ferrar said. 'What happened?'

'Nephew Belesz telephoned from Budapest, he wanted to laugh at me in person – which is typical nephew.'

'He actually laughed?'

'A sort of theatrical snarl, not a real laugh. "Ha-ha, Uncle" was the way he put it.'

'Oh.'

'Then he said, "What do you take me for? A fool?" Which I was tempted to answer but didn't. He went on and on, he did. It seems the lovely Celestine could never write such a letter, or *any* letter, but he had a pretty good idea who *had* written it.'

'And you said?'

'Naturally I had no idea what he was talking about. "Did somebody write you a letter?" I was terribly confused, and that made him mad, and he actually *sputtered*.' Polanyi was amused at the recollection. 'Then he raved for a while, at one point he used the word "chicanery", and slammed the telephone down.'

'Time for a new approach,' Ferrar said. For a few minutes they rode in silence, the horses' hooves clopping softly on the packed dirt. Ferrar was thinking hard, he had to come up with something.

Finally, Polanyi said, 'The letter was a fiasco, no doubt about it, but I think I learned something we might use. Yes, he was angry, but there was more to it than anger, and after he'd hung up I found myself thinking, *He's scared*. That I had tried to attack him and would again. It was somewhere in his voice, you know how some people are? They get frightened and they cover fear with bluster.'

'And so?'

'We find a way to threaten him.'

'Physically?'

From Polanyi, a brief but informative silence.

'I would hate to have a client drawn into an act that would compromise him, legally. It's my job to protect you, from yourself if necessary, Count Polanyi.'

'You're right, Ferrar, I won't *do* anything. Still, a properly conceived threat will prey on the mind. This isn't theory – at the darker end of the diplomacy business it's done all the time.'

'Let's not do that yet, Count . . .'

They were riding along a lane bordered by Lombardy poplars, which opened to admit an intersecting path and there a woman had dismounted and held her horse by the reins. What had stopped

Ferrar in mid-sentence was the woman's golden hair and, as Ferrar stared, he realized who he was looking at. 'Maria Cristina?' he said, bringing his horse to a halt.

'Cristián!' she said. 'I thought, what a beautiful day, I shall go to the Bois, and here you are!' Her riding habit was fancy and new, the look on her face anxious.

Ferrar said, 'Marquesa Maria Cristina, may I present the Count Janos Polanyi.' Maria Cristina acknowledged the introduction with a gracious nod.

'*Enchanté,*' Polanyi said, bowing in the saddle.

Ferrar turned to Maria Cristina and said, 'Would you care to ride along with us?'

'Oh I wish I could,' she said. 'But I am expected for luncheon.' She raised a foot, slipped it into the stirrup and, as Ferrar held his breath, successfully mounted her horse. '*A bientôt,*' she called out. 'I hope to see you soon, Cristián,' and rode off with a flip of the reins. Which the horse understood to mean *speed up*. Maria Cristina jerked backward, then got her horse under control, turned halfway around and saluted them with her riding crop.

When she was out of sight, Ferrar and Polanyi went trotting off down the bridle path. Polanyi said, 'A friend of yours? A . . . good friend?'

'Yes, she is.'

'And she is a marquesa? A Spanish marquesa?'

'She was married to a Spanish marques, she is of French and Italian descent.'

'For a Spanish marquesa, Ferrar, she doesn't ride very well. Was she waiting for you?'

'I believe she meant it to seem a coincidence.'

'Did she? Well, if you don't mind my saying so, she is in serious pursuit of you, my friend. I hope you will invite me to the wedding.'

'Early for that, Count.'

Polanyi cleared his throat, a version of the comic-book *harumpf,* and said, 'Forgive me, Ferrar, if I say *damned strange.*'

'I don't mind, you aren't wrong. I suspect that my being with a friend surprised her.'

'Well, I didn't mean to disrupt a seduction, but I suppose love will find a way.' After a moment, he said, 'Ever done it on a horse?'

'I can't say I've had the pleasure.'

'A bad idea. The horse bolted and I wound up on the ground with my trousers down and damn near broke my pelvis. Of course, Hungarians believe they can do *anything* on a horse.'

'What happened to the woman?'

'She hung on, went galloping away over the fields, bare bum bouncing in the moonlight.'

The best part of the incident in the Bois de Boulogne was that Polanyi forgot his nephew and went on to tell Ferrar saucy stories about his youth. Thus, reprieve. For the time being, anyhow. But Ferrar was now troubled, what the hell was Maria Cristina doing? She had been so stately, so poised, until the night at the Windsor. And how had she known where, *precisely* where and when he would be on that Saturday morning? *What do I really know about her?* he asked himself. He still wanted her, very much wanted her, the evening at the hotel might have been a failure but it had whetted his appetite; he could still see her, almost undressed, and remembered every detail. And he intended to try at least once more. So went the weekend, and Ferrar was glad to return to work on Monday.

Where he put suspicion aside until the late afternoon.

And found himself in the office of the law firm's notary. Every international law firm in Paris had to have a notary, to sign and apply an official seal on legal documents and, since the notary had to be a French citizen, it also fell to him to do research into French public records. The notary at Coudert was a man in his sixties and, wounded in the Great War, walked with a cane. He had a small office, where the shelves were crowded with dossiers holding the documented history of the law firm's clients.

'I am interested in the dossier on,' – Ferrar consulted his notes – 'the Marquesa Maria Cristina de Valois de Bourbon y Braganza.'

The notary found the dossier, untied the ribbon, and opened it up. 'What would you like to know, Monsieur Ferrar?'

'Do I have the title right?'

'Yes. Born in Angers, the eight March of 1896, thus forty-two years of age.'

'And married?'

'To a marques with that title, her maiden name Palestrin.'

'Were you able to discover anything about the marques's financial circumstances?'

'Very little. He did hold title to estates in Spain, but conducted much of his business in cash.'

So the story about the theft of loaned money could well be true. Ferrar thanked the notary and left the office with elevated spirits. *There, you see?* he chastised himself. Nothing quite like distrust to burden the romantic heart. Now relieved, Ferrar thought hard about what strategy might bring Marquesa Maria Cristina to remove her satin undergarment, and then into . . . bed? On the couch? On the soft rug before the fireplace? On the sweet grass of a meadow?

Where?

NIGHT
WATCH

27 May, 1938. It wasn't easy for Ferrar, taking the little train up to Louveciennes. He didn't look forward to what he had to do there, and the spring day was a hard lesson in what would be lost. The region of the Seine, west of Paris, was the ancient preserve of the aristocracy – Saint-Germain-en-Laye, Versailles – and who could blame them, there was no lovelier countryside. And the season made it worse – long *allées* of plane trees shaded the winding roads, so that the carriages of the nobility did not overheat in the summer sun. Ferrar had brought along the morning newspaper but he never opened it, his eyes following the vista unfolding slowly out of the train window.

At the house, the usual excitement; everybody had something they just had to tell him and the patient Ferrar listened with unfeigned interest and, when appropriate, sympathy. Ferrar had a big, warm heart, people were drawn to him, the family no less so. When the welcome calmed down, he took Abuela outside, where they could speak privately; much of the effort to make the news less painful and lead the family to accept the inevitable would fall on her.

A gnarled old tree stood at the border of the property and, long ago, someone had built a circular wooden bench around it. There they settled. 'This will not be easy, Abuela, but it must be done,' Ferrar said.

'Is there trouble, dear one? Your mother hoped you were visiting with news of the marquesa.'

'Trouble is coming, Abuela, it may not arrive for a time but, if it does, you will have to leave here.'

'You mean the war, don't you?'

He had never seen his *abuela* cry, and he didn't now; nonetheless, he could see sorrow darken her eyes. 'The war, yes,' Ferrar said. 'If it comes to France it will come to Paris, and I could not bear to see my family hurt.'

She looked away, took control of herself, then said, 'Again.'

'I fear so. While I was in New York for meetings I rented a grand apartment. For the moment, only you need to know about this – we will read the newspapers, and we will decide when it is time to leave. We'd best decide early, Abuela, so I can make arrangements for travel. The trains will be crowded, the roads impassable.'

'And will we never return here? I know you hear complaints, from everyone, about this or that little problem, but we have come to love it here, Cristián.'

'I know, it is the same for me. I would like to think that the war will be over in a few months, and that France and the other allies will win, and we can return. I will keep this house while you're in New York.'

'New York. What is it like?'

'It is a city for commerce, lively, with lots of different kinds of people.'

From Abuela, a sigh of acceptance. 'I don't want to leave, with all my heart I don't, but we won't survive a war, we are too peaceful for war.'

'For now, dear, not a word.'

She nodded. 'I will wait until you tell me the time has come, and then I will do my best to soften the blow.'

They walked together slowly, back to the old house, where midday dinner was in preparation.

As the first week in June arrived, Ferrar worked on legal matters and, also, when he looked up from the dreary papers, on matters of the heart. He looked up often. The decision, when it came, was sensible. *Tradition* – that would be his ally in the chase: he would call Maria Cristina and propose a weekend at a small, fancy hotel in the country. By the sea. This meant a lovers' retreat, a shared room, but, if what went on in shared rooms was not what she wanted to do, she could gracefully decline; *be busy,* or *have a cold.* At five in the afternoon he telephoned her at the Windsor and, after preliminary chatter, said, 'I have a suggestion. I know a very nice little hotel up in Varengeville-sur-Mer, on the Normandy coast. Would you like to go for the weekend?'

'Oh, Cristián, what a good idea!'

'The hotel is called the Auberge Normande, it's quiet, and looks out on the sea.'

'When shall we go?'

'This Friday evening, if you are free.'

'I am.'

Now he would have to wait, but anticipation was likely good for them both – on his part sharpened by certain plans he did not share with her, which he turned over in his mind, then over again. The only drawback was that he would have to drive, and he did not drive happily. He had taken driving lessons, and he knew he could manage, and she would read the map – still, he worried. Ideally, he would have borrowed de Lyon's Morgan sports car but he didn't dare, so settled for the rental of a small Renault as arranged by a travel bureau. Friday evening, having taken its own sweet time, finally did arrive and Ferrar, in corduroys and sport coat for the country, reached the Windsor a half-hour early and, to a chorus of horns bleating at his sorry efforts, parked.

Carrying a small valise, she came downstairs, he led her to the car, opened the door, and, once she was seated, was rewarded with a wicked smile. Up on the coast, the Deauville area was so popular with Parisians going away for *le weekend* that it was known by the smart set as the Twenty-First Arrondissement, but Ferrar was heading well east of there and so had clear roads for the drive north – about ninety miles or, for Ferrar the snail, just under three hours. A warm, intimate time in the front seat; Maria Cristina looked ravishing, her light summer dress eager to be taken off, the Normandy fields at their lush best in June.

She did go on about her friend Benita, not that he minded. He liked hearing about the schoolgirl Benita. 'What times we had,' Maria Cristina said as they approached Rouen. 'Naughty pranks, you know, Benita could be a real imp when her mood was right. And when she was sad she would climb into bed with me and I would hold her until she felt better.' Innocent as dew, Maria Cristina, as she told her stories.

'I will try to help her,' Ferrar said.

'If you can, Cristián, then she could travel up to Paris and we will all spend an evening together.'

'I promise to do what I can.'

'Oh look, that poor man has a flat tyre! Should we stop and help him?'

'I don't know much about automobiles, I'm afraid.'

'Then forward. I'm sure someone else will stop.'

'And we should reach the hotel in time for dinner.'

They came to a village where their road wandered here and there through the local streets, Maria Cristina looked desperately for signs, Ferrar tried not to hit anything, and eventually they reached the village's main square for the second time. A local *garagiste* finally put them right. 'Nobody goes that way, you'll get nothing but lost. Now, here's what you do.' Directions, complicated directions, followed, but in time they left the village, though not on the road they'd been using. Then, after driving in what they were sure was the wrong direction, their road suddenly reappeared.

'Ah, here it is!' she said. 'The D155, where has it been?'

At last, Varengeville and then, at the end of a gravelled driveway, L'Auberge Normande; a three-storey house, half-timbered, the boards warped by time, the plaster freshly whitewashed. As Ferrar drove up to the door, the sound of breaking waves could be heard above the crunch of tyres on gravel, and voile curtains stirred at the open windows. Inside the hotel, a hushed silence and the smell of furniture polish. Ferrar registered at the desk, a young man in an apron took their bags upstairs. Their room was at the top of the house, in fact two rooms, a small parlour and a bedroom, with everywhere the same blue-and-cream fabric – lords and ladies in a pastoral scene.

When they were alone, Maria Cristina embraced him and said, 'It's lovely, just lovely.' Downstairs for dinner, they had an apéritif in a room with plants and wicker chairs. There were, of course, other guests, but they walked quietly and spoke in low voices, if they spoke at all, like courteous ghosts. The dinner was probably good but Ferrar never noticed; soup, trout boned at the table, a salad, and the requisite Norman Camembert. Followed by a walk on the beach in lingering daylight.

Then, back upstairs.

They sat in the parlour, smoked cigarettes, and talked about nothing in particular, idle conversation, no sensitive subjects. When it got to be ten-thirty, she said, 'I would love a bath.'

'I'm sure there's plenty of hot water,' he said. And off she went.

To return after forty-five minutes wearing emerald-green, silk pyjamas. 'I thought it might be chilly up here by the ocean. Do you like these?'

'I do like them.'

'Perhaps I should have chosen something more, provocative.'

'You are beautiful. In pyjamas or otherwise.'

'Kind of you, monsieur,' she said, making light of the compliment. 'May a lady sit on your lap?'

'She is welcome, of course, but perhaps not right away. Why don't you curl up in bed and I'll stay here for a while?'

She hesitated, more uncertain than alarmed, said, 'Very well,' kissed him on the forehead, and went off to the bedroom. Through the open door he could see her climb into the bed, then turn off the lamp on the nightstand. Lying on her back made her look expectant, so she turned on her side, slipped an arm beneath the pillow, and closed her eyes.

In truth, pausing at the edge was something Ferrar quite liked. He stood, had a last look at the white combers rolling up the beach, then closed the curtains and turned off the light. In darkness, Ferrar returned to his chair and waited. In the bedroom, Maria Cristina opened her eyes, saw that Ferrar remained in his chair, then turned on her other side and drew her knees up. They'd had an abundance of wine with dinner and Ferrar now worried that Maria Cristina might actually fall asleep, so he rose and stripped down to his shorts.

In the bedroom, he sat on the edge of the bed, counted to twenty, then lowered the quilt. Maria Cristina started to roll onto her back but he put a hand on her shoulder and said, 'Silk is pretty to look at but it feels even better.'

'To me also.'

'May I rub your back, madame?'

'Well . . . all right.'

He began to stroke her, using the backs of his fingers, sometimes the nails, sometimes not. A responsive lover, he listened carefully to her breathing, thus she led him to those places where she liked to be touched: her shoulders, her calves, the backs and insides of her thighs, her hips. Now and then he toyed with her, taking her waistband in his fingers, but went no further. In time, he stopped teasing her and, slowly, slid the trousers of her pyjamas down to her ankles, and took them off. And if the silk felt good, bare skin felt even better, and she breathed a soft *oh* every time she exhaled. When he slipped his hand under the vee of her legs she raised her hips, then lowered them, pressing herself against his up-turned palm. This felt very good indeed so she did it again and again, the rhythm gradually becoming faster. With his other hand he encouraged her, until she shuddered and lay still.

With effort, she turned on her back, then reached up and tugged at his shorts, which meant *take these off.* He did so, unbuttoned her pyjama top, then bent down and kissed her on the mouth. A long kiss, first this way, then that way, as he took her nipple in his finger-tips, a kiss that ended only when he entered her. He had wanted the lovemaking to go on at length but it didn't – he was overexcited. And the way her hands felt on his back, urging him on, didn't help. He lit a cigarette and shared it with her as they lay side by side, staring up at the ceiling, listening to the waves on the beach.

He had known, since the *chance meeting* in the Bois de Bou-logne, that he had to find out what was really going on. 'I was won-dering . . .' he said, but she cut him off.

'Don't, Cristián, not now.'

'Don't what?'

'Don't make me explain anything, please don't. Tomorrow maybe, but for now we are having a lovers' weekend.'

'All right. It's just that . . . all these questions . . .'

She was silent, shook her head and pressed her lips together.

So, a lovers' weekend. The sea was too cold for swimming but they waded together, or sloshed through ankle-deep water and held hands on long walks. She was restless at night, tossed and turned, had bad dreams, and mumbled in her sleep. He never asked his question, but then he didn't need to. He knew. Knew what she was doing but didn't do very well. They had the grand lunch on Sunday, the classic veal with cream and mushrooms, then drove back to Paris.

By preference, Max de Lyon did not have an address. He stayed here and there; in pensions and residence hotels, sometimes in the apartment of a woman friend. When, on Monday morning, Ferrar reached him at the Oficina Técnica, he suggested a meeting after work, at a café on the south side of the Luxembourg gardens, where the Boulevard Montparnasse traces the border of the Sixth Arrondissement. De Lyon often stayed in this neighborhood, one of the hidden *quartiers* of Paris, quiet, and far from the honking taxis and marching communists of Saint Germain.

De Lyon had chosen a fancy café, with polished brass and tiled floor, the waiter was quick to arrive and Ferrar ordered brandies. As de Lyon sat down he said, 'From your phone call, I had the impression that something's gone wrong.'

Ferrar nodded, then started slowly. 'I met this woman, as a law client, and we began a love affair, but she is a spy, I think.'

De Lyon raised his eyebrows. 'Really? What makes you think that?'

Ferrar told the story of his time with Maria Cristina, concentrating on her campaign to meet a senior diplomat at the Spanish embassy.

'And then, a new love affair begins,' de Lyon said. 'It *can* work that way, it has, often enough. Are you in love with this woman?'

Ferrar's *no* was tentative. 'It was desire, a *folie,* I couldn't stop thinking about her.'

'A condition I know well,' de Lyon said. 'And when you made love to her, was she, umm, *practised*? The sort of woman who will go to bed with a man to get what she wants? A courtesan?'

'No. The first time we tried, she was suddenly in tears. Then, last Friday, it happened.'

'And so you wonder, what now? Well, perhaps she is being coerced. Somebody somewhere might have a lock on her and she must do as he says, so she tries, and fails, and will be disposed of. And that's just one possibility. If you follow the rules, you have to tell Molina about this, as well as the embassy security officer, Zaguan, and if they accept your suspicion she will be interrogated, and then disposed of. Either way she won't survive.'

'You make it sound hopeless,' Ferrar said.

'It is.'

'What should I do?'

'End the affair, never see her again, and, if you care about her, give her an excuse – tell her you've fallen in love with another woman. She can try that on her controller, maybe he'll believe it. She can't run and hide, because the terrible consequence, whatever is being used to coerce her, will take place.' He thought for a time, then said, 'You know, I might just have an idea who she is.'

'You do?'

'Your predecessor, Castillo, had a woman spy, a volunteer, or so he believed. She was supposedly spying for the Republic, but that's an old game – misleading information for the enemy, and discovery of what the enemy wants to find out. This woman entered Madrid but she was being pursued and she was trapped, in hiding. Somehow she got a message to Castillo and asked for help. Castillo found himself a set of false papers and went to Madrid to save her. And there he disappeared, and the story ends, but it doesn't. Now she's sent after you, likely by Franco's secret service. They have her hunting a diplomat, but she's also after information from the Oficina Técnica, such as the date for the Ebro offensive.'

Ferrar lit a cigarette and finished his brandy. 'Max, can anything be done?'

'I don't think so. You may want to save her, but I am afraid she's lost.'

'I can't accept that,' Ferrar said.

'You'll have to,' de Lyon said. 'She is a casualty of war, Cristián.'

'There must be *something*,' Ferrar said.

'Give her an alibi for losing contact with you, maybe it will work.'

'And if it doesn't?'

'She will vanish. And they'll go after the next name on their list.'

To return to the Place Saint-Sulpice, Ferrar made his way through the Luxembourg Gardens, glorious on a day in June but Ferrar, head down, saw none of it. When he opened the building door she was waiting for him by the mailboxes in the lobby. 'Your concierge is a good soul,' she said. 'And he let me wait in here.'

She was different now, he saw: a blue spring suit, a sensible handbag. 'May I come upstairs, Cristián?' she said. 'I am here to say goodbye.'

In his apartment, he offered her a brandy, and they sat in his study. 'I think you know what's going on,' she said.

'I know,' he said. 'You are spying for Franco's secret service.'

'Trying to. But that's over now.'

'What will you do?'

'I can't say, but it doesn't matter. I wanted to ask your forgiveness.'

'You have it.'

'I had no choice, Cristián. I was forced to do this; they have my younger sister at Nationalist headquarters in Burgos. She is kept in a guarded house, and she is allowed to write once a month. To remind me of what may happen.'

'How long has she been there?'

'About eight months. She was abducted in Lisbon and taken to

Spain. She said in her first letter that they would kill her if I didn't do as I was told. So, I tried.'

'Was I your first . . . target?'

'No. Castillo was the first. Then you.'

'Other than the letters, are you in touch with them?'

'Oh yes, they must have their reports. Her captor telephones me, arranged calls to a public phone at the Gare du Nord. And asks the most intimate questions, in order to humiliate me. This excites him, I can hear it. I don't know who he is, but I know *what* he is, a señorito, as they are known, a "little gentleman". He speaks the most particular Castilian Spanish, with a kind of lisp – *thinko* for *cinco*. So very upper class he is, and arrogant beyond belief.'

'I know the breed,' Ferrar said. Impeccably dressed, hair perfectly combed, a superior being, the señorito was known for his imperious stare, *you offend me by your very existence*. Of the señorito a French journalist remarked, 'He judges the poor man's worth by his servility.'

'They will rule Spain, when Franco wins the war, sad to say.'

'Do you have any ideas – about what to do now?'

'I might try to play them along for a while. After that, I don't know.'

'You'll tell them you're still working on me? A friend of mine suggested that I break off the affair, having fallen in love with another woman. Do you think they might accept that?'

'Maybe so, maybe not. But, if they don't . . . I've thought of ending my life. A sacrifice. It might free my sister.'

'What if you pretended to die?'

'Pretended?'

'Perhaps a traffic accident – a statement by the police, reported as such by the newspapers.'

'How would one even *attempt* such a thing?'

'The French authorities could do it if they wanted to. By which I mean the Sûreté. They might be willing to help you if they thought you could be useful to them.'

'From one master to another, is that what you mean?'

Ferrar nodded. 'You will have to work for them – they will not help you otherwise, sympathy is not what they do. On the other hand, as a marquesa, you would have entrée into certain circles that interest them.'

'I am not a whore, Cristián.'

'There's no need for that. Female spies don't necessarily have to sleep with male targets – they can go to parties and hear gossip. Remember, the love affair with me was the señorito's idea.'

'I actually thought I could do it – I found you attractive. Then the moment came, at the Windsor, and I couldn't. And I meant to do something similar in Varengeville, but you tricked me. I'm not made of stone, and when you touched me it began to feel good and I didn't want to stop.'

Ferrar sighed, then shook his head in sorrow over what had happened. 'Would you care for some more brandy?'

'No, my dear, I have to be on my way. I know I shouldn't ask you, but this is the last time we'll ever talk so, is there any chance you know someone at the Sûreté?'

'I don't, but I believe you can find your own way to approach them.'

He led her to the door and they kissed goodbye, left cheek then right. Ferrar returned to his study, refilled his glass and lit a Gitane. De Lyon was right, he thought, he could have nothing further to do with her, and that included easing her way to someone at the Sûreté. *Complicit* was a prosecutor's word he did not want to hear. Still, he had to do something for her, and he would find a way. Secretly, so that she would not know what he'd done. Of course, if the Sûreté accepted the scheme, she couldn't remain in Paris. The more he thought about it, the more complications he discovered, so he stopped thinking, found the dog-eared page in *The Road to Oxiana* and joined Robert Byron where 'A mountain freshet had cut the road outside Isfahan.'

*

In Odessa, Lieutenant Commander Ivan Malkin, the assistant director of the Red Star Armoury, was reaching the end of a busy day. He planned, after work, to take his wife and children for a picnic – ride the train a stop or two, then walk out into the woods. The country around Odessa reminded visitors of Provence; gentle hills, blue skies, serenity. Malkin badly needed a dose of that. He had been running the armoury for almost a year, ever since the director, a victim of the Stalin purges, had been taken away at night. It was a difficult job, but Malkin worked hard and had so far survived. Munitions for the Black Sea Fleet were now manufactured in nearby Tiraspol and shipped by rail to the naval base at Odessa, and that made Malkin's job easier – he had to warehouse the shells, then have them loaded onto the warships.

Outside the office, one of his sailor-workmen was moving three crates with a forklift; the engine pumped out clouds of black smoke, burning oil, and Malkin could hear the bad piston. The forklift wouldn't last long, he thought – he had five or six dead machines rusting away in the cinder yard behind the armoury. He did make the ritual requests for replacement parts and repairs, and the requests were always approved, but, after that, nothing happened. This was a type of Soviet theatre, the theatre of bureaucracy.

Malkin stared at the clock on his office wall – *how much longer could this day possibly go on?* Then the telephone rang and he answered it. 'Lieutenant Commander Malkin.'

'Comrade Lieutenant Commander, Comrade Zhenitev speaking. I am a supervising officer with the Port Facility Inspection Bureau, Southern Ukraine Division, and this evening the Red Star Armoury will receive inspection.'

Malkin's heart pounded. He thought there might be an organization with that name but it didn't matter – these people would find evidence of some crime against the state and the Cheka would come and arrest him. In the USSR, bureaus and committees multiplied like rabbits. Lethal rabbits. 'Thank you for informing us, Comrade Zhenitev, we are prepared for inspection.'

'The committee will arrive in forty-five minutes. We expect your workers will have left for the day, make sure that they do. Only you are to remain.'

'Yes, comrade, I understand, I will be waiting here for the committee.'

The comrade supervising officer hung up.

Malkin looked death in the face. Once the authorities showed up, that was that. He telephoned his wife and, trying to keep his voice steady, told her there would be no picnic that evening. She sensed that something was wrong but, Russian phones being what they were, did not ask for fear he would answer and say the wrong thing. 'I see,' she said. 'Perhaps tomorrow, we can go.'

They would find everything, it couldn't be hidden – corroded metal, broken machinery, holes in the ceiling, there was so much he'd been unable to repair. Unable? No. *Unwilling,* in the eyes of the state – and so guilty of that form of sabotage known as *wrecking.* He saw the grisly word in the newspapers every day. Malkin held his head in his hands and said a prayer. A short prayer. He leapt to his feet and hurried out to the armoury floor and began to pick up cigarette butts. There were signs everywhere, smoking was forbidden. Imagine, all that explosive going up at once.

He was halfway through this task when the committee arrived. There were four of them, three were pure apparatchik types, lumpy men in lumpy suits, accompanied by a terrifying woman – small, mean eyes, a hatchet for a face – who carried a terrifying briefcase; it meant authority, it meant power, it was a weapon. 'I am Comrade Inspector Kostova,' she said, her voice as dry as a bone. Malkin, trying to conceal his shaking hands, greeted them. Offered them vodka from the bottle in his desk. They refused, eyes narrowing, *are you trying to bribe us, comrade?*

The old armoury, built by Czar Alexander II in 1861, was three storeys high and packed with munitions; torpedoes, depth charges, anti-aircraft shells, heavy machine-gun bullets. 'Shall we begin on this floor?' Malkin said.

'Top floor, comrade,' one of the apparatchiks said.

'I will inspect the office,' Kostova said. 'Are these all the filing cabinets?'

'They are, comrade inspector.'

As Malkin led the rest of the committee towards the wooden ramp that served the upper floors, they produced notebooks and pencils to record the sins of the soon-to-be former assistant director. In the office, Kostova, using the technique common to thieves, opened the bottom drawer of the first filing cabinet, finding it packed with official forms, pages interleaved with carbons. Kostova knelt on the floor, thumbed through the forms, and under her breath said, *'Poshol'*, which meant 'fuck'. She'd thought at first that the forms packed into the drawer were duplicates, but they weren't, there were a dozen of each variety, then K566-Q gave way to C-49 HH. She began to go through them, selecting three of each type – God only knew what they were for. She slid them into her briefcase, then went on to the next, and the next.

While she was at work, Malkin and the committee had finished the inspection of the third floor and descended to the second, walking along aisles where crates with stencilled identification markings were stacked to the ceiling. Midway down an aisle, one of the apparatchiks paused and said to Malkin, 'I will take a count of some of these crates, you go on ahead, I will catch up with you.'

'As you wish, comrade inspector,' Malkin said.

But the apparatchik didn't count anything, he worked his way back two aisles, where a certain marking had caught his attention. He found the camera in his briefcase and began to take photographs, focusing on the stencilled identification: 76MM MODEL F-22. When he was done, he went off to find the rest of the committee.

They were there for an hour, by which time there wasn't much left of Malkin, who wiped at his brow with a handkerchief. What unnerved him was that they didn't *say* anything, never asked a question, simply looked here and there and scribbled little notes in their notebooks. What had they found? When at last they returned to the office, Inspector Kostova was waiting for them. 'Have you finished your work, comrade?' said the apparatchik who seemed to be in charge.

'I have,' she said. 'The office appears to meet the standard.'

The lead apparatchik turned to face Malkin and said, his voice angry and hard, 'But the armoury does *not* meet the standard.' He let that sink in, then said, 'Listen to me carefully, comrade, there are many things wrong here, I won't read you the list, but it is obvious that little effort has been made to maintain this facility.' Malkin winced, these words meant he was to be accused of *wrecking*. 'Some of it we may report – the committee must meet and decide what to do with you. But, until that decision is made, you may not discuss this inspection with *anybody*, is that clear? The work we do is considered a state secret and, if you talk about it, you will be guilty of *revealing* a state secret. And what happens next is just what you think. Do you understand?'

'Yes, comrade inspector, perfectly I understand, completely.'

The apparatchik stared at him – for a long time, perhaps twenty seconds, an even sharper threat than could be put into words. Then the committee left the armoury, driving away in a large, official-looking black car. So, what he'd feared had come to pass, he would next face investigation by the Cheka, then they would force him to sign a confession. Still, the committee hadn't taken him into custody, which meant he was safe until two in the morning, the hour when the Cheka came to call. Or perhaps that would happen the following night, or the one after that.

Malkin went back to his office and telephoned his wife, 'I will be home soon,' he said.

She knew what that meant – he was still a free man. 'I will have dinner waiting,' she said. *Thank God.*

At the Oficina Técnica, Max de Lyon received a telephone call from a man called Morand, the Odessa gangster's confidential agent in Paris. 'I have a telegram for you,' Morand said. 'I assume it's important so you may want to come over here and collect it. I'm at 12, rue de Liège, one flight up.'

De Lyon took a taxi to the address, and found the office easily enough – a sign painted on the pebbled glass door said J. P. MORAND, CONFIDENTIAL INVESTIGATIONS. De Lyon knocked at the door, which opened to reveal a man who, as Vadik had said, looked something like Oliver Hardy – the resemblance evidently appealed to the detective because he had grown a duplicate of the comedian's little moustache. Standing at his side was a woman dabbing at her eyes with a handkerchief. Morand acknowledged de Lyon with a glance and said to the woman, 'Now, now, my dear, don't cry, I'm sure it will all work out for the best.'

Trying to hold back the tears, she nodded, and closed the door behind her.

As Morand showed de Lyon into the office, he said, 'That's the *worst* part of this job, but it pays the rent. So, you are Monsieur de Lyon?'

'I am.'

'Here is a telegram from Vadik – I didn't want to use his name on the phone. It supposedly comes from a Soviet trading company in Odessa.' Although Russians didn't have enough to eat, the state needed hard currency so they sold wheat abroad. Thus the wire was addressed to a grain brokerage in Paris, and said: *We have found the variety of wheat you requested stop In future we will specify date of shipping stop signed R. Szapera for SovExportBuro Odessa.*

'Make sense?' Morand said.

'It does. Vadik has found what we're looking for. If we want to wire back, can you do that?'

'Whenever you like. The reception of the telegram will cost you a service fee, three thousand francs.'

'Very well, I just happen to have the cash.'

'Money on hand,' Morand said. 'Always a good idea.'

*

In Odessa, Vadik's people began to shadow the armoury. At a late-night restaurant across from the entry gate, a man in workman's clothes took a window seat for three nights in a row. Drunks staggered past the gate at midnight. A woman in a kerchief sold meat pies from a wicker basket. They were interested in the quality of the armoury's security and the news was not good. There were eight guards, sailors with rifles, who arrived at eight in the evening to relieve the day shift. The sailors showed up for guard duty, on time and apparently sober, and did not sneak away for a nap, and the officer who supervised the guards was young and brisk and seemed to take his job seriously. In a tenement room, Vadik met with one of his lieutenants and said, 'We can't do it by force, there would be a bloodbath.'

'No, we can't. They would send Chekists down here from Moscow, hundreds of them, and some of us wouldn't get away.'

One of Vadik's people entered the armoury, dressed as a sailor, with the crowd that arrived in the morning. He found the aisle where the 76mm ammunition was stored and began to count the crates. The shells weighed twelve pounds apiece and were packed twenty to a crate, to be managed by two loaders – which meant twenty-five hundred crates. But all he could find were one thousand nine hundred and thirty crates, which reduced the anti-aircraft ammunition to thirty-eight thousand, six hundred shells. This he reported to Vadik, who went off to see his friend at SovExportBuro and sent a telegram revising the order and the price.

Meanwhile, the woman who had played the part of Inspector Kostova, in fact Vadik's sister-in-law, was hard at work on the forms she'd stolen. This was not easy; the language used on the forms was strange and stilted, created by bureaucratic gods in a distant heaven. A form requesting a resupply of pencils asked for all sorts of information, that is, if a *hand-managed writing tool – lead* even *was* a pencil. Still, what else could it be? But an hour at the task taught her to deal with the language, and it was then she came upon *E-781 L2. Authorization for Emergency Distribution of Inventory*. Three pages of it. Asking, again, for unimaginable volumes of detail. She walked over to Vadik's tenement-room office and showed him the form.

'Is this of use?'

'What is it?'

When she told him, he was delighted.

'Will it work?'

'Normally, it wouldn't. There isn't a naval officer in the world who would act on such a request without at least a telephone call. You can't just send weapons out into the night. However . . .'

'Yes?'

'This is the Soviet Union, and here it may not be smart to ask questions, here it is smart to obey a directive while finding a way to protect yourself. And, in our case, we know who we are dealing with, and that *will* make a difference. Maybe.'

'And, dear Vadik, if maybe not?'

Vadik shrugged. 'Run like hell. I know all about that.'

Working with Morand, Vadik arranged for a telephone call to the detective's office and spoke with de Lyon. 'We may have found a way,' Vadik said, 'it depends on the individual approving the paperwork.'

'Some money, perhaps.'

'In this case, no. But we will use another approach. Do you have transport?'

'We're working on it. Any idea of the date?'

'Not yet. Could be a week from now, maybe ten days.'

When de Lyon hung up the telephone he remembered Professor Z and the particular way he'd said the word *diversion*.

Ferrar had met, through involvement in a legal matter, one of the more respected shipping brokers in Paris. Dupre's office was close to the heart of the financial district, up past the Bibliothèque Nationale and near the Bourse, in a genteel, elegant building served by a very slow elevator with a cage for a door. Dupre was a dignified old gentleman, courtly, often amused. Leaning against the walls of his office were large squares of green felt tacked to thin boards where Dupre, by means of notations on slips of paper pinned to the felt, and a telex machine in the corner, kept track of much of the world's merchant shipping. As Dupre would explain, the liners, which ran on schedule between two ports, kept their cargo and location up to date, not so much the tramp freighters – sometimes they reported, sometimes not.

Dupre had a vast, antique desk with a ship in a bottle set on a wooden trestle. 'Have you been working hard?' he asked Ferrar. His smile indicated that he knew the answer.

'Yes, it's the war.'

'Here as well, and curses on the man who invented the torpedo. What can I do for you, Monsieur Ferrar?'

'I'm here to find a ship.'

'Plenty still afloat. I would imagine you are representing a client.'

'The client is the Spanish Republic.'

Eyes to heaven, Dupre said, 'Something tells me to put my fingers in my ears.'

'I wouldn't blame you, Monsieur Dupre.'

'You will have to find a way to deal with the Non-Intervention Pact, but some of the tramp freighters will carry anything, if somebody fiddles with the shipping manifest. Of course I can't recommend that. Why not a Spanish ship?'

'We inquired at the office of the naval attaché – no shipping available for two months. And, if we started a fight over that, it would take weeks. We want to ship as soon as possible.'

Dupre found a clean sheet of paper and uncapped his fountain pen. 'From where to where, Monsieur Ferrar?'

'From port of Odessa to port of Valencia.'

'I see. And the cargo?'

'Anti-aircraft ammunition in wooden crates.'

'You'll pay a price for that, Monsieur Ferrar; hazardous cargo. You're buying from the USSR?'

'No one else will sell us ammunition,' Ferrar said. Which was true, but not the answer to Dupre's question.

'What's the tonnage?'

'Two hundred and thirty tons, more or less.'

Dupre stood, and began to walk around the room, peering at his paper slips. 'We should be able to find something, there are always merchant vessels working on the Black Sea. And just about every port is two days from Odessa, even for the older ships that do ten knots an hour.'

As Dupre moved to a different board, the telex machine printed out a new length of tape. 'Let's try your allies first; South American countries, and Mexico, they carry tons of oranges and bananas up to Odessa – you don't want to get between a Russian and a banana. Aah, here's what you need.'

He unpinned a slip of paper and returned to his desk. 'The *Santa Cruz,* out of Tampico, Mexico, thirty-two hundred tons, built in 1909. She's at the dock in Constanta, Roumania, waiting for a tramping contract. Shall I get you a price?'

'That's the usual thing to do, but we'll pay whatever they ask.'

'Then I'll wire. *Santa Cruz* is owned by the Compañía Aguilar, in Tampico – you'll have to pay in advance of course; ammunition, submarines, time of war.'

When Ferrar returned to the office, Jeannette told him that Barabee wanted to see him right away. Then she gave him a certain look, a warning. As Ferrar sat down, Barabee stood up and closed his door. He wasted no time and said, 'My contact at the Sûreté called this morning.'

'Now what?'

'It seems they have an interest in the marquesa, he didn't say why. So I told him that I don't know much about the case but that you were representing her. He asked that you call him at his office – you don't mind, do you?'

'Not at all.'

'Do we have anything to worry about?'

'I don't think so, but I'll let you know after I speak with him.'

'By the way, he's the one who helped you out with the Poles, so you should do the best you can.'

'I will,' Ferrar said.

Barabee gave him a telephone number and the name of a colonel.

Ferrar took the information back to his office. Barabee had been brusque, not his usual style, but Ferrar couldn't blame him. Calls from French security officials could be handled, but Barabee clearly didn't like dealing with them. Ferrar dialled the number, which was a direct line to the colonel's office.

'Monsieur Ferrar? Thank you for calling. I should say first of all that this is something of a sensitive matter, so your discretion would be appreciated.'

'I ought to inform Mr. Barabee if it concerns the law firm.'

'Very well, but nobody else.'

'No, only Mr. Barabee.'

'This matter concerns a marquesa, Marquesa Maria Cristina with plenty of title after that, Bourbon, Braganza, and so forth. Husband's title, I believe.'

'That's my understanding.'

'Well, she came to see us. Talked to a junior officer, who sent her on to a senior officer, who sent her on to me. So, the nature of your relationship, please.'

'The marquesa was a Coudert client – she was seeking to recover a debt owed to her deceased husband's estate. Then, we became friends, if you understand what I mean.'

'Intimate friends.'

'Yes.'

'We had a long and serious discussion with the marquesa, and in the course of that discussion she told us she was a Coudert client, so I telephoned Mr. Barabee, and he suggested I speak with you. Now, the marquesa came to see us with the intention of freeing herself from a connection with the Spanish Nationalist secret service, she had some harebrained scheme involving a faked automobile accident. Did you know she was a spy?'

'Not at first. When I figured it out I ended the relationship.'

'You didn't tell her anything, did you? I mean, perhaps by accident?'

'I did not. She tried, I'll say that for her, and she's a very seductive woman . . .'

'Indeed.'

'. . . and I liked her, but, beyond that . . .'

'I understand your feelings for her. She sat in my office, well dressed, very prim and proper, but you could feel the heat from across the room. Technically, she committed a crime on French soil, although not against France. Still, I was obliged to arrest her.'

'I regret you had to do that.'

'Don't feel too bad. She is comfortable, not in a prison, and in the end it all turned out for the best.'

'It did?' *How could it?*

'Well, the more I spoke with her, the more I felt she might be someone who could help us, and she agreed she was willing to do that. Our work here is *comprehensive*, as I like to put it, national borders don't mean all that much in this office but, as you would imagine, we are especially concerned with Germany and Italy. I believe this influenced her decision.'

'Did she tell you about her sister, who is held in Burgos?'

'Be patient with me, Monsieur Ferrar, I'm getting there. Yes, she did tell us about her sister, so we had to do something about that. Here at the Sûreté we find it's best, often, to work in the upper regions of the various services we deal with, so I made a telephone call to my counterpart at the SIM, the Nationalist secret service, and we worked out a deal. The marquesa will no longer be controlled by the SIM, and her sister will be freed. In return, we agreed that nothing of this affair would appear in the press.'

'Please don't think I'm being flippant, Colonel, but you should have been a lawyer.'

'Oh but I *am* a lawyer, monsieur, or rather I was.'

'Did you tell your counterpart that the marquesa will now work for you?'

'I didn't need to tell him that. He knew. European nobility is of particular interest to us, all of us. They ruled every country in Europe for generations and they are still influential – politicians cannot resist them, especially if they look anything like the marquesa.'

'Truthfully, I am more than glad that you were able to save her.'

'We do what we can. I wonder, now that the marquesa is no longer a threat to you, perhaps you would like to resume the affair.'

'No. Not after what happened, I couldn't.'

'Monsieur Ferrar, I will remind you once again to keep this matter secret, and then I will say good afternoon.'

What, Ferrar wondered, was that certain note in the colonel's voice when he asked about resuming the affair? Did his interest in the marquesa extend beyond a professional concern? No, impossible! Really? Why?

In Odessa, the Cheka came for Malkin at two in the morning. There were three of them; they told his wife to go into the bedroom and shut the door, then waited while he dressed. At least, Malkin thought, they had not arrested her, which was common practice. When he was done, they took him out to their car – the black, boxy Emka, manufactured for the NKVD and driven exclusively by them. Malkin, rigid with fear, knew his future; he would be taken off to a basement in an NKVD prison and interrogated. Reaching the Emka, he was shoved into the backseat and one of the Chekists, who wore glasses and a hat, sat next to him. He was, Malkin sensed, one of those Bolshevik operatives who truly *believed;* relentless, merciless.

But then, Malkin did not go to the room in the basement.

The Emka stayed where it was, while the Chekist sitting next to him said, 'Comrade Malkin, you are in grave difficulties. You are, the inspection committee has determined, guilty of the crime of wrecking. For that you get twenty years in a Siberian gold mine. Not a good place, Comrade Malkin, a place from which very few return.'

The Chekist waited for a response, but Malkin could only nod.

'A sorry fate, comrade. But then, there might be a way out for you.'

Malkin stared at him – had he heard correctly? 'A way out?'

'You are a very lucky fellow, because just at this moment you are in a position to help us and, if you do that properly, your crime will be forgotten.'

'What can I do?'

'We have under way a very important and very secret operation, I can't tell you *what* we are doing, but I can tell you how you might play a part in our efforts. Are you familiar with the form E-781 L2?'

'No, what is it for?'

'It's called *Authorization for Emergency Distribution of Inventory.* Have you ever used it?'

'Never.'

'It allows you, as the acting director of the Red Star Armoury, to ship ammunition if there is an unexpected crisis. No written orders are required, and no signatures needed other than your own.'

Malkin swallowed. This was worse than wrecking – there *had* to be an order from the office of the navy, at least a telephone call from a senior official, he couldn't do this on his own. When the shipment was discovered he would be shot. 'Where is my authority to do such a thing?' he said.

'A verbal instruction from the NKVD, and a signed copy of the form I mentioned.'

'Of course I will do as you wish, comrade officer, but can you tell me how it would work?'

'As usual. You will direct your workers to transfer the ammunition to the dock, where it will be loaded into the hold of a ship. Basically what you do every day.'

'Yes, but . . .'

'Very well, you refuse. Mischka, we're on our way.' The driver started the car and began to pull away from the curb.

'Wait!' The car jerked to a halt as the driver hit the brakes. 'Of course I will do what you ask – if it's for the good of the nation, I'll do anything you say, anything at all.'

'Ah, a wise choice.'

'When will this happen, comrade officer?'

'In two or three days, whenever our ship gets here. It is our own ship, by the way, used by our service. It is not a naval vessel.'

'All right, two or three days, yes, just tell me when.'

'We will. Meanwhile, you can never speak of this because, if you do, we'll be back and then you won't be such a lucky fellow.'

'And, later on, if a senior officer should question my actions?'

'You will show him the form. But it won't come to that, the navy knows better than to question our operations. You will simply request that a replacement stock of ammunition be provided. And you will be a free man.'

'Thank you, comrade officer.' Malkin glanced out the window and saw the silhouette of his wife as she watched from the darkened bedroom.

'We will contact you,' the Chekist said. 'And now, comrade, go home.'

*

In Spain, where the river Ebro provided a line of defence for the gathering of the Republic's forces, the Army of the Ebro prepared to cross the river and attack Nationalist positions on the other side. The new army had been made up of the Republic's last reserves, thus the conscription of sixteen-year-olds and middle-aged men with families had been ordered, to be supplemented by Nationalist prisoners of war and technicians of the Republic's hydroelectric plants, now behind enemy lines. Altogether, some eighty thousand men, supported by one hundred and fifty field guns – some of them manufactured in the nineteenth century – and twenty-six anti-aircraft cannon.

The crossing of a river by combat assault troops under fire was complex and difficult, so for a week the soldiers trained, using ravines and rivers along the coast in an attempt to keep the operation unobserved. Much of the training involved practice in the use of pontoon bridges, some of which had been fabricated in Barcelona, while others were purchased in France by the Republic's arms-buying agency in Paris. In addition, the Army of the Ebro would employ rafts, and small boats that each carried eight men.

But the formation of the new army and its training was no secret. German reconnaissance aircraft, unopposed by the Republic's dwindling air force, observed the preparations, and Nationalist spies confirmed the observation reports. Franco and his generals knew what was coming but, at first, could not believe the Republic would attempt such a foolhardy operation. Did the Republic's military leadership not understand what dive bombers would do to an army trying to cross a broad river without air cover? Perhaps they chose not to understand: a battlefield victory was now the only thing that would save the Republic, so it had to be tried.

Odessa, 3 July. It had been a hot day in the city but now, in the lingering summer dusk, warm air on the coast met the Black Sea's cooling water, resulting in a mist that hung over the naval base, drifted through the glare of the port's floodlights, and obscured the tops of the cranes. At ten in the evening, just as darkness gathered, the small trucks used by the Red Star Armoury began to carry wooden crates to a ship waiting at the dock. This was the *Santa Cruz* out of Tampico, Mexico, though the name of the vessel was hidden from view by a tarpaulin hung over the side of the freighter. An unusual visitor to the naval base; built long ago, hull streaked with rust, the paint on its smokestack blistered and crumbling.

Leaning on the railing of the *Santa Cruz,* the freighter's captain, Juan Machado, smoked cigarettes and watched the loading under way. A merchant mariner for thirty years, he was a compact man with grey hair and wore an old, blue suit jacket, had been in every port there was, had seen his share of storms at sea, had lost one ship but saved many others. Now he watched as the holds of his freighter were filled with pallets of crated ammunition. Did the owners of the Compañía Aguilar know what they were doing? He supposed they did, they usually did, it was a matter of money, though Machado could only imagine what the insurance for this voyage had cost.

Some of the crew, many shirtless, a few wearing peaked caps, stood at the rail and watched the cargo handling. Normally they wouldn't have bothered but their curiosity was provoked by certain unusual circumstances: the tarpaulin hiding the ship's name and, down on the dock, guards in civilian clothing maintaining a wide perimeter as the trucks were unloaded. Guards? Well, why not, nothing quite like Russia for unnamed threats and dangers. The crew had been looking forward to spending time ashore – good whoring to be had in Odessa, as well as good food and well-run gambling dens, where it took them a long time to steal your money so the excitement could last all night. But, Machado had told them, not this time.

At the armoury, Lieutenant Commander Malkin had stationed himself by the open doors of the building and kept inventory by counting truckloads, while at his side an apparatchik from the inspection committee kept his own count. An hour into the cargo loading, a workman showed up at the doors and told Malkin there was an urgent telephone call for him at the armoury office. When he picked up the phone it was the port captain, calling from home, wanting to know what the hell was going on. Malkin said he wasn't sure but he had filled out and signed an emergency authorization form.

'At whose request?'

'State security, this is their operation.'

'Oh,' said the port captain. Then he hung up, swore a vile oath, and went to bed. This was the only challenge Malkin would ever hear. The best thing, in such situations, was to file a form and forget about it – nobody wanted to investigate what the secret police were up to and nobody did. As for the real NKVD, their officers were busy that night. Their officers were busy *every* night, treason was everywhere, and they cruised the streets of the city in their Emkas, going from apartment to prison, then starting out anew.

At dawn, the rising sun struck the clouds a fiery orange and the *Santa Cruz* steamed slowly out of port in a heavy sea. On the dock, Vadik, hands in pockets, watched her go.

In the Roumanian port of Constanta, Max de Lyon and Cristián Ferrar were having dinner on the terrace of the best restaurant in town. To de Lyon, the USSR was now forbidden territory, with such intense security he no longer dared to go there, so he waited with Ferrar in the Black Sea port and they would board the *Santa Cruz* when it docked, later in the evening. Which meant that for ten days they would be eating whatever was produced by the freighter's galley. 'We'll manage,' de Lyon had said. 'But we might as well have a good dinner tonight.' That it was, pork fillet stuffed with ham and mushrooms, and a bottle of dark, heavy Roumanian wine.

'What did they say at the office?' de Lyon asked.

'Not much. I told the managing partner I was taking two weeks of vacation and he didn't seem to mind. 'Be careful,' he said, 'if you're doing work for the arms office.' Nothing more. He has no idea what I'm actually doing – better that way.'

The terrace looked out over the port, and they could hear music coming from the waterfront bars – an accordion, Gypsy violins. Out at sea, steamship lights twinkled in the foggy night air. De Lyon laid knife and fork on his plate and lit a brown cigarette. 'When the *Santa Cruz* docks,' he said, 'we'll have a look at our cargo, just to make sure, and then I'll signal Molina to wire payment to Vadik, using the SovExportBuro in Odessa.'

'So, no Swiss bank account.'

'Too complicated; Vadik has to share out the payment with his people, and he can't sneak out of the country every time he needs money.' He paused, then said, 'I hear it's getting tighter every day in Russia, much tighter, and if Vadik shows up in Paris one of these days, I won't be surprised.'

They took a walk after dinner. On a summer night, the streets were crowded: people of the town, couples of all ages, sailors on their way to the next bar, prostitutes strolling arm in arm. Ferrar couldn't stop looking at the beautiful Roumanian girls; small, dark, and lithe, they flirted with him, all shining eyes and pretty smiles.

The *Santa Cruz* made port at eight-twenty. De Lyon had paid a clerk at the customs office to let them know when it docked and he came to their hotel, then walked them to the wharf. De Lyon and Ferrar climbed the gangway, found a sailor, and asked to see the captain. Machado was in his tiny office, perhaps a former cupboard, with just enough room for a desk. After they introduced themselves, he looked them over for a moment, then said, 'You must be the passengers, the company wired your reservation.'

'We are,' de Lyon said. 'All the way to Valencia.'

'Maybe you have something to do with the cargo,' Machado said.

'It is ours,' de Lyon said. 'We are serving the Spanish Republic.'

'Well, that's all right with me.' He stood and said, 'Let me show you your cabin, it isn't much to look at, but better than hammocks in the crew quarters.' At the end of a narrow passageway, a small room with a porthole and two cots.

'Just right for us,' de Lyon said.

'Good,' Machado said. 'Passengers don't work on freighters, but I wonder how you would feel about standing a watch? We're two hands short, so it would help us out.'

De Lyon and Ferrar glanced at each other, then Ferrar said, 'We'll be happy to help out.'

'I had in mind the midnight-to-eight, split in half, four hours each and you can trade off if you like.'

'Anything special we have to do?' Ferrar said.

'Stay awake. I expect it will be a quiet voyage.' Machado looked at his watch. 'We'll be sailing in a few hours, we only came here to pick you up.'

Machado returned to his office. Ferrar put his small valise at the foot of the cot next to the wall. He'd gone shopping in Paris for clothes to wear at sea – a long-sleeved cotton undershirt with three buttons at the neck, canvas trousers, and canvas shoes with rubber soles. When he started to change clothes, he saw that de Lyon was doing the same thing. 'I'll take the midnight-to-four,' Ferrar said.

The *Santa Cruz* carried a crew of seventeen; mostly ordinary seamen and stokers – the ship was coal-fired – a bosun who served as second officer to the captain, a radio operator, and a cook. Like many merchant marine crews, they came from everywhere: a few born in Mexico, others were Portuguese, Algerians with French passports, two Germans, three from Venezuela. They had signed on at various times, from seamen's hiring halls in various ports, and spoke, like almost all merchant seamen, a kind of pidgin English that allowed them simple communication, especially in areas of work at sea.

One of the Germans was called Horst. He'd had a number of last names over time, a conspirative necessity, because he'd been a member of the communist seafarers' union in Hamburg, which had fought it out with the Nazis in the early thirties. That war they lost, and the survivors had fled the Reich. Horst had managed to ship out on a Turkish freighter and then, two years later, had found a berth on the *Santa Cruz*. He was in his thirties, a thickly built stoker, his face scarred from fighting on the Hamburg docks.

In Constanta, where the ship often called on its Black Sea voyages, he favoured a bar in the port where you heard German spoken and the beer wasn't bad – it wasn't German beer but it wasn't bad, and you could fall into conversation with other German sailors, many of whom had the same history as Horst. When Machado gave his crew a few hours' liberty after they returned from Odessa, Horst made for his favourite bar. Soon enough, a fellow seaman, speaking German, settled down beside him at the bar and bought him a beer. 'Just come into port?' he said.

'Yes, about an hour ago.'

'From . . . ?'

'Odessa.'

'I've been there, not a bad place for sailors. But you have to watch out for the Russians; they drink and they look for a fight. And, if they hear you speaking German . . . well, you might have trouble.'

'We didn't have liberty in Odessa, not this time.'

'Really? Why not?'

Horst shrugged. 'I don't know, we weren't there long, maybe twenty-four hours.'

'Delivering goods?'

'No, loading cargo.'

'Really? Want another one of those?'

'I wouldn't say no.'

'I'm called Emil.'

'And I'm Horst. From Hamburg.'

They turned on their barstools and shook hands. Horst had a hand that for years had held a shovel and his skin was like sandpaper. Emil, however, had a soft hand.

'Not much gets loaded in Odessa,' Emil said. 'Sometimes grain. Was that your cargo?'

'No.'

'Then what?'

Horst knew perfectly well what the *Santa Cruz* had in its holds but he wasn't going to discuss that with a stranger. 'I don't know, some kind of machinery, in crates.'

'Not the usual.'

'Oh, we carry every damn thing there is. Not cattle. I did that once and I'll never do it again, I'd rather get a job in a factory. Ever work on a cattle boat?'

'No, so far I've been lucky.'

'What ship are you on now?'

'I'm waiting for a berth – that's hard in Constanta.'

'If you say so.'

'Anything on your ship, the . . . ?'

'*Santa Cruz,* out of Tampico. We're short of crew but we aren't hiring on, as far as I know. It's the owners, saving a little money.'

'That's how they are, the bastards.'

'You're a socialist? You sound like one.'

'I gave up on politics when I left Germany. But, before that, I was in the union in Rostock.'

'So you had to leave, like me.'

'That's what happened, but maybe I did the wrong thing.'

'Thinking of going back?' Horst said. Then he said, 'My turn' and waved to the bartender.

'Thanks. Pretty good beer they have in this place, right?'

'I like it. Are you thinking about going home?'

'Sometimes. I hear it's not so bad, the wages are good, and all you have to do is say you're sorry for your sins and that's that. They need seamen, no doubt about it, so if you mind your manners it's like you never left.'

'Sounds like you've decided.'

'Maybe I have. What about you?'

'No, I'll stay with my ship.'

'Someone told me they even pay a bonus.'

'Is that right?'

'Yes. You ought to think about it.'

'I'll have this beer, then it's time to be off. Nice meeting you, Emil.' *You're a spy, Emil, a Nazi spy.* Now Horst was glad he hadn't said anything about the cargo. Then he worried – maybe 'machinery in crates' was too much, but he hadn't wanted to lie, and he wasn't good at it.

The knock on Ferrar's door came at ten minutes to four. From the passageway, 'It's Silva, I'm the bosun, watch in ten minutes, you awake?'

'Be right there,' Ferrar answered, wrestling his way into the pullover shirt.

Silva was waiting in the passageway, holding a hooded, rubber rain jacket, a pair of binoculars, and a flashlight. 'Here's what you'll need,' he said, then led Ferrar up to the deck where an iron stairway climbed past the wheelhouse to a small platform with a railing. 'You won't see much at night,' he said. 'Best to watch a three-hundred-and-sixty-degree arc. Also, once an hour, open the hatch above the holds and make sure of the cargo. We worry about fires in the holds, especially this trip, and that's about it. There's a helmsman and a radio operator in the wheelhouse, if you have any questions you can ask them.'

Ferrar needed the rain jacket, even in July it was cold at night on the open sea, and the steady wind made it worse. Just below his feet, above the window of the wheelhouse, a searchlight cast a white beam on the black swells ahead of the ship. Now and then, when a rain squall blurred his vision, he wiped the droplets from the binocular lenses with his shirt – he would have to find a rag somewhere before his next watch. He swung the heavy binoculars left and right, then turned around and did it again, but the sky was overcast, there was no moonlight, and all he could see was darkness.

Istanbul had forever been a magnet for clandestine operations. Here, east met west and they spied on each other. A year earlier, the Abwehr – German military intelligence – had purchased a hotel with a view of the Bosphorus Straits and now used the top floor as a lookout point, watching traffic in the sea lanes that led to the Sea of Marmara and then to the Aegean. There were two observers that night, a lieutenant and a sergeant, who sat side by side in front of the window and tracked the busy strait with their binoculars. Some time after five o'clock in the morning, the sergeant said, 'There's an old tub for you.'

'Where?'

'Twenty degrees north, single stack.'

'I see her, she's the' – he worked to bring the name on the hull into focus – '*Santa Cruz*.'

The sergeant thumbed through the shipping register by his side. 'Out of Tampico,' he said. 'Wonder where she's been.'

'Could be anywhere; Bulgaria, Roumania, Russia.'

'The way she rides in the water she's hauling cargo,' the sergeant said.

'So she is.'

'Is she worth an inquiry?'

'Why bother? She's just a freighter, headed for Greece probably.'

'Look at her stack.' Grey smoke boiled from the mouth of the stack then blew away in the wind. 'She's doing the best she can.'

'In a hurry,' the lieutenant said. 'So what?'

'I don't know, I guess we'll let her go.'

'Hmm.' The lieutenant squinted through his binoculars. 'Oh, what the hell, we might as well inquire.' He laid the binoculars on the ledge beneath the window and filled out a form for the wireless operator: date, time, name of ship. 'I'll take this down later,' he said. 'I wouldn't mind knowing the cargo and where she picked it up. Probably nothing we should worry about, but still . . .'

On the *Santa Cruz*, there were two seamen in the wheelhouse, a wireless operator and a helmsman. The radio operator wore headphones, a wireless key close at hand. When the Morse code started up, he wrote the message down in the radio logbook. 'What is it?' the helmsman said.

'An operator in Greece, naval base at the port of Salonika. Wants to know what we're carrying and where we're going.'

The helmsman moved the wheel a few inches until the compass showed the correction. 'Sounds official,' he said. 'What do we say?'

'I don't know.'

'Better go ask Machado.'

The radioman, moving quickly, descended to the captain's cabin on the deck below the wheelhouse. When he knocked at the door, the captain called out, 'Come in.' He was on his cot, propped up on a pillow, reading a book.

'A message from the naval base at Salonika. They want to know cargo and destination.'

Machado thought it over.

'What do I tell them?'

'Acknowledge reception, nothing else. If they try again, do the same thing. We're in international waters, we don't have to tell them anything.'

*

Piraeus Coaling Station, 1:30 A.M. In a light drizzle, a tug boat manoeuvred the *Santa Cruz* to the dock where she would be resupplied with coal and fresh water. Silva came up to the watchman's bridge above the wheelhouse and found Ferrar, who was standing the twelve-to-four. 'Your job in port is to guard the head of the gangway,' the bosun said. 'So you carry a side arm.' He handed Ferrar a leather belt bearing a holstered revolver. Ferrar buckled it on, then went down to the lower deck and stood by the gangway, where Machado was talking to a stoker called Hector.

The port of Piraeus was adjacent to Athens, but the coaling station was a long way from the commercial edge of the city. Thus an enterprising merchant had opened a small store, about a quarter of a mile down the road, that served the steamship crews as they docked for resupply. Machado was in the process of going over a shopping list. 'Twenty canisters of loose tobacco, rolling papers, and get us a few tins of aspirins.'

'What kind?' Hector said.

'It doesn't matter. Maybe fifteen tins ought to hold us. Buy a few bottles of ouzo, every man will get a drink once a day while it lasts.'

'Anything else?'

'No. I don't have Greek drachma, so here's some Turkish lira, I'm sure they'll take that. You have plenty of money, pay what they ask and bring the rest back to me.'

'Aye, sir,' Hector said.

'Off you go.'

Hector descended to the dock, then, flashlight in hand, walked away down the dirt road that served the coaling station.

Ferrar stood by the gangway, hood up in the rain. At the bow of the *Santa Cruz*, coal rumbled down a long chute attached to a bulky wooden storage tower with a ladder to the top. Machado said, 'I have to update my logs, so I'll be in the office if anybody needs me.'

At three-thirty, the coal and water resupply completed, Machado reappeared. 'We'll be getting under way,' he said. 'When did Hector get back?'

'I haven't seen him.'

The captain was annoyed. Looking at his watch he said, 'What the hell is he doing?' Then, 'Take Silva with you and go find him.'

Ferrar and the bosun went off down the road. As the lights of the coaling station receded, it grew very dark and Ferrar kept the beam of the flashlight on the ground ahead of them. In fifteen minutes they reached what looked like an ancient stone hut. Inside, illuminated by a single lightbulb hanging on a cord, the shelves were packed from floor to ceiling with everything that merchant crews might need. Since the ships being serviced were from many countries, the owner spoke a few words of several languages, including English. When Ferrar and Silva came to the counter, the owner seemed anxious and frightened. 'What is?' he said. His voice quivered and his eyes darted back and forth, from Ferrar's face to the revolver.

Silva said, 'We're looking for a man from our ship. A big fellow, did he show up here?'

The owner nodded. 'Is gone,' he said.

'How long?'

'Long time now. I saw it.'

'Saw what?'

'He left, then robbers take him.'

'What?'

'I watch him go away, then his light went . . .' With his hand, the owner imitated the wild path of the stoker's flashlight, up and down, side to side. 'Put him in truck,' the owner said. 'Drive away.' He slid one hand across the other, the gesture meant *gone*.

'We better get back to the ship,' Silva said. They searched the road on the walk back to the *Santa Cruz,* but found nothing.

*

Machado was waiting for them at the head of the gangway. Silva recounted what the store owner had told them, and Machado, mouth grim, said, 'There's a telephone in the port office, I have to call the police.' He paused, then said to Ferrar, 'This is a simple robbery, nothing more, is that what you think?'

'Yes, what else could it be?'

'Something to do with the cargo and where it's going.'

Ferrar hesitated, then said, 'It's possible.'

There was an anxious crowd of sailors gathered on the deck. When Silva and Ferrar had returned, no Hector to be seen, the news had spread quickly. From the crowd, the stoker called Horst emerged and hurried towards the captain and the others. 'Captain,' he said, 'I don't know if it means anything, but they tried to get me to jump ship.'

'Who are "they"?' Machado said.

'A German, in a bar in Constanta. He pretended to be a seaman, but he wasn't. He offered me money, to go back to Germany.'

Machado looked directly at Ferrar and said, 'I'm going to have to tell the police everything, I hope you understand.'

Ferrar nodded. 'Yes, you have to,' he said.

De Lyon came down the passageway and he and Ferrar moved away from the crowd to speak privately. 'What do you think?' Ferrar said.

'This was no robbery,' de Lyon said. 'This was an abduction, they've figured out what we're doing, and what they don't know they'll find out from Hector.'

It was dawn by the time the detective showed up; tired and weary. Tired because he'd been called from his bed before dawn, weary because he'd spent his life looking at the bad side of human nature and that wasn't going to change. He was swarthy and broad, and reminded Ferrar of Stavros. In the passenger cabin, de Lyon and Ferrar sat on one cot, Machado and the detective on the other. As

Greece and Great Britain were long-standing friends and close allies, the second language in the cities was English. The detective listened carefully as Ferrar told the story, made a few notes, then said, 'They robbed him, but it might have been more than that. Why take him away? Why not just hit him on the head?'

De Lyon said, 'There's some chance this was an abduction.'

'That *does* happen, you know, in ports. Some captain is short a crewman, so they go out to the bars and find a sailor on liberty . . .' He spread his hands, *so life goes around here.*

'There's a possibility he was taken by the German spy service,' de Lyon said.

The detective, incredulous, stared at him, then, for a time, at Ferrar, and said, 'Who are you, sir? Merchant seaman? Owner's representative? What?'

'My friend and I are taking munitions back to Spain.'

'Which side?'

'The Republic.'

The detective said something to himself in fast Greek. Then, 'Thank you for telling me but, I hope you understand, if I report what you've said, then the government will have to get involved. And you'll be here forever.'

'Yes, we know that,' Ferrar said.

'What do you want me to do?' the detective said.

It was Machado who answered. 'I'm responsible for Hector, whatever happened to him has to be investigated. Maybe you can even find him but, no matter what, his family has to be informed and so does the company.'

'And then? For the rest of the story?'

'Our soldiers need this cargo,' Ferrar said.

The detective put his pencil away.

Two nights later, some time after nine in the evening, it began to rain; at first a summer shower, then a steady, windblown rain and the *Santa Cruz* began to rise and fall as she fought through the heavy swell. On the platform above the wheelhouse, the seaman keeping watch tried to use his binoculars but it was hopeless. When the waves hit the ship's hull, a cloud of spray burst over the deck and was caught up in the wind, so he had to wipe saltwater from his burning eyes. The ship had now entered the Mediterranean and was ten miles off the town of Licata, just below Sicily.

The watchman kept trying, squinting into the night, then turning aft and looking over the ship's stern. Where he thought he saw a light, just for a second, then it was gone. Was he seeing things? That happened on the night-time watches; a phantom, a mirage at sea. The watchman lay flat on the platform, the spray blowing over him, and tried to find the light with his binoculars. A minute went by, then another. At last he gave up, told himself there was nothing to be seen, and started to rise. Then he saw it again. Off the aft beam, then gone, or hidden when whatever was out there plunged into the trough of the rolling waves.

The watchman, hanging on to the railing, went down to the wheelhouse, its interior lit a faint green by the light of the compass on its post. 'Wet out there,' the radioman said. On the table by his transmitter was an enamel coffee pot. 'It's cold as hell but you can have some coffee if you want.'

'There's a light out there, somewhere astern of us.'

The radioman shrugged. 'Another ship. Want me to see if I can raise her?'

'Try it.'

The radioman tapped out some code, then listened to his headphones. 'No answer.' He tried again, using this frequency and that, but there was only silence.

The watchman flipped the hood of his rain jacket back on and said, 'I'm going to have another look.' He worked his way up the metal steps, and again flattened out on the watchman's platform. The wind was singing now, and he could hear each wave as it slammed against the hull, then burst into spray. He almost missed the light, because he hunted for it where he'd seen it earlier but the positions of the two ships had changed. Now it was on the other side of the freighter's stern. A tall wave towered to the level of the lower deck and the freighter shuddered as it hit her. But there it was again. Brighter. And now it didn't disappear.

The watchman once again returned to the wheelhouse, where the helmsman struggled with the big, spoked wheel, trying to keep the *Santa Cruz* on course. The wheelhouse window streamed with water. The radioman said, 'Well, see anything?'

'There's a ship out there, and it's catching up to us.'

'In *this*? What the hell is he doing?'

'I better go find Silva,' the watchman said.

'What'll *he* do?'

'That's what he told me, report anything at all. And, whoever she is, she's keeping radio silence, right?'

'I guess so. Or they're drunk or asleep.'

A few minutes later, the watchman returned, Silva by his side. The bosun asked the radioman to keep trying the usual frequencies, then the two climbed up to the platform. The storm was growing worse, the wind now howling through the deck cranes of the freighter. Silva and the watchman focused their binoculars on the stern. 'There it is,' the watchman said. 'Fifteen degrees off the starboard beam.' When Silva found the light he said, 'It's getting closer. He should be changing course, moving away, but he isn't.' A minute later he said, 'Closer now, and staying on our aft beam. The sonofabitch is *chasing* us.'

Down in the wheelhouse the wireless came to life. Through the crackling static the signal was fast, then repeated as the radioman translated the Morse code into words and wrote down the message. 'Is that him?' the helmsman said.

'On the emergency frequency.'

'What did he say?'

'They're the Italian naval launch *Spezia* and they are ordering us to make for the port of Licata.'

'Go up and tell Silva,' the helmsman said. 'He'll get the captain.'

By the time Machado reached the wheelhouse, the motor launch *Spezia* was running two hundred yards off their starboard side and the powerful light held the *Santa Cruz* in its beam. 'Send this,' the captain said. 'Cannot follow your order. Captain Machado. *Santa Cruz.*'

The radioman tapped out the message and the *Spezia* operator was back immediately: the words 'we repeat' and the same message as before. Machado said, 'All right, let's try this: "We are *Santa Cruz* of Tampico, a Mexican vessel in international waters."'

The radioman sent the message, but there was no reply. The men in the wheelhouse were holding onto whatever they could reach as the ship pitched and rolled. From the *Spezia,* the wail of a siren cut through the howling wind. 'Helmsman,' Machado said, 'put the light on her.' The helmsman worked the control by his wheel and the illuminated *Spezia* turned from grey ghost to white motor launch. On the bow, a machine gun set in a metal shield was aimed at the wheelhouse of the *Santa Cruz.*

Then a naval officer, his oilskin coat open to reveal a white uniform, appeared on the deck of the motor launch; in his hand a loud-hailer. The officer raised the device to his mouth and, his voice amplified, said in slow, halting Spanish: '*Santa Cruz,* we are ordering you to change course and make for the port of Licata. We will follow you in.'

The freighter's loud-hailer was hung from a wire loop by the light control. Machado grabbed it and stepped outside the wheelhouse. '*Spezia,* you have no authority to order us to do anything.'

From the officer on the *Spezia*: 'We will fire on you if you do not obey our order.'

Machado stepped back into the wheelhouse and said, 'He's threatening to shoot at us.' Nobody answered, this was the captain's decision to make. They all knew about the tons of ammunition in the holds, one bullet would be more than enough. Suddenly, a stream of sparks flew across the bow of the *Santa Cruz*.

'*Filho da puta,*' Silva said. *Son of a whore.*

'That's tracer,' the radioman said. Bullets made an impact, tracer ammunition set a target on fire.

'Silva,' the captain said. 'Go find the gangway watch pistol, then get the ship's rifle from my cabin.' When Silva hesitated, the captain said, 'We've been caught up in some kind of secret operation – they've been after us since we left the Black Sea. Which means that if we follow this order there is more than a cargo at risk. We are at risk, we'll be locked up in prison, or worse. So we're going to shoot out his searchlight and make a run for it.'

Silva was back quickly with the weapons – the rifle was an old German Mauser from the 1914 war. As he handed the captain a box of bullets, another stream of sparks whizzed over the bow. From the officer on the *Spezia*: '*Santa Cruz*. That was your final warning.'

Silva took the big revolver from its holster, Machado put a handful of bullets in his shirt pocket, worked the bolt of the rifle, then slid a round into the chamber. Together, crouched low, they ran out of the wheelhouse and lay flat on the deck. Machado, following target shooter's protocol, wound the strap of the rifle around his upper arm to steady his aim.

Then the *Spezia*'s machine gun fired at the freighter – they could see the tracer as it hit the hull. That was the end. The radioman mumbled a prayer and the helmsman crossed himself as they waited to die. The *Spezia* fired again, a buzzing orange flash lit the wheelhouse as the round punched through the wall, the helmsman said 'Unh' and sank to one knee. Just by his side, there was blood on the wall.

Ferrar and de Lyon, both breathing hard, came running into the wheelhouse. The radioman was trying to stop the helmsman's bleeding and was tying a belt into a tourniquet above the wound in his thigh. De Lyon ran out onto the deck where, using two hands, Silva was firing the revolver. De Lyon lay down next to the captain. 'Let me try it,' he said.

Machado, voice raised above the wind, shouted, 'It's impossible to hit anything – the target is moving and so are we. But maybe you're better at this than I am.' He handed the rifle to de Lyon.

'What do you want, Captain? The officer or the light?'

'The light. Our only hope.'

De Lyon fired at the light, the bullet hit the wheelhouse of the *Spezia*. The officer, offended that someone had the nerve to shoot at him, shook his fist and ran for cover. Once again, the *Spezia*'s machine gun raked the hull of the *Santa Cruz* but the deflected tracer flew away into the night.

As de Lyon reloaded the rifle, Machado said, 'The iron hull is too thick for a light machine gun.'

'What about the wheelhouse?'

'That's thin steel. I'd better get everybody out of there.'

The captain clambered to his feet, the *Spezia* gunner fired at him, one of the rounds hit the deck in front of de Lyon and sailed away over his shoulder. Concentrating hard, de Lyon exhaled, then held his breath and put slow pressure on the trigger. The light stayed on.

Machado took the helm, Ferrar and the radioman carried the helmsman out of the wheelhouse, headed for the stairway that led down to the second deck and the crew quarters. Meanwhile, the officers on the *Spezia*, realizing that their machine gun would not penetrate the freighter's hull, sent out a sailor with a high-calibre rifle. Ferrar, having left the helmsman to be tended in the crew quarters, reached the deck by the wheelhouse. 'We were on fire,' he said to de Lyon.

'Where?'

'Storage room. A tracer came through the porthole and hit a pile of tarred rope. The crew took care of it.'

Silva was putting the revolver back in its holster. 'All done,' he said. 'No more bullets.'

'Let's go back to the wheelhouse,' de Lyon said. 'Maybe there's one last thing we can try.'

Machado was at the helm, trying to keep the freighter on course. When the others arrived and stood next to him, he nodded at the motor launch. As the sailor on the *Spezia* fired, they could see an orange muzzle-flash. 'Captain Machado,' de Lyon said, 'I think all we can do is run for it.'

'He's a lot faster than we are.'

'If you change course so that our stern is facing him, he can shoot all he wants.'

The captain nodded and used the engine-room telegraph to call for full speed, then turned the wheel to bring the *Santa Cruz*'s stern around.

It took time for the motor launch to react, then, when it did, it also sped up, giving chase. Faster by several knots than the freighter, the *Spezia* closed, in a few minutes, to thirty yards off the aft beam.

'He'll hit us if he doesn't slow down,' Machado said.

'I'm going back to the stern,' de Lyon said. He left the wheelhouse, Ferrar followed him. The two lay flat on the deck, de Lyon slipped a round into the rifle's chamber. The *Spezia*'s searchlight was a lot closer now, de Lyon made sure of his aim, then squeezed the trigger.

The light exploded.

In the wheelhouse, Machado turned off the *Santa Cruz*'s searchlight and ordered Silva to put out every light on the ship. The machine-gunner and the rifleman on the *Spezia* took this as a challenge, now firing at a dark, bulky shape in the driving rain. But the upward angle made it difficult to aim and the tracer flew up over the wheelhouse. The captain of the *Spezia* kept his position for fifteen minutes, then gave up and set course for Licata.

*

The Nationalists and their allies tried once more. Two fighter planes were readied for action at the Nationalist airfield on the island of Majorca. The pilots sat in their planes, ready to take off when the *Santa Cruz* neared the island, but the order never came, because the storm rolled west across the Mediterranean and nothing was going to fly in that. The *Santa Cruz* steamed into the port of Valencia on the twelfth of July and the ammunition was loaded onto trucks bound for the river Ebro. On the twenty-fifth of July, the Army of the Ebro began to cross the river, an air attack soon followed. The anti-aircraft gunners brought down some of the Messerschmitts strafing the men on the pontoon bridges but it didn't matter, the Nationalists had plenty of reserves. The battle went on for a month, the Army of the Ebro was destroyed, and columns of refugees headed north, seeking refuge in France.

26 July. In the garden of the Hungarian embassy, Count Polanyi mopped his forehead and grumbled about the weather. 'I don't like the summer,' he told Ferrar. 'I'm not built for the heat, can't get to sleep, no appetite.'

'It's the same with me,' Ferrar said. 'My apartment doesn't really cool off at night.'

'And these, poor beasts . . .' He referred to the vizslas, who lay stretched out on the gravel, panting, eyes half closed. 'I take them out to the Bois for a run, and they just sort of mope around, sniffing the bushes.'

'Will you go away in August?'

'We'd all like that, wouldn't we?' he said to the dogs, who knew when people were talking about them and looked up to see what was going on. 'But I'm afraid not – damn this fucking war, it won't start, yet it won't go away. Anyhow, spies are busy when there's a war coming, so I have to be here, talking to people, sending cables, bah. Where will you go?'

'I'll be right here, our clients are having all sorts of problems, so no August vacation for me.'

'That's a kind of sin in this part of the world, Parisians don't believe in much but being out of town in August is sacred. By the way, whatever happened to your lady on horseback?'

'I'm not seeing her any more.'

'The best choice, I think, though she was something to look at.'

'That she was.'

'I wanted to see you because we've come to a decision about our legal problem.'

'Which is?'

'To do nothing. And we will let nephew know about it. The holding company will stay as it is, the bank in Budapest is open for business. Stalemate. Of course if the board can't function, it can't vote to pay its shareholders, so no money for us, no money for him. He may grow tired of that, in time. It's the fight he enjoys.'

'You'll deny him the pleasure of being hated.'

'Why are some people like that? Who knows, I don't. Anyhow the fascists are taking over in Hungary, he's one of them, so when the war starts he'll have to join up. Then we'll see who likes a fight.'

'And the dogs?'

'They'll stay with me, and my niece. She was having difficulties in Budapest, political difficulties, so I found her a place in my neighbourhood. And what happened next is that we became a family, a family of five. Very domestic, the dogs; meals on time, a last walk at night, they arrange your life.'

Ferrar smiled. 'I envy you, Count Polanyi.'

'One of these days we'll breed the bitch, would you like a puppy?'

'I would, but I'm away too much of the time.'

'Hmm, yes, you're probably right. Still, let me know if you change your mind.'

*

On a hot night in late August, Paris was deserted. Ferrar and de Lyon found an outdoor table at the brasserie near the Oficina Técnica. They took off their jackets and hung them on the backs of their chairs, loosened their ties and rolled up their sleeves. When the waiter appeared they ordered Pernod, poured some of the yellow liquid into their glasses, then added water, which turned the drinks a cloudy white. De Lyon was reflective, staring out at the empty street.

'Are you busy?' Ferrar asked.

'We're closing down the office, any arms-purchasing will now be done by the embassy. And they won't be doing much.'

'No? The fighting goes on.'

'The Republic is out of money, and the war is lost,' de Lyon said. 'So I guess I'm out of a job.'

'Not for long, Max. By September, Hitler will march into Czechoslovakia and Europe will be at war. Someone will want you.'

'Likely they will. Actually I have a chance to buy Le Cygne, and maybe I'll do that but, whatever happens, I want to stay in Paris and help in the fight, if I can. What about you?'

'My firm will find ways to be active on the anti-fascist side, and I'm too old for combat infantry. When it starts I'll move my family to New York, France will be in the thick of it and I expect we'll be bombed. Even so, I will stay in Paris.'

'Another Pernod?'

'Yes, thanks. What about your friends?'

'You mean Stavros, Nestor, and the rest?' He smiled, thinking about them. 'Gangsters don't do badly in war; a lot of money about, black market everywhere, police busy chasing spies. Anyhow, they will survive, I think, it's really all they've ever done and they're good at it.'

They stayed at the table for some time, drinking Pernod. A cooling breeze sprang up as the long dusk gave way to darkness and they smoked cigarettes and talked until, after midnight, the waiter came to their table and told them that the brasserie was shutting down for the night.

*

In September, Ferrar had to go to New York for meetings at the Coudert office. On his first night at the Gotham, he tried to read a magazine but he kept looking up, thinking about what he meant to do the following day. He had been brooding about Eileen Moore for weeks, especially so since the end of the affair with the marquesa. Yes, he missed being with Eileen but there was no point in that. Now he wanted to know what had become of her.

Eileen Moore made characters of the people in her life; would tell Ferrar stories about them, and it was as if he knew them. For example, Miss Feingold, Eileen's boss, who supervised the book reshelving workers at the New York Public Library. Poor Miss Feingold. She had, in late middle age, tender nerves, and was prone to hysteria over small things. Thin as a rail with caved-in shoulders, angry at the world – how could such ferocious energy be packed into that small frame? Taxi drivers, waiters, her workers; all wondered about that, and tried to avoid setting her off.

Late the following morning, Ferrar was at a meeting, and when it came time to take a break, he left the conference room, found a telephone, and called the library. Was Miss Feingold available? They would go and see, please stay on the line. Ten minutes went by, then the phone was picked up and a shrill voice said, 'Yes? Who is this?'

'Miss Feingold, my name is Cristián Ferrar, I was a friend of Eileen Moore . . .'

'Are you the lawyer?'

'I am.'

'Are you the lawyer who helped her with the divorce?'

'I didn't. I would have been happy to help her but I am in Paris most of the time. I was told she was married and was having a child.'

'*Eileen?*'

'Yes.'

'Well, there's no child that I know about. She did have a

passionate fling and, foolish girl, went and got married, then had a terrible time getting out of it. New York State is difficult about divorce, and she hadn't the money to go to Reno.'

'How is she doing?'

As Miss Feingold started to answer, a secretary looked into the office where Ferrar was using the phone and said, 'Mr. Ferrar, they're going to need you in the conference room.'

He thanked Miss Feingold, and returned to work.

Ferrar left work at five-thirty. He couldn't be sure, but from his conversation with Miss Feingold, it sounded as though Eileen Moore was still working at the library. So he took a taxi up to Forty-Second Street, climbed the stairs to the entrance, and sat on the top step. What, he wondered, had she done? Lied about the pregnancy? She might have, not wanting him to know that she was crazy for a new man. Rather like, he thought, his mad passion for the marquesa.

A warm, September evening, the library was busy; a flood of people going up and down the stairs. All kinds of people – teenagers, college students, artists, old men and women, and those strange eccentric types who'd spent years doing research on some subject, likely esoteric, that preoccupied their lives. All sorts they were: people who went to libraries.

He kept his eyes on the crowd. Did she come to work at six? That was his recollection. Six o'clock came and went. And yes, there she was, auburn hair, redhead's complexion, mind a thousand miles away as she took the stairs in a hurry, late, having to explain to Miss Feingold. But then, she happened to glance up, and stopped dead, mouth open in surprise, staring at Ferrar. They stared at each other for a time, and, as they did, the loveliest look came over her face, a kind of warm light. Not so very different from the look on his face. Really, much the same.

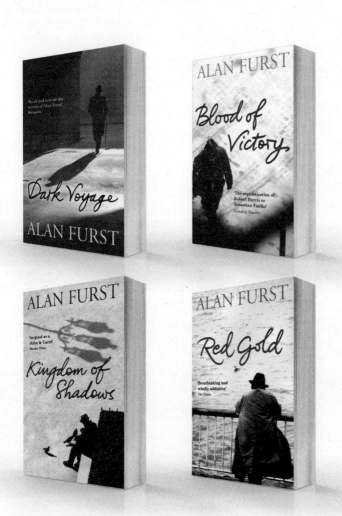

'In a class of his own' William Boyd

Available now from W&N in paperback and ebook

The World at Night

'A brilliant piece of atmospheric writing'
Daily Telegraph

ALAN FURST

The Polish Officer

'One of the best novels of the year ... brilliant'
Robert Harris

ALAN FURST

'Furst's wartime thrillers have set new standards in the genre'
Sunday Telegraph

Dark Star

ALAN FURST

ALAN FURST

Night Soldiers

'Intelligent, ambitious, absorbing'
Literary Review

'America's pre-eminent spy novelist'
New York Times

Available now from W&N in paperback and ebook